LOOK WHAT THEY DONE TO MY SONG

Look What They Done To My Song

A NOVEL BY
John McCluskey

Random House  New York

For my Parents (Helen & John, Sr.)

Library of Congress Cataloging in Publication Data

McCluskey, John.
    Look what they done to my song.

    I. Title.
PZ4.M12668Lo [PS3563.A26218]   813'.5'4   74-8654
ISBN 0-394-48818-0

Manufactured in the United States of America

98765432

First Edition

LOOK WHAT THEY DONE TO MY SONG

Aimless tracks in the sand, gulls across the sun. Mack-on-Mack. I close my eyes and I am juju priest to Shango, knower of black magic eternal. Understand that it is no lost art and did not vanish when black people buried their bones in southern yards and trusted to luck in great cold cities or huddled here along the sea. Words and needs—these tools, yes, for blues and roots. In quiet dawns I seek the sea and ponder black magic. Create chants to destroy the curse sealed with the first native betrayal when slaves, though it was long before the captives knew the real stink of submission, were exchanged for bracelets and rusty guns and the Bible. The blind curse that can put black hands to shredding black throats. I want to get back to that moment, to erase it, for the death and the pain even, but not the life and the joy.

I realize all that can live for me and trust the wisdom of such realities. I am ageless Du Bois stilled in thought. I am frozen by responsibilities for futures not yet birthed. I make possibilities of thin suns above me. I rap out a gift of love along the way.

I am black, and human and must not deny my heart. In tune, certainly, with the rhythms reserved for me. (Mack, your great-great grandpa was a big black man and his wife was real light with good hair and your scars come from a ugly old cross-eyed man your mama looked at when you was still inside her belly.) I am the sum of possibilities, lost, found, approaching.

I close my eyes and shut out the bleached side of this moment. To get back along the road of good times, to pick up scattered pieces of me. To deep and silent loves passed by, now like reeds bending in the wind. Love is a series of holy acts. The first act is to see. Aimless tracks in the sand, gulls across the sun . . .

One

SOCIAL pressure is a drag. It stoops to peek under blinds or stalks with cutting eyes past the small house where I'm staying. It complains that I play my horn too loudly. Or it sits, fat and ugly, on the porch when I ease by whistling.

When I come to the beach and woodshed in easy isolation, the restlessness of the ocean breaks every strait jacket of the puritans. Here time is only the growth of my shadow.

This is America, make no mistake. A tiny village on Cape Cod. Television antennas above cardboard houses. Behind me the traffic is moving in spasms. All this after Santa Fe and rides on boxcars, inching across the plains toward the end of long runs. After countless jobs in anonymous towns. Here, the cradle.

I stretch on the sand, leaning against the horn case. A chilly wind blows off the water, darkening it with ripples, sending bits of paper scraping over the sand. An ill wind blows no good, as my father would say. And he should know. That afternoon he stood among the snickers of country folks, his gabardines ballooning and fluttering. He wore a pair of silk wings that he had worked on for months. From the fourth floor of an apartment house, he would try his leap to freedom, his backhand at natural law. The neighbors poured out, wise guys laying bets. Then he mumbled a few words, checked his watch and leaped. A strong breath of wind buoyed him for a moment. As the first screams shot up from the crowd, he turned once, his arms pumping sadly there two hundred feet above. I was too young to consider the possibilities of a broken neck. I could only feel ashamed watching those arms beat the air in desperation. A tree limb offered itself and dangled him by a shredded wing. Amid the laughter of freedmen and thin Indians.

He worked as he thought, in fit after brilliant fit, deaf to the jibes of the neighbors, blind to their grins. His world still spins dizzily in his head, uncontrollably sometimes, as it must have that night in Ohio when he announced that we would move to Santa Fe and no one spoke at first or questioned it, since his dreams were not to be doubted. "I know things will be better out there." My mother, once a semi-popular blues singer, hummed while packing and kissed my head with remote smiles on her face. "I believe yo' daddy done gone stone crazy this time."

And I chased the years hunting and learning under the deep blue of the New Mexico sky. Sitting in parks and slapping out the "hambone" on my thighs, or sucking the last drops of wine from bottles found behind the baseball field. Perfecting my dozens repertoire: "Your old lady wears combat boots." Roller rinks and right halfback on the all–New Mexico high school team later. Rubbing up against little girls of all shades. There was one girl I called Pocahontas and worshiped in my shyness. She came up pregnant before graduation and ran away with a man no one seemed to know. She returned years later with three children and new ugly flesh.

Then there was the Sunday night, hours after Malcolm's death, when I awoke screaming, wiping from my cheeks what I had taken to be his blood. Mama stayed near me that night, as she did with all her children when nightmares or illness broke our sleep. From the next room a sliver of light shone all night beneath my door and I could hear her moving around, humming, finding things to do to make it appear as though they had to be done in those early hours and knowing I was going through something I couldn't talk about yet.

By the next morning I knew that I would have to leave. I had known it for three of the five years we had been there, but I was waiting for the moment that the truth would get hold of me and shake me every way but loose. Word of Malcolm came from refugees pushing through town to L.A. I counted his death with that of so many others around the land as assassinations of spirit, a spirit whose only peace needed to be fury. I wanted to grow in that spirit and I guessed that growth needed its right place. I wanted to be a man and a musician, or what I thought a man and a musician should be, and Santa Fe wasn't where it was at. I blamed it on the Indians, the dull whites, black folks from Alabama who thought the West would be best—on everybody huddling under those night winds off the desert. When those excuses failed, I had the letter from Boonie, an old friend who was drumming steadily in Columbus, Ohio. He said he needed a strong sax man. My money would stretch only as far as Kansas City and I would have to work myself east.

A month later when I hit the road, neither of my parents went through the tearful good-bye changes. They were smarter than that. My father was proud that some of the dreamer had passed down and Mama gave blessings with the knowledge that dreams must be tested. Her only advice at the door: Don't trust strangers. But she must have known that everyone is a stranger out here. She is convinced that I will return a minister.

A ship moving slowly toward the canal. The sluggishness in this morning. Jupiter Sims, the ragman, is whistling "Stormy Monday Blues" as he shuffles up the beach, stooping under his burlap sack. His eyes are red from wine and his face heavily creased. He might be forty-three. Or twenty-six like me.

"Look like this beach yo' home, man," he says. "I could hear you playin' clear on the other side of the road."

"What you know good?"

"Nothing, except that some folks still tryin' to figure you out even though you done been here a month. I guess they's trying to figure out what you lookin' for here and when you gone get it and how. Brother Jesse just swear you hidin' out from somethin' cause you stay to yourself and ain't got too much to say to nobody."

"Tell them that what they don't know can't hurt them." I toss him a cigarette before he asks. His rusty knotted hands clasp around it, breaking it. Fumbling, he tries to fit the ends together. I hand him another.

Jupiter drops his bag and settles sighing next to me. "Say, remember that band cat you told me to talk to about a job? Well, I saw him yesterday and he say he done told you once already that he got enough mens . . . Then he say as long as you can read a sight . . ."

"Sight-read?"

"Yeah, if you can do that, he can take you on when somebody get sick."

"Tell him thanks." A fat crippled dog chases gulls to the water, spins and darts back for others. A couple in faded coveralls follow, clapping at him when he rushes back ahead of a wave. Clawmarks on his ear. Coon probably. They nod as they pass. Half the ship lost in mist now.

"Jupiter, your hustle doing you any good here?" It's the type of question that a prostitute fields countless times while smoothing wrinkles in her skirt and touching up her hair before going out the door. Or a petty thief while stroking his chin and grinning over the stereo he copped. Freak accidents of luck can do it every time. Never knock another brother's hustle. But it's too late this time.

"Well, you can't exactly make yourself a millionaire picking up rags, but I do all right for myself. Folks in town look out for me. But you got to keep scufflin' or you begin to tell yourself it's somebody's charity you livin' on rather than anything you can do for yourself." He stands. "You got any more whiskey?"

"I knocked that out days ago."

He waves and starts off, slowly as he mounts a dune, then over, his cap bobbing, dropping away as he nears the road. He wastes no time.

> *"I cried, Lord have mercy*
> *Lord have mercy on me*
> *I'm trying to find my baby,*
> *Won't somebody send her home to me."*

Tightroping a crooked line of rusted seaweed and debris. Broken bottles, stiff condoms and charred wood sprout in the sand. The sun's sting is canceled by sharp gusts off the ocean. Traffic sounds sweep more strongly off the road. Ahead of me there are figures idling across the dunes. Slow-moving backs dropping out of sight. Destinations waiting.

I was delivered here one cold rainy night by a lady wrestler. Her name is Big Tina and she is heavyweight wrestling champion of New England. She was my third ride that day, offering herself in a small Connecticut town as an Indian summer sky grayed and threatened, finally breaking as I stepped out of her Cadillac at a rotary just outside of the village. She invited me to one of her matches, a tag-team affair in New Bedford. I couldn't handle it.

"What's wrong?" she asked. "You got a little chick waitin' here for you?" She raised her arms behind her head, breathing deeply to show off her oversized breasts.

"Not yet," I told her.

She frowned and laid rubber getting away.

Minutes later I was dozing off in a phone booth and only vaguely aware of the sound of the rain before the honks from the old Ford a few feet away. An elderly couple took me to their home where they fed me and asked me to stay on for a few days. That was a month ago. A month and the Sledges are paying their dues. Their few friends are more scarce than ever, they boast. There are questions in the stares of the signifying neighbors: Who is this man who drinks too much and plays his horn too loud and looks too long at the behinds of pretty women and does not work? The Sledges saying little and making it as best they can, not even hinting that I move on or get a job, but proud, it seems, to have me there. ("Never turn a stranger from your door. He might be your best friend, you never know.")

Between light furniture deliveries and trips to the super-market each week, their car sits collecting dust and memories. I know few people bored with their daydreams and certainly not Reba Sledge. Afternoons she will stand watching the car from the window, a headrag on her short gray hair, a mop in her hand. The Old Ship of Zion, they have named it. At one time they used it for annual trips to Bessemer, Alabama, but friends there now rest in the back rooms in the homes of relatives, nursing homes, cemeteries. ("Seem like every time we go down, somebody we know gettin' funeralized.") Sons and daughters have married and have strayed to Chicago and Detroit and Cleveland. And the ship is docked on a silent street in the shade of skinny trees.

Reba Sledge is stooped now, peering into the oven. "Any calls?" I ask.

"Hunh, them biscuits been in there for an hour and ain't doing no good. I done told Dupree a million times we need a new stove." She wipes her hands on her apron and looks up. "Yeah, that girl called again. She say to call her back."

Behind the house the door to the shed bangs shut. Mr. Sledge is a rail-thin man who speaks only when spoken to. He was a blacksmith and farmer in Lowndes County, Alabama, before he moved to the steel mills in Bessemer. Klan raids on his land wore him down over the years. The battles were lonely ones and he couldn't save enough crops to feed his large family. So he salted the fields and left. He makes it here as a carpenter. We exchange nods over the roast chicken, rice and black-eyed peas.

"Find anything yet?" he asks, moving in on the biscuits. Stains of sweat on the long-sleeved underwear he has rolled to his elbows.

"Ain't nothing moving here but the wind. No music, anyway. I hear that people go out and pick cranberries and make a decent bit of change."

He flags away the idea. "You don't want that."

"It's money. Beggars can't be choosy."

"That's no money to speak of. Five dollars a day, what's that? When I was a boy, I wouldn't chop cotton for that. Now I say that to say this. People around here been acting damned funny since you come and I ain't never had no use for funny-acting folks. But they still keeping the business coming in and I got so much business I can't halfway turn around back there. I could pay you to help out in the shop and haul things to folks in that piece of iron out front."

"Don't call it that, Dupree," his wife says, laughing.

"But I don't know anything about making cabinets," I tell him.

"Don't have to know. I'll take care of that. You got a good head on your shoulders, strong hands and back." He settles back, picking his teeth with a matchbook cover.

"The last time I tried to drive a nail, I smashed up two fingers. Neither of them mine."

"Then I'll wear boxing mitts when you start hammering." He laughs. "Ain't nothing to it, son. It's easy, like chunkin' rocks at a big barn." He knows he has me. The job will not hurt, I know. My money has grown short and I do owe them more than the little I've been paying at the end of each week. I nod.

"Attaboy," he says with that quick nod that old people use to signal approval. My father's advice: Mack, a nigga ain't nowhere unless he can work with his hands. A brain can't build a house.

From the beginning I've tried to speak only when necessary. They have the habit of stopping everything when I start to talk. Forkfuls of food will stop just short, Adam's apples will stop working. At first I took it to be an extreme form of hospitality—make the stranger feel special. But it's more. They hang onto my every word and look disappointed when I stop speaking. Do I sound funny? No, they will answer. Saditty? Not at all. "Sound like a natural-born leader, don't he, Dupree?" Reba Sledge asked one evening. If she had raised the same question behind the horn, then I'd have something to jump about. After all, the horn is the only voice I want to move folk with. To say I'm like a leader in any other way is to place a heavy weight on me. Just say I'm the one who woke folks up to themselves one dawn, blowing wild and beautiful changes.

I can't get angry at them, though. The Sledges listen to me and, in their strange childlike way, are steps ahead of my buddies in Santa Fe. My buddies only blinked when I mentioned my faith in my music. They'd change the subject to football. Or asked how I expected to eat. I hope the Sledges don't pour any more special favors on me because my voice makes them get happy. I can't repay any investment of hope except my own and I must keep free for even that.

Agreeing to take the job has been enough for one evening. I excuse myself and slip outside. The sidewalks are rolling up fast. Downtown, hotrodders gun their motors for passing girls. Jupiter Sims toms with a fat-bellied cop. Portuguese girls in long dresses glance at me with neutral eyes. Distant bells tonguing out vespers. Michelle will call again later. It might do her some good, this hide-and-seek game. Streets dappled with the last flecks of sunlight. Looks. Passing through conversations and leaving them dangling. You people, you square guilty people. Near Omaha a small town boasts of John Brown's Cave. I have taken the tour with farmers and their wives, with high school teachers in white socks and Hush Puppies. At the end of the tour there was the child pointing at me as I came into the light. "Mommy, is that a nigger?" People here seem a bit more cool about it. "Are you an Indian?" or "Where are you from?" Perhaps it shouldn't bother me. I should use it somehow. Become SuperBlood. Grin a lot at their corny jokes. Move in next door.

I drift to a street where three black families live in three small houses. Unfriendly, they seem unaware of the code. Convinced of their place on the Mayflower, no doubt, or of exiles like me, who will remind them of too much. The well-greased legs on one of their girls running after a boy, his legs slowed by stiff dungarees, shouting something with his head turned. He slams into me and bounces off, unhurt, stalking around me in casual surprise before breaking away. They weave their way around a corner. The sun dies on Bay Street, and turning back to the Sledges', I notice the dark figure of a girl frozen to a window, a dull light behind her, before the quick closing of the blinds.

A man can usually find out where he's at and where he's going by the type of women he is messing with. I'm convinced of this now. It's usually the low-lifers that get the ball rolling. When I was much younger, it was the warm-blooded widows who enticed my friends with bubble gum and packs of Mary Janes and fruit pies, who had sweat mustaches and slipped their hands so slowly across the shoulders of my backward buddies. They told also of dry-eyed schoolteachers who burned incense, lectured and hummed Billy Eckstine tunes while they made ready. They were for the others, but not for me. An Indian did me in. Her family had left the reservation for good. An Indian even before the day my father snatched me by the wrist and stormed out of the house. "Ain't no son of mine gone be a punk!" and the adobe whorehouse where I stood in the door and explained that I was already a man. At sixteen, two years a man and not doing so bad for myself either and him going upside my head right there in front of two hillbillies. An Indian girl and we twisted stiffly, thrashing like spastics, while her little brother was digging it all from behind a tree. I told him I was a magician and could turn him into a speckled rock or a panther or a black man unless he hatted up and kept quiet. That gagged him for good, started him shaking. His sister not liking me so much later.

Since then there have been cream-colored girls from the Hill. I was a change of pace for them. In the clubs where I've played, they would sit in a corner nursing a Scotch on the rocks. Away from sweaty loud nigras, they would watch me on the stand and shift on their cute behinds. With them it has always been very public like that. Picked up in sports cars, I was, and dropped off that same way.

I think to my early plots on Michelle. Two weeks ago, as a favor to Sledge, I was simply to deliver a set of shelves, but the pretty girl smiled too long. Nice breasts, wide-set eyes. In the doorway we made stabs at conversation, hitting on fat tourists she couldn't stand and her recent trip to New York. Her mother listened from the next room. Somehow I made it into the room and coffee was mentioned. I relaxed after taking the first round with little trouble, though feeling clumsy in spite of everything. Her voice was velvet rain.

"You really from Santa Fe? That's weird. What's it like?"

"Not too much different from this place," I told her, keeping an eye out for her mother.

"That's not saying too much, you know. Let's see, I think the farthest I've ever been away was that trip to New York. We saw Harlem. You ever been to Harlem?"

I nodded and listened to her words whistling by as I thought up various plots. "Why do you stay in this nowhere place?" I asked.

"You're still here, aren't you?"

"I'm broke. I can't leave."

"Uh-uh, you probably expected something nice like me to happen to you." That caught me off guard. She smiled when I reached for her hand. "What's your hurry?"

She has softened even more since then, and when she called this morning to tell me that her mother would be in Providence for a three-day neo-suffragette meeting, I wasted no time getting over. In bed, Michelle smiles her smile and watches Bobo, her cat, move curve-careful over her hip, then down up her side, nosing her face. She strokes it, then shoos it off the bed.

"Even Bobo knows we don't belong here," she says.

"Maybe he wants to get into the action."

"Clown!" She looks off for a moment. "Suppose my mother walked in now."

"Suppose the world stopped turning." My fingers lost in her hair.

"You're missing the point," she says.

"You worry too much, Michelle. Your mama is probably wheeling and dealing in some meeting this very minute." I move off to the kitchen and she doesn't bother to pull the covers to her chin.

Before I came along, she claimed that she was afraid of her body, rarely studied it, since it was hooked so closely to memorable sin: the nights she undressed before a mirror, high from three beers, after her boyfriend had wrestled with her in his car. The one time before the mirror in a doctor's office when she thought herself pregnant. Other times it belonged to a stranger. She watches me as if through a distant window, the covers across her knees. She is silent for a few moments as I resettle next to her.

"My mother is still giving me the third degree. She wants to know your plans. Whether you're in the Army and just passing through or whether you're going to be here for a while. She doesn't believe what I told her."

"What's that?"

"That you're a musician, and you got this crazy idea about music saving the world." Her mother guarded the door the next time I dropped by. Her fish eyes coldly frisking me like a cop's. She pulled off her glasses and wet her lips, tossing question after question.

"Does that bother her?"

"My father was colored, you know. He was in the Merchant Marine and used to sneak over here when his ship would come into New Bedford. He had been a musician for most of his life and still played once in a while. He always promised to buy me a trumpet for my birthday or for Christmas. When he came home it was always good times because he'd take out his trumpet and make me a tambourine or drum out of something and we'd just play our heads off. It was good for Mama, too. I don't doubt that she loved him once. At least she loved him until she found out she couldn't change him into some meek little something. The last time he came around was when I was six years old. That's fifteen years ago, Mack. She even tried to make me hate him, but I've gotten to know my mother a lot better. She must have driven him crazy with all that respectable mess. He probably couldn't stand it. Anyway, what I've been trying to say is that she's been down on musicians and colored men ever since." Then she laughed. "If she saw you here now, she'd have a fit."

"You ought to come with me when I leave town," I tell her.

"I can't."

"Still being respectable?"

"Don't play." She props herself on an elbow, looks off. "No word in the last two years from him. Though he never comes back, he sends me presents. And Mother tells the world she's a widow. Do you like me, Mack?"

Self-portraits in two colors. Red was our setting, then sad browns. The couch, the rug, before sand, flesh, eyes. Trust the first impression, its limits. Smoke from our cigarettes thins, unravels, out. And this will end as it began. The black man in their lives, the easy riders. "A nigga ain't shit"—these words as pablum, though the mothers left behind will wait. Will always wait.

"Michelle, you call yourself black or white?"

"I settle in the middle. Portuguese."

"With your mix, that's black."

"That's Portuguese here, sweetie."

I run through a few sentences with a broken accent. "See, I can be Portu just as easily. It's all in the mind. Like 'nigger,' it's a frame of mind. I could have you thinking black in no time." It's a sore point with her. Yet perhaps pain, precise pain, can accomplish what compromise cannot. She can be neutral here from now until times get better. Black men will call her high-yellow. White men will call her Eurasian.

"You ever coming back to see me?" she asks.

"I'd be insane to stay away."

"I guess my mother will keep her eye out for a rich young man for me. You know, I can't take you too seriously about running away together. I think you're pretty much a one-man show on the road."

"Geniuses are always one-man shows," I tell her, hoping to get both of us off our hooks.

"Maybe I'm asking for too much too soon, huh? I mean, I just want you to remember me. I don't want you to walk on water, Mack, or blow out the sun. But you make me feel beautiful." She slides away and moves to the window to look out at the morning rain. "I've never felt beautiful in any way that I could believe for long."

The love I first saw. Home. Running with the rest of the Royal Priests after throwing rocks at passing cars. Pumping hard through alleys, awaking dogs, before the screams from Big Shorty's house. All of us crowding up to the porch to dig on it. His wife on her knees in the middle of the room, her hands to her ears, her head snapped by hard blows from Shorty. Spittle at the corners of his mouth. (Stop it! stop it! someone screamed. No one did.) He cursed and hit her again and again and she just stayed on her knees. Then the siren and the fuzz. We ran for cover. The grays found nothing, only Shorty's dry-eyed wife kissing him and telling them they must be mistaken. Wrong house, she said. The second time it happened. Love, I called it both times.

"You still messin' with that girl, huh?" asks Reba Sledge, straightening up. She must have seen me all the while, known that I had paused watching through the back door, though her head has never once come up from the hoe. The rain hasn't lasted, barely wetting the ground. Clods fly from the hoe like sparks off a grindstone. Her mouth works to shoot out snuff juice and her look is an innocent one.

"You got to look over a old lady sometime. She always thinkin' every youngun is her own. I guess I ain't got no right meddlin' in your private business. That's yo' business. But I just knowed a whole buncha colored men who done got messed up fooling around with them Gitchee women."

"She's not Gitchee, Mrs. Sledge. She's Portuguese."

"That ain't the same as Gitchee, huh? Well, I'm glad of that. Them's some wild heifers. But watch yourself, you never know. There's so much happening these days."

She turns back to her garden. Up at dawn, scratching, kneading, chopping at the earth, she will scold it as she would a child, yet pet and spoil it since the mother in her will not let her do otherwise. The land was brought along too as if the sight of neat rows of vegetables was as needful to them as laughter. As if that need was as easily transferable from place to place as their scarred Bible and a photograph album and recipes long memorized after a grandmother and mother who were slaves and never cooked for any folks except their own after one momentous day. Momentous since they became free to take new names, make new gods, yet sweating the same sweat, working the same land, almost the same land as during slavery, because life had to be the lazy procession of suns and the silence of the earth they owned.

She talks while working, not looking up. "While we was still living in Lowndes County, there was a boy once came to us, 'bout like you did. Not to say we wasn't expecting him the morning that he walked up to the house, 'cause Cousin Mattie had called and told how he walked straight up to her in town. She say she thought straight off that he was a teacher just like her boy what went off to school and got educated and got him a good job teaching school in Atlanta. The boy talked like white folks, she said. He wanted to come out to the country because he was looking for some roots or something. Mattie didn't know no better and she started remembering the times I used to fool around with herbs and sent him straight to us. Early next morning he come a-struttin' down the road, just as straight and tall and handsome. He walk right up to the house like he been there a thousand times and knowed all about it and knowed the dogs too, 'cause they didn't even bother to bark much.

"Then I gave him some breakfast and listened while he went on talking about roots. I told him the best roots were over Black Ridge near the creek, but he say he was lookin' for some different kind of roots. He asked me if I knowed all sorts of people who I never heard of before. By that time Dupree done come in and we didn't know what he was talking about and wondered if he was just out there signifying around. We told him that he was welcome to stay on. 'Course now, we always did help out our own kind.

"He stayed with us four days, wakin' up with Dupree every morning and working the peanut patch before the shop opened, grinning and working like it was fun. In the evening we would talk some more and he'd be writing down real fast everything Dupree and me be saying. Some of the things

Dupree said I ain't never heard him say before. I never did say too much 'cause you never know what they taking it down for. People funny these days.

"Then the girls around there decided they just can't keep away, so they come just a-switchin' and carryin' on with they fast selfs. Some of them fools brought him pies and cobblers, but he never paid them no mind. Fact he didn't pay too much attention to nothing except what we said, like we was big stuff sitting around in the evenings talking about where we came from and all that. Sometimes he would go walking and talking to himself, but a man got a right to do that, I guess, if he got so much knowledge his head always about to bust. That boy was smart as a whip and spoke right up like he knew just what he was talkin' about. You can tell when somebody know what they talkin' about 'cause they don't start licking they lips and shuffling they feet and looking all up at the sky. He never did say what he did, but me and Dupree figured he was a professor and reading just about everything there was to read. When we'd ask about his work, he'd start lookin' all funny like we done just told him some bad news. And I don't know what in the sam hill made him do that. You know and I know, some people made to do something while others ain't. God didn't tell the spider to make honey or the bee to spin webs and he didn't tell some men to study books who should have been farming or singing all along. We never did find out if he found those roots he was looking for." She leans on the hoe and adjusts her headrag.

"Did he ever come back?" I ask.

"Naw, but we hear from him from time to time. Last we heard he was still moving around up there in Boston. Y'all young peoples ought to settle yourselfs down."

"You have to keep moving while you're looking."

"Looking for what?"

"Looking for places where you don't have to look any more." More than once they have opened their doors for a drifter, at least that one before me, who can only accept more than he can ever give these people as their sole reward, probably that reward marked and memorized from somewhere in their Bible.

"You tell him hello for us when you see him," she says.

"Who?"

"Andrew. The boy I was telling you about."

She must have forgotten that I need to know his last name to find him. Then again, she's probably let that slip her mind too, like the way she sometimes calls me Roy, her son's name.

"You like it here?" I ask.

"Do a blind man like the dark?" She studies me as I move outside. "Besides, it don't matter now whether we like it or not. Dupree can make a little money here doin' what he like to do and we lives pretty good. We couldn't do that for too long down South. The kids wanted to help out, you know, but I just didn't think it was right to stop folks from gettin' on in life and depending on them for everything, even if you done raised them.

"One day we just started riding in that old piece-a car. We was trying to get to Boston 'cause we know some folks there. But the car stopped on us right here in this town and Dupree took that for a sign. So we cast our buckets here. Now, between you and me, it ain't been no picnic with the peoples around here. Even our own kind ain't too friendly, thinkin' they so high and mighty. Most of them came through with a tiny circus four years ago and stayed on and thinkin' they been here all they lives."

"People can be cold like that," I offer.

"Can't they, though?" Her face twisted in a sad frown. "Be particular, son. People gone scandalize your name. They gone

ERRATUM

twist up most things you say and do. They gone misunderstand you sometimes, no matter how good your intentions be." She looks briefly to the sky, then pulls an ear of corn from one of the dozen or so stalks in the garden. She shucks it and pinches a few kernels. "Corn don't seem to take to this sand so good."

It has been a neat picture so far—the old couple and me, the prodigal son. I haven't minded their concern. But something's up. After dinner, Mrs. Sledge has left the room and Dupree has brought out the wine. It isn't every day that he dips into his home-grown wine. Only Sundays and holidays so far. His face grave as he runs it down.

"Mack, you know what I make this wine from? Cranberries. Now most folks know you can make wine out of most anything, but I use cranberries in mine because it taste the best . . ." I shrug, waiting for him to go on.

"Mack, you like my wine?"

I nod. Something is on his mind, but he is stumbling. I knock out some more of the wine. It's certain that when he's making his wine he isn't playing. It is strong enough to bring eyesight to the blind. He shakes his head and settles back and we tell stories into the night. I suspect that I haven't heard the last about his wine.

As days belong to the deserted beach and the stutters on my horn, the streets own my nights. A bag of blues will always leak the same scenes. Wet streets and stillborn days and the blur of faces, voices. An empty bottle bouncing too loudly in an alley can. I kick along a pebble or wind my watch like any good citizen, looking off to steady myself as the last sip begins to take its warm effect. Stray cars for traffic. A cruising cop. The mooing of a tug. My reflection in a display window and the rattling cough of a drunk swaying on a corner. The sidewalk lifts me beyond the bright windows, sets me down in

the village green where a janitor stares at my horn case. I run
to the beach.

> *I keep drifting and drifting like a ship out on the sea*
> *I keep drifting and drifting like a ship out on the sea*
> *I ain't got nobody in this world to care for me.*

Perhaps I can get away before the snow. I'd hate to be
stranded here in the winter. A quiet place to steal away to was
all I wanted, borrowing time to practice. Promises always
complicate things. Michelle. Snow, lost and falling on sand, the
town settling suffocated. Square scene, it must be. Where will
everyone be then? Where is everyone now? Are the pilgrims
on strike?

I assemble the horn and drop to the sand, running through
the scales. The notes speed off flat and metallic over reed
squeaks. I slip on a new reed and fix my mind to a simple
melody.

Two figures are approaching. A deep voice humming
"Sweet Georgia Brown." The smaller figure, a girl's, breaks
away and darts about in circles with arms windmilling. Several
times she nearly trips, but manages to stay up.

"Play some mo', man," comes the voice. A huge black man
is standing over me, grinning like crazy. "Some mo', man. You
was sounding damn sweet."

He drops down next to me, pulling the girl with him. "Go
ahead and cook. We just sit here and listen." His hand
gripping the back of the girl's neck. He wears a small earring. I
have seen neither of them around town.

"I would like to play some more, but it looks like I'll have to
borrow wind from somewhere because mine is all gone."

"Don't sweat it. While you was going, you did sound
outasight. Didn't he, sugar?" The girl nods, smiling with heavy

eyes. "This is my woman Ivone. Stone fox, ain't she? She a little drunk now, but she togetha. You ain't from here, I know," he says. We shake hands. "My name is Ubangi, man. Jones. Ubangi Jones. I stay over in New Bedford. Came up here in '61 on one of them reverse Freedom Rides."

"No shit?" I try to make out his face. Favors Otis Redding, this gypsy out of the South. Swears he sings like Johnny Taylor.

"Uh-huh. It seems that folks in my town—little town name of Calypso, North Carolina—seem like all the folks thought that things would be a lot better if I wasn't around. So this big tobacco man bought me a ticket and asked if I wanted to leave. I said yes quick as a bird can blink and caught the first thing smokin'. Where you from?"

"Santa Fe. I've just been around here for a month. I would leave if I could."

"But you can't so you ain't, right?" he adds. "I think I know what you sayin', home. Fresh off the train they had a job all ready for me showing folks around Plymouth Rock. Pay wasn't too bad and I didn't know that place from any other up here so I stayed."

"You're drunk," the girl says. "Don't talk so damned much. You don't know this man."

"He looks okay to me. Look like a righteous homeboy to me. Want some?" A half-empty bottle of muscatel. I take two long swallows and hand it back. He kills it.

"My name is Mack. I'm just here to get myself together."

"Problems, huh? I guess that ain't too much different from most people."

"No, except what I sometimes hear in my head makes me different."

"Yeah? Well, I got that under control. When I wants to dream about women I eats red beans and rice, and when I wants to dream about more women I eats catfish." The girl is out of his reach now, throwing her arms wildly, moving to the water, then away like a water-shy bird. She claps and begins a majorette strut when I start playing behind her. Ubangi brings up the rear, tapping out a rhythm on the case. We move through the wet sand over the dunes to the highway. The shots of wine have turned my legs to rubber.

A car occurs on the highway. It veers to the middle of the road and rocks to a stop directly ahead of us. A citizen cop with eyes wide open for couples wrestling in the cold or wandering hoboes.

"Out the way!" Ubangi warns as we march past.

The cop shoots back in reverse and steps out. He taps my arm. "Look, I don't know what the hell this is all about, but you'd better tell your friend there something about respect for the law." He stares at me for effect.

"Don't mind him. He's my cousin from Mississippi and just visiting for the weekend." He nods at this and stands his ground, watching Ubangi. His eyes show the intelligence of dead space.

"Come on, home," Ubangi calls. "Tell the dude to jump in the wind. We ain't hurtin' nothing."

"Cool it. He's the law." Ivone is strutting far up the road. I try again to smooth it over with the cop.

Ubangi shuffling back. "I feels like going upside some cop's head anyway. Just on a humble." The nervous man collars Ubangi and goes for his stick. "Unhand the threads, mutha-fucka!"

Before I can reach them, Ubangi has the stick and is bringing it down. The cop ducks, then slips and hustles around the car. Ivone screaming and running back.

"Go-ud damn, man! You made me miss." He glances from the ground to the dent in the roof of the car. I try to shove him against the car. Ivone screaming, "Not again, not again!"

The cop is climbing in the other side of the car, reaching for the intercom. Ubangi pushes me away and lunges into the car. I manage to trip him and he catches himself in the door. The cop crawls around the car in wide-eyed panic, finds his feet, sprints down the highway.

"Let's make it!"

Ivone is sitting against the car crying. "Not again, not again!" Leaning upon one another we shuffle away. At the final curb before town, the cop has slowed to a stagger and is shouting something. Three coming by sea. The niggers are coming! The niggers are coming!

Two

THE HEAT's off now. Any fool can see that. I must confess that we haven't lost much sleep over our little run-in with the cop, but we haven't expected things to be this cool. He must have buddies, friends in the right places. But none of the gray empty faces moving past the cafeteria have even bothered to check us out. From time to time we might catch that dull look that grazing cattle give to passing cars, a look with no spark of recognition.

"That cop ain't no fool," Ubangi says. "He don't want no parts of me."

"I didn't want to break this to you yesterday," I hear myself lying, "but I ran into the cop the day after you left for New Bedford. I told him you had slipped back to Mississippi on the first thing smoking. But I really shut him up when I asked him if he went back to get the shoe he left on the highway. He just walked away then. Anyway, it was probably a good idea for you to split and let things cool off. How was New Bedford?"

He snorts. "It wasn't much better, I'll tell you. I had to stay out of sight with some partners. The reason I left there in a hurry the first time was because I busted some cracker in the mouth. Come to find out he was a rich man's son."

"How did you get into that one?"

"I used to be a bouncer in this discotheque, you understand, and one night this drunk dude starts acting silly. We're at the bar and he claims I'm mocking him or something because he stutters. Well, I stutter too when I get excited, so the more he hollered at me the more I stuttered until I finally had to bop him one. Sugar Ray couldn't have done no better."

A jab stops inches from my nose. "You box, man?"

"A little," he says, his dukes still up. The cat might be a punch-drunk heavyweight on top of everything else: would-be con man, strong arm. Eventually it always comes down to a test even among the best of friends. Who's the better man? He can outcuss, outeat and outdrink me. But on a good day I could dance him silly and keep him off guard with lightning jabs and combinations. No contest. I duck a right cross he's thrown at three-quarter speed.

"You ain't bad," he says. "What's your best punch?"

"My best punch is whatever knocks a chump down." And he's again impressed by the left that shadows his face before he can think to snap his head back.

"You got to come on to Boston with me and be my bodyguard."

"Who will do the thinking then?"

"Who you think, nigga?" he says. "Me. Besides, I'm the one with the contacts up there and it's the contacts that do it, Mack. I know them all up there. Anybody will tell you if you ain't got contacts, you ain't got a pot to piss in."

Boston is clearly his idea. Before I've run into him, I've toyed with the idea of turning south to Philly or D.C. The weeks here have taught me the rhythms of this corner of the land and it's dragging me. Even the idea of New York has edged its way back into my mind. I can get work there again with a decent combo. But Boston? All I know about it is what a sailor once said: "Pilgrims and queers mostly." Prophets like that you don't take too seriously as you go along, though. He might have carried his bad luck with him.

Ubangi claims that I might have hidden talents and that the scramble for quick money might bring those talents out. A pimp, he says. He can tell by the way I carry myself, the smooth way I rap.

Everything is everything, all things are possible. What should I expect? Out of the cottonmouthed South he's run, believing the farthest point north the closest thing to heaven. Follow that thinking and the North Pole should be what's happening. At least I've known better than that. It hasn't been a picnic, drifting across this land of the free and funky. And stopping in this town, where most people have never heard of grits. I'm still not a lot of places I'd rather be: gigging at decent clubs, cutting an album once in a while. He knows all of this and he's started to play on it.

I look around. Except for the man in the back corner, we're still the only ones in the cafeteria. Ivone misses our little daily routine since she works afternoons at a drugstore. She doesn't hear our heavy plans to get on easy street and stay there. She knows better, and she must know that plotting anything with Ubangi is an act of faith. But with the wine and nothing else to do these dreary afternoons, it can be a good way of not letting this place get you down. We've been here two hours. It's always the same, the conversations drifting easily with the only dependable scenes, the angry winds or showers to blink at over coffee. Ubangi hasn't stopped talking for the past half-hour.

"Quiet as it's kept, Mack, rocks been the natural story of my life. Before I moved to New Bedford, there was that rock at Plymouth. I was there two years and only God knows why."

He snorts again. He will say liquor and women. The simple arithmetic of our need is the same.

"But it was pride, a stupid pride that kept me there. At least that's what I called it then. You see, I was the hippest guide they had. Folks would break their necks just to stand in line and let Ubangi show them the statues and the ship and jive. I'd give them a slick little speech about how the dudes beat the Indians out of their corn and said thank you by naming rivers and towns after them. I'd spice it up a little to keep them laughing and I'd cop me a whole bunch of tips in my pilgrim's hat. Talk about a boss rap! I'd have them going, but after a while it got to be something else. Rich women would practically toss their drawers at me, pointing out their motels and stuff to me. I stayed away from that, though. I done heard too many stories about cats hemmed up in them hotel rooms and the husband coming home early. Most of them didn't look like they could cut the mustard no way, so I played it cool, got some nice knit shirts out the deal, and found out where their daughters were. Want some more splo?"

We've sneaked some of Sledge's wine out in a Mason jar. He pours a heavy dose into his coffee, tastes it, smacks his lips. "This stuff gone make us rich," he says.

"Get on with the story."

"Yeah, yeah. Now, I was explaining to you about rocks. See, rocks was what I busted from dawn 'til dark in the stinking workhouse in North Carolina. Most folks don't know this, but the sun in North Carolina can get hot enough to fry your brain like an egg. That's what we had to work in! And if the sun didn't get you, them big gray walls would. They'd be loading you onto a truck to take you out on the roads and you'd look up and it seemed that the walls had just gone up a foot. Then you start to thinking of all the balling and fingerpopping you used to do and maybe a fine woman, too, who's probably with someone else at the time you be thinking about her and you standing there looking up at them walls and that sun and knowing all your cussin' and thinkin' and cryin' won't do a damned bit of good because that sun and them walls don't know the first thing about slacking up. Then if that wasn't bad enough, you'd get out there on a rock and bring your hammer down and boom! . . . What you thought was a rock is really a piece of steel. So you hit and you hit and you hit, but don't nothing happen. So you keep hittin' and it's just you and that rock until you think you can't go no more. Then it cracks a little here and a little there and you bust it wide open, going to town on it 'cause it seemed like one rock was about to end all your troubles. Plus everybody in that place was just as sad and mad as you. Course there were some a little bit luckier. I can remember just like it was yesterday when they made this ugly one-eyed nigga a special guard. We used to call him Goldie. They gave him a horse and a rifle and told him to follow us out to the road and shoot the first nigga who even thought of running away. If he let anybody get away, they'd kill him. There wasn't enough crackers to go around, so they got a few more like Goldie and turned them on us. Shit, they had us more scared than the peckerwoods."

"Those the kind you have to watch, man."

"Damn straight, Mack. I know. I done seen enough of them, in and out of prison. But those walls . . . those walls could make the average man trade in everything he ever knew except what he had learned about killing, lying and cheating. Even your kinfolks stop coming around after a while. People just don't want to have shit to do with you. Sometimes you see them driving along and you be working on the road and one of them calling himself nice might toss you some cigarettes. Man, we'd run after those cigarettes like crows after grass seed. But the man would just get a kick out of that and drive on. He just wanted to see us like animals out there because it made him feel better. After a while you stop trusting everything, even your buddies, 'cause you don't know who done turned sissie on you and who ain't. Naw, you don't stay yourself for long."

Grizzled old men of the sea have collected in front, hoping some lost tourist might take their pictures and slip them a five. A woman running a knock-kneed run to a waiting taxi, her opened coat ballooned by the wind, her child in her arms.

"How long were you in?"

"Three years. Someday I'll tell you about it. I killed a man once." He pulls a cigarette from my pack, looks off. "Yeah, when I gets on rocks and what they signify, I know what I'm talking about. There were rocks in our front yard when we used to live on the plantation. We would tote big bushels of them to the ditch that ran alongside the road. Sometimes we'd draw the white boys to our side of the plantation and put a few knots on their heads."

"Ubangi, while we're sitting here remembering things, let me tell you about the time I caught a rock on my back. It was during the Detroit riot and I was checking out some shoes when somebody who couldn't aim straight got me instead of the window.

"Did you get the shoes?"

"Uh-huh, a couple of pairs. Then there was the time I was running out of this chick's back door and her boyfriend was dead on my butt, poking at me with the longest knife in the world. I was making it when I fell over this rock and heard the fox scream. I thought it was all over, but I threw dirt in the cat's face. That stopped him, man, and I got three steps on him and he never got close again."

He laughs loudly. "I guess you got rocks in your head too. Come on, let's hat up."

It's a mistake to go to the docks. The day is deadest here, an anchor for the spirit. The water is ugly with the colors of oil and sludge, slapping against the dock timbers with the roll and heave of a fleshy woman's belly. Hurry sundown so we can meet Ivone in front of the drugstore where she'll be standing, hopping from one foot to the other, her hands pulling together the ends of her coat collar. Hair drawn and tangled stiff in the wind. Tonight I'll avoid the reruns of sitting in Ivone's living room sipping beer while she and Ubangi make whoopee in the kitchen. I'll go by Michelle's, surprise her. She won't speak to me any more. Lately when I call, it's a polite "hello," then nothing happens and I fall headlong into the silence. Nothing I can say brings her to life. Has a phantom back-door watcher who caught me easing out the other day told everything, about the rose in my lapel, my coolness? Has her mother threatened to take the silver from her spoon? I'll have to be very slick, though. A woman like that can have me tortured at high noon in front of the bridge club. The cops are pansies next to them. They're the real backbone of this town. They're the ones who can put idiots up to burning other witches. Yes, evil eyes and ears are everywhere and I'm a long way from Santa Fe.

The Peeping Toms should have keys to the city. Without them there can be no conversations, no dreams. To them I'm like the hitchhiker I picked up the other day. She shot up at the side of the road in men's clothing and a knit cap, like she had just pulled a shift on the docks. As soon as she was in the truck, she jabbed hard with questions.

"You at the base, I bet." She was a little like Big Tina, oversized titties, big bones.

"Just passing through, huh? I figured you for one of them pretty soldier boys from up there on the base. Well, when you get over there, pick out a cute one for me and tell him there's a lonely lady out here."

"I'll do that."

"Will you? Oh, you're just playing. I can tell. Look, you know you don't do me no favors by lying." Hawking, spitting out the window, she was a hard one. "That's me on the hill there. Been there alone for years and I'll tell you, it ain't much fun for a lady." All I saw were the trees, but I let her go on her way. Her heavy-thighed walk.

With the Sledges, Michelle and everyone I can talk with, I'm just another weirdo in this bleak place. All-seeing all-hearing gossips can feed off the scraps of our dreams during the winter, but I won't go through any changes.

The next day, High Priest of Country and Mojo Man playing tonk on the village green. A slip of sun has put hope in the afternoon. It is the day after the master plan has been run down. We are to sweep into Boston and rip off all the loose change, leave chumps dizzy and scratching their heads over their empty pockets. Which means, I've warned him, hitting on those just like us. He says it doesn't have to be that way.

I cut the deck, then show forty-nine after the deal. Two kings, a joker, a ten and a nine.

"Get away from me!" he shouts. "You a juju man for true!"

"Be cool, 'Bangi. Keep talking like that and someone might come along here to take you away to the funny farm. You're the one who dealt the cards. I just touched them."

"I'll try you one more game, man. If you hit again, I know a trick."

I talk him out of the next game. He has no bluff and his face is a mirror. I tonk out on him, leaving him with a pair of twos. "Where you buy these cards, Mack?"

"Cards are cards, man. You always trying to shift the blame. How are you going to make it in Boston and can't even play tonk right?"

"It ain't the same thing. People trust me, they talk to me. I'll just be my sweet self and the money will find me."

"Hell, leave it up to you and we'll be on street corners with tin cups. Just remember I want to try it my way first. With the horn."

In my horn case I find some smudged papers. No one has seen all of them, though Sassie Mae, an old girlfriend, has read one or two and told me I should be a poet. A piano player has read a blues I've written and has used it on slow nights. On these scraps of paper are souvenirs of past changes. It's an old habit. In junior high I composed short formal notes to God with a buddy who wanted to be a preacher. Who still sits on a porch in the small Ohio town trying to convince others there is nothing outside their beauty. A nut, they called him, fodder for the funny farm. The vacant eyes and the slowness of his words put them off, you see. The way he went around screaming at things, then my screaming too after I convinced myself that he was too far gone. The way I huddled close to the black angel with my name. Except for a few, most of the notes have been lost over the past three years.

His attention wanders as I read to him. The notes make no sense to him, no wonder, since each time I read them now, they make less sense to me. I cut it short and put them back in the case. "You going hunting with Old Man Sledge and me on Saturday?"

"Shoot yeah. Y'all just bring an extra gun along and I'll outshoot both of you. I wouldn't miss that for nothing. But here's something for you to check out." Then he whips out his wallet and finds an old yellow newspaper clipping. It is a picture of King in a crowd at a conference in Raleigh, North Carolina. An arrow points to a head behind him, Ubangi's.

"You? In a march?"

He nods sadly and shoves his hands deep in his pockets. My friend is full of surprises.

"You ain't the only one who done been around," he says.

"I see that."

"The thing wrong with a dude like you is that he figure he know it all just 'cause he done seen a few places. Ubangi been around too. What you learn doing all that traveling?"

"I learned a few things, more than I knew. As you can see, though, I still ain't making it too tough. I mean, nobody's calling me the greatest tenor player on the planet. They thought I was good in Kansas City, that's where I stopped first after leaving Santa Fe. I stayed there six months. My folks kept writing and asking why it was taking me so long to get to Columbus."

"What about when you got to Columbus?" he asks. "You hook up with your homeboy? The one who wanted you to play in his band?"

"By the time I had gotten there Boonie had disappeared. I must have turned that town upside down looking for him, but they just claimed he walked off the set one night and they never saw him again."

Just then a bad thought trips me up. I'm playing the opening notes for a grand ceremony. The air is thick with frankincense and myrrh. I hear voices, though I'm alone. Shadowshapes dance to a different rhythm and they whisper that my fingers move so slowly over the keys because I think so slowly. Work yourself free, they whisper fiercely.

Three

THE FIELDS are north of town, just off the highway. A dirt road leads us back a mile or so where Sledge claims the rabbits are as thick as flies on sugar. On the way out he's warned us about stepping on pheasants, since they've gotten so fat and bad in these fields that they don't run from hunters any more.

"Old man talks a lot of smack, don't he?" Ubangi says as we climb out of the car.

"He's been listening to you."

"Well, anyway, I'll take him at his word about all them rabbits running around out here. That means I'll be one shooting fool this morning."

"You probably shoot like you play cards, slow and sloppy. Don't let me catch you hitting one of the dogs, now."

Whistling among the low pines that stand at our backs, a nasty wind has slapped me awake. The brown fields stretch as far as I can see in one direction. I loosen my belt another notch as the heavy breakfast settles. I've overdone the grits bit so bad that Reba has started calling them my birthmark.

"Sledge, how did I let you get me out here in all this cold?"

"You act like I held a gun on you to get you out here," he says, dropping shells into his double-barrel. "All I said was you could start looking for another place to stay if you didn't come. Besides, forget the weather. As long as you think on the cold, it'll stay cold."

"I'll think on my woman, then."

"You won't hit a thing that way," he says, offering his Bull Durham to us. Ubangi bites off a chunk, but I pass.

The two hounds we've brought are sniffing at our guns and boots, playing ahead of us. We've awakened the fields with the sun. Sledge claims we'll stay until one of us reaches the limit of five rabbits. If our shooting matches our woofing, we should be out of here in an hour. But behind all the noise we've made readying ourselves, any animal with any sense would be miles away by now.

"Them's good young dogs," says Sledge, expecting my question. "Once they stop playing, they can run a poor rabbit to death. Heh-heh." In his element, this old man is king. Closely matching his movements, paying attention to his silence, we start through the field on either side of him. Ubangi has offered me wine as antifreeze, but that will dull me. I want to stay on top of things now that I'm here. Overhead are three crows calling shrilly, and once we settle down to take care of business, that's all that can be heard.

The dogs run far ahead, sniffing, backtracking in tight circles, then racing on. Though my eyes have begun to water and my fingers are growing numb in the thin gloves, the biggest problem will be the boots. They're two sizes too small. They've been the only pair he could borrow for me. I try it on my heels for a while, but that don't get it. Then I go flatfooted, spreading my weight over the length of my feet. That goes okay until we reach softer ground. This has the makings of a long, long day.

The first hound-cry is a moan that quickly dies out. "THERE!" Sledge's gun is up and his shoulder is knocked back twice. I've only heard one shot, the second coming so closely behind.

"I got him, son. Ain't no use in you aiming." He grins as he brings up the big rabbit. He guts it quickly, leaving its steaming insides for the dogs to sniff at.

Ubangi and I trade looks. This man doesn't play. It's easy to see that this first kill has his blood boiling. Ubangi takes another sip from the flask.

"Told y'all what them dogs can do," Sledge says, dropping more shells into his gun.

"I hear you talkin', old man."

Minutes later a man with yellow blotched skin has come out of nowhere to join us. Sledge says that the man's all right and mumbles something about hunter's courtesy, though everybody's not a hunter and every hunter doesn't pop out of nowhere looking like hard times.

"Who is this funny-time dude?" Ubangi whispers to me.

"Daniel Boone, my man."

"He looks old enough to be some kind of Daniel Boone."

The man has a strange toothless grin, like the widowers I've known as a child who've always lived alone in dark houses at the end of the block. You'd hear them along the alleys around midnight, waking the dogs. That kind. His laughter must ring the same bell with Ubangi because he's paying more attention to the stranger than he is to his hunting. The man is silent now as he moves familiarly through the shrubs. We learn later that he owns the land.

Then Sledge gets another rabbit with no trouble, and the

echo of his shot is fading when a dozen quail are flushed. With one shot I bring down two of them and, later, with a straight face, I will call that good shooting. Ubangi brings down one and the thin man manages to get one, too. The fields are alive now with the dogs squealing like children at a picnic, but there is no more shooting for another hour.

We stop at a clear fast creek and Ubangi brings out the brown bag that Mrs. Sledge has stuffed with ham sandwiches. Iron Man Sledge gets a sandwich, barely breaking stride as he moves on. "This ain't no time to stop, y'all. Y'all couldn't be no soldiers."

"I wouldn't want to be. Who said this was supposed to be war, anyway?"

He frowns and starts toward the creek. We let him go on. Strike while the gun is hot must be his motto. Catch the animals napping. These fields have changed him into a different man, spittle at the corners of his mouth. The way he looks now he might strong-arm a bear. But I have my blistered feet to worry about.

Ubangi picks on the quiet man. "Say, man, you Portuguese or what? You speaka English?"

He gets dark gums for his trouble. The man sips quickly from his thermos, then hurries off. We're surprised, though, to see Sledge back. He smiles strangely as Ubangi and I sip his wine from a Mason jar.

"Men, an idea just popped up on me down there by the creek. You wouldn't believe that it's got something to do with that wine y'all drinking now. A young fella called me from the air base a couple days ago and he asked me if I had some wine to sell. It kinda took me by surprise, since I ain't never thought too long about sellin' any of my wine. You see, one of his buddies had come over to pick up a table I made for a major over there. I gave him a little sip of the wine and he said it was some of the best stuff he had ever had. Better than the moonshine they brew down in Tennessee. Well, he must have told his buddy 'cause they claim they can sell it real good on base. I told him I'd think about it for a while. You men know I ain't a person to rush into anything too quick, especially at my age. I figure it be easy as hell. We could get a flat three dollars on each bottle."

"Mr. Sledge, how well do you know either of these dudes?"

"Not too well. Like I say, I just see the one when he come to pick up the table. We sat around and I listened real close to him. He seem like a man you can trust. Just don't trust the majors and colonels and stuff. All we have to do is deliver the bottles, pick up the money, and keep our mouths shut."

"What's the catch?" I ask him.

"Well, Mack, you know how the Army is set up to keep the men from having fun. So if it's known by too many folks that we're bringing in joy, they might put you in jail and throw away the key."

"That's a pretty big snag, Mr. Sledge."

"Y'all some choosy beggars," he says. He sees that neither of us has cared for that crack. He starts to speak again, but the sound of a shot rolls back from the field. The dogs have jumped something for the silent man.

"Just think about it," Sledge says as he trots off into the field.

We move in behind him and I see there's something which must be explained to Ubangi. "He was wounded pretty badly in the back during the First World War. They gave him a pat on the back. He stayed in for three years after that, and when he came out, they claimed they had no record of him even being in the Army. He had his uniform and gas mask but that still didn't do him any good. They said he could have bought them anywhere."

"Mack, you mean they ain't gave the old man nothin' for almost gettin' hisself killed? Shit, I would have done a job on them suckers."

"Which one, though?" I ask.

"I don't know, but somebody would pay."

When we pull even with Sledge and the phantom, a pheasant takes off in front of Ubangi. The phantom has seen it too, and their guns go off together.

"Leave it alone," the man says as Ubangi rushes up to the fallen bird. "That's my bird."

"Your bird? You ain't hit nothin' but air, old-timer." Ubangi straightens up.

"No sense in arguing," I offer. "Cut it in half."

"I ain't cuttin' nothing, Mack!"

They stand facing each other, their guns up, though they don't seem to be aware of them. Would they shoot one another over the bird whose blood is threading down its wings? Sledge and I trade looks. Then he moves over to whisper something to the man, who doesn't take his eyes off Ubangi's.

"Cool it, Ubangi. Let the sorry dude have the bird. It's probably so loaded with buckshot it ain't worth it."

He chuckles and kicks the bird toward the man. The man looks uncertainly at me and Sledge, then picks it up.

After that, it's all downhill. I try to get Ubangi talking about the wine-running, and he perks up enough to tell me how he's already had the base cased for something like that.

"But I don't know if I'll help Sledge or not. I mean, he called us beggars and just took up for that goofy dude . . ."

Things really fall apart when all of us miss a rabbit breaking toward the thick woods bordering the field. Ubangi has gotten the first and last shot, and cursing old and bitter hunters, throws a handful of shells among the trees.

. . .

We get over in no time. Our contact's name is Corporal Eddie Lidge. "Call me Fastback for short," he said the day I went over to finalize the operation. The brothers were playing poker and Lidge was winning righteously, letting the world know it. Then he noticed me, knew me to be the runner of joy. His quick bowlegged walk. He pumped my hand and introduced me around.

The next day we backed the truck to a warehouse, and with three soldiers, quickly unloaded a dozen bottles of wine stashed among the furniture. The pieces of furniture would go to the homes of officers. Myers, Fastback's right-hand man, hummed like a man with a new pair of shoes and a pocketful of money. They told us to come back Friday night for the dance and celebrate with them.

Everybody and his mama comes over for the Friday night dances. The saditty townfolks suffer through drive-in movies or reruns in their musty living rooms. Their virgin daughters toss in their early sleep and priests yawn over their opened scriptures. In September, the tourists take everything, leaving these timid souls to sweep up and sit in the front windows of their souvenir shops and wonder about the long winter ahead. Now they are where they are supposed to be.

On the stand are Cool Eddie and the Icemen. They have ambitions to be bad in their black see-through shirts and white bell-bottoms. Booker, the trumpet player, standing off to the side, appearing lost. He pops his fingers and waves to one of the dancers. We've been introduced earlier and he's asked me to bring my horn with me. I'll have to take him up on it sometime. Though the sax man can't play a lick, he can honk up a good breeze. *Ahhboo, ahhboo, ahhboo.* Eyes closed, bent forward from the waist and shaking his knees. From the old school he is. All his solos are the same, but nobody seems to care, too busy balling. What moves you is good. Even the white boys get into the act, dusting off last year's dances.

"Mack, why you just sitting here by yourself grinning?" It's Myers, in shades as usual. Generally called "the Major," I'm told, because he acts and talks like one. Too bad he's in the wrong Army. We haven't hit it off too well, but we can speak.

"What's happening, Myers?"

"You got it, slick. Where's that wild Ubangi?"

"He's casing things in Boston. We'll be going up there next week."

"You going to cut loose this gravy train you got down here?"

"It can't last forever," I tell him.

"I know what you mean, slick, and this ain't soul town either. I got four mo' months in this hole and I'll be long gone. But look here, if you gone move on these women you better hurry up and make your move now, 'cause the brothers on these bitches like white on rice."

Myers ain't jiving. The WAC's and the young chicks from town are getting all the action they've come for. They're enjoying it, taking their time about choosing. It's still early. A big muscular WAC has been giving me the eye. I've seen her around before. She's a sergeant or something, and the first day we met her in the commissary she wanted to talk about the places she's been. Ubangi's laughed his ass off, spreading his lies later in the barracks. ("Mack's old lady got a heavier beard than he got, y'all . . .") I've tried to avoid her ever since.

Myers is restless. Near us dances an MP with a short woman, slowgrinding. Her fingers running up and down the back of his neck. Myers guzzles his beer and belches, staring. "I'll check you later." He's mentioned that a crap game is in the john where the smoke is thick enough to choke a mule. But I won't be dropping any money there. We're leaving in a week. I'll take the reefer and the liquor they offer, but they won't see my money tonight.

Then Fastback slides up to the table and hands me a fresh drink. He has a big one of his own. Sledge certainly has this place pegged. Without alcohol, the entire base would be A.W.O.L. They'd go out of their minds in this prison, generals included.

"Mack, I been thinking. After I get out, I might stay here and open me up an American Legion or something. It couldn't miss. I mean folks around here ain't used to good times."

"You right, Fast. But you need money to make money."

"The way you selling that old man's wine, you don't have to worry long. I got a dozen more orders for you. I dropped a little on the pattie dudes and they done gone crazy over the stuff. We'll need more bottles next week."

I nod. Things are looking better than ever. Maybe Myers is right. Why run when you're on top? It's something to think over. The band has gone into a James Brown number, matching the original tune blow for blow. A clown does the splits for his woman. Fastback gets into the action, dancing behind the woman, while the Scotch works its spell on my head. I won't even try to join the action.

Jupiter Sims, first contact and guide, bebops into the room. He's laid out in a dazzling dashiki with a huge tiki around his neck. His fox is Afroed back and very fine. She can't be more than seventeen. Jupiter has a good eye, no doubt about it. Old "buddies" who've put him down for sweeping streets troop over to slap him on the back, and grin at the fox. That's how tight things are among them. "Hey, Jup," they go, "what you doing for yourself? And Jup, my man, why don't you introduce me to this fine tender young thing?" After a while he gets tired of that mess and just waves to them.

"I hear you making big money over here," he says to me. "I don't see you playing on the beach no more."

"I ain't doing that much. A little change of pace helps the soul, you know."

"Uh-huh. Mack, this is Rita. Rita, meet Mack." She turns, her eyes wide and lips parted right out of the last flick she's seen. But she's a sweet girl and we hit it off right away. Later Jupiter and I slip to the bar.

"You like them young and ripe, don't you?" I ask.

His eyes come alive. "You goddam right I like them young. What's wrong with it? I'll let everybody know that young womens is my weakness. Every man got a weakness and young pretty girls is mine. Now, Mack, we been friends so far, so don't go messing up by dipping too much in my business."

"I didn't mean no harm and I'm sorry if it came out the wrong way."

"No harm done then," he says, still salty. "I expected you to be up there on the stand tonight."

"I might get up there later, after things get warmed up a little . . ."

"You look like you warmed up now," he says. "What you been drinking?"

He orders me another drink, and when I get back to my table, the big WAC is sitting there as if nothing's happened. "Hi" comes her throaty greeting. Then she asks me to dance and I try to keep space between, knowing what the cats will say later. She's a lot stronger than I've thought.

"You know, I've missed you," she says. "I thought that you and your friend would be gone by now."

"Gone where?" I ask, wondering at the blond streak in her hair.

"Oh, just gone. This place seems a little slow for you. It's not doing your health much good either. I think what you need is a woman around to cook you a good meal every day . . ."

But by the music's end I've broken the clinch and escaped to the john.

I wait there until I'm certain I've shaken Sergeant Wilma Johnson off my trail. Then I ease out and get up on the stand. It's best I play and stay out of trouble. The group is loose and there is no strain among them when I start to blow. We jam hard the rest of the night, a natural ball. I couldn't know that it would be the last time for a long time that I'd feel so contented playing. Nor could I know Ubangi and I would be leaving in a hurry three nights later because we'd gotten sloppy. One of these new soldiers Fastback has brought into the fold will turn out to be a company man and he will go to a general and blow the whistle on all of us. No, I could not know so much, so I play until the dancers can't dance any more.

Four

FIVE NIGHTS ago we landed at the Hotel Deluxe. By the name, a flophouse. When we walked in, the desk clerk put down his girlie magazine and scratched his stubble. We were obvious murderers who had split from Harlem in the stolen car belching smoke out front. He pulled our coats to the fact that he was used to sudden invasions in the night, that we could trust him. Then he gave us a large room on the second floor, near the fire escape.

We had rushed out of Falmouth as the sun died. Word had leaked and the finger had been put on us. Fastback tearing into the commissary: "The MP's on their way, man. Y'all better hat up!" We hustled out to the truck and roared past the gate where one of the sentries had just picked up the phone. Five minutes was all we needed to pack and explain to Reba Sledge, who, though slightly surprised, fixed us a bag of sandwiches at Dupree's command, five minutes in which the MP's could contact the village patrol and send them tripping to Ivone's to ambush us. "Whiskey peddlers and dope dealers," they put over the wire. In the old Ford, warmed up and loaned by the hip Sledge, we by-passed Ivone's. They spotted us near the edge of town, but we lost them at a fork, made the bridge, then really opened up. Not for long, though. The last five miles of the trip were hell and, wheezing, the car quit for good in front of the hotel. Ubangi has called that a sign.

The sign has only worked for the hotel, since Boston has turned us a cold, cold cheek. In the past few days I've shaken a dozen hands in employment offices and watched a dozen faces play sad. No work, mister. It's bad all over. As if I'm to understand that, along with all the other men in line, most of them with large families to support. Hospitals, post offices, pretentious restaurants—all of them in the same sad shape, full of help and not hiring. By night, horn in hand, I've made the rounds of the bars, the ones with the classic organ-sax-guitar and drum combos pushing noise on the night. Most of them have simply made no room for me. Others have allowed me one set on the stand, then forgotten to invite me back. Now I leave the horn in the room, sit quietly at the bars and consider other cities.

It is the fifth day and I'm following a lead on a dishwashing job at a downtown cafeteria. In these streets, these streets of ancient dirt, Ubangi is somewhere peddling surplus clothes that he's copped from a warehouse. He's looking over his shoulder and telling a chump that he's ripped the vines from Filene's, but keep it under your hat, my man, because there's a lot more coming and I know I can do you some good. He's come in each day with a thick roll of bills that he's counted out in front of me. ("You got to see the light one of these days, Mack. Every fool do. If they don't like the way you blow, make a little money with me and buy your own club. You ain't got to kiss their ass, let them do some kissing. See where I'm coming from?")

I cross the wet street and push into the large cafeteria, squeezing my way to the back. It's the lunch hour and the place is packed with the secretaries, the clerks, the junior salesmen. In a small office a red-haired man looks busy at a desk. He pumps my hand, then shoves some papers at me.

"Fill these out," comes the hillbilly whine. "You ever wash dishes before?"

"Yes, I have."

"Good. We get a lot of boys in here who don't know the first thing about working in the kitchen and halfway scared to get their hands wet. Then we have to let them go, just likat." He hardly looks at me. Out the window, over my head, at the door. Maybe it's something he's seen career bosses do. He looks more like the type that operates a rig between St. Louis and Pittsburgh. A naked woman tattooed on the back of his hand: "Rose." He's been ready for me, all the same.

"Can you start now?" he asks. I tell him I can and he smiles up from the papers. "Okay, I'll take you to the kitchen to meet Good. He'll fix you up. We got an extra-heavy crowd today, so you can start at two o'clock. That'll give you plenty of time to meet most of the crew. We've got a good crew here, Mack. You'll like 'em. By the way, my name is Sykes, Harvey Sykes, and next week you'll start on the night shift if things work out okay today."

He introduces me to his man, Good, a nervous scrambler with a thin mustache and shined shoes. Good is wiping his hands on his dirty apron as he moves up to welcome me, his broad grin more for Sykes than for me.

"What's to it, Cool Breeze?" he asks, relaxing considerably after Sykes has left. "You here to scuffle fo' a piece of change too?"

"I'm taking what I can get right now."

His look is a knowing one, the heavy look thieves might

trade on the street. He tells me I can call him Crackerjack, since everyone else does, and he shows me around, explains how dishes are to be stacked.

"You learn fast, Cool Breeze. We have you up front in no time." I meet a scar-faced man called Spoon, a ripe plum of a woman named Bettie, and a red-eyed dude who answers evilly to the name of Fuckup. All of them nod silently, except the woman, who claims I look like Luke.

"Luke was a no-good nigga who used to work here," Crackerjack explains. "One night he ran off with a whole truckload of T-bone steaks and we ain't seen hide nor hair of that nigga since. We don't need them kind around here, you know, though Luke didn't never seem to mean nobody no harm. I'm sho you ain't like him, but y'all do kinda favor 'bout the nose and mouth."

All afternoon the kitchen is a sweatshop with short breaks out to start a cigarette or sip cans of beer that Crackerjack has sneaked in from the cooler. Bettie operates a portable from where she's scraping carrots, moving her head with the music. From time to time she's shown me a righteous smile. I weigh my chances of getting next to her, but she knocks a hole in all that, talking endlessly of her men during breaks.

"What's a woman to do? I mean, really? You see, I'm in love with two men. One of them is already married and promises me he will leave his wife if I just say the word and the other one, the other one used to go with my best friend. You can just imagine how I'll stand with her when she finds out."

So much jive, her rattling off like that. She'd probably like my head as number three in her little collection. She's Sassie Mae, my ex-foxy Columbus woman, without the legs and dimples. Older, maybe. I soak up her talk only to stay away from Crackerjack's prying questions, but he corners me during the last hour before quitting time.

"You're a musician, huh? You got to check out those Sunday sessions at the Tiajuana Lounge, jim. They jam up a storm. I know all them cats over there too."

Immediately I go to work on him, asking him about the music scene, pumping him for leads. He promises that he can get me into solid work with no trouble. He's cocky as a champ, but something about his smoothness, his know-everybody talk bothers me. He's too friendly. The type whose hands are always going for your pocket, or your woman.

"I haven't heard you play, but that ain't no big thing. I can recognize a cat with soul by just talking to him a little while. But what kind of bag you in—Yardbird, Pres?"

My sound has been described many ways. The Eldorado drive of Stanley Turrentine, the swift glad comedy of Sonny Rollins, the steady quest of Coltrane. Yes, I've been all those attitudes, but I wonder if Crackerjack knows them. "I play me as much as possible."

"Well, whatever, you just give me a couple of days and I'll have you out there on front street doing your own thing. And, look here, you'll have to come over to the crib sometime and have dinner with us. My old lady invented cooking, jim."

"I can dig it," I tell him, "because I invented eating."

We go our separate ways: he to a pro basketball game that he has twenty-five dollars riding on; I to the hotel. On the way I try to order it all in my mind, this starting everything all over again, the buddies you see through early, the ones you know only after it's too late, the whole kiss-ass thing with club managers to stay on a gig. The questions of club owners: "Are you a junkie or some kind of freak?" Everybody has his weaknesses, but the musician's freezes him out of funky clubs where the cops and Italians have their stubby fingers. This weird map of respectability.

When I enter the lobby of the hotel, the clerk puts down a

new stag magazine and hands me a note from my box. Ubangi wants me to meet him at the bar across the street. Something good is up. Come clean, he says. I wash up, splash on some of his cologne, and make myself ready for anything. A job at a big club? A studio set? The clerk is smiling as I rush out. He's read the note, of course. There's nothing you can keep from him.

Ubangi is entertaining two women at a small table. He has them taking turns giggling on each other's shoulders. They're drinking beers and are beyond the noise in the crowded bar.

"What you know good, Mack?" he says. "Give me some of that good skin, yeah, and meet my friends, Phyllis and Yvette." The one named Phyllis giggles hello, while Yvette is a little slower about it. She wears a red wig which has cost her a good amount of money. Phyllis seems like a new arrival to the big city.

"I'm showing these women a bad watch, man, baad! But as bad as it is, it can't begin to match their beauty."

Ignoring this, Phyllis gives the watch to Yvette, who tries it on, holding her arm up to let the dim light bounce off the cut glass. "It's beautiful, child," Yvette says to Phyllis. "I can't understand how come he only want ten dollars for it." She hands it back to Ubangi, searching both our faces for clues beyond the obvious: he's pushing them a cheap watch in a velvetlike box. He probably bought it for three dollars from a costume jewelry warehouse.

"Look, I been out there all day selling these watches for thirty dollars apiece. But that ain't nothing in my book because I consider it a pleasure just to have you two fine foxes take a little time out to rap with me."

Yvette ignores the gaming. "When you steal these?"

"I was lying when I said I stole them. You see, I run me a jewelry store not too far from here. Sometimes it's hard to tell some black folks that 'cause they don't want to believe no black man can own a jewelry store and they afraid if they buy from his store they'll make him rich. So I front like this to keep everybody happy."

Yvette and Phyllis trade looks. "Excuse us for a minute," Phyllis says before they head for the back.

"Mack, Phyllis is mine," Ubangi says, his eyes following the taller woman. Yvette, in white boots, is shorter, fuller. My type. I don't argue with him.

"I just bumped into them on the bus coming over here from Grove Hall. Just thought I'd mix a little business with pleasure, heh-heh. Where you been all day?"

"Washing dishes at a cafeteria downtown . . ."

He frowns. "That ain't for you. You're too smart for that mess."

When they come back, Phyllis announces that she will buy the watch. Ubangi quickly takes her money and buys another round, as a far-out sign of good faith, as celebration. He tells Phyllis how happy she will be with the watch, that he guarantees all merchandise. Then he leans closer and begins to whisper things that get her laughing again. Edging closer to Yvette, I try to make conversation, but the sudden surprise of her thighs and the way she wets her lips let me know that time isn't to be wasted on the small talk. When I look up again, Ubangi and Phyllis have vanished, no fronts, no lies, just vanished in a hurry. I search too for that magic word, but Yvette takes my hand and tells me that I must walk her home.

Her place is very close, a small apartment where she lives alone. She relaxes me, fixes drinks and turns on the Temptations. I notice her high-school prom picture, four years old, on a coffee table. Her last moment of glory, she has said.

"Who's the dude grinning with his arm around you?"

"My boyfriend. We still see each other a lot, but it isn't like it used to be. We was supposed to get married after we both had worked a year and saved a little. One thing led to another and we still ain't married yet."

While we knock out our drinks she wants to hear about my life, but all I could do would be to complain. It would drag both of us when we don't need that now. She pushes me away from her and smiles, her tongue playing at the corner of her mouth. "You sho in a hurry, ain't you?" she says. Turning out the single light, she comments on my grin, my sweaty palms.

Her nervous snicker. Then I can hear her breathing, the fall of her skirt, and later the purr of her flesh on the sheets. Silently, our crazy games played out, we are ready for the wild, wild ride in the night.

The next morning I lie alone in her bed, enjoying the thought that it's Saturday and I'm not due again at the cafeteria until Monday evening. I remember waking briefly to the hard suns of Yvette's eyes and her whisper, "You must be hungry," and her closing the door. Now I can hear a key in the door and I freeze. It's her boyfriend! I look around for a weapon. But she steps in with an armful of groceries.

"Where have you been?" I calmly ask.

"Where do you think? I just robbed the corner grocery store for you. We're having ham and eggs this morning, baby." Her face, though it will never shine out from the cover of a magazine, is fresh and cool and necessary this morning. Her white boots, her imitation-leather white coat, the long wig.

We have little that will go beyond the half-opened blinds and we don't even try to lie about that. I turn on the radio and watch her move around the small kitchen, wanting her again, knowing that after this day we will go our separate ways and leave last night's fun as an isolated track in our memory.

"Can you spend the day here?" she asks over the music from the radio.

"I got until Monday, Yvette. I ain't in a hurry to get anywhere else."

The phone rings as she hands me a small glass of juice. She talks low, giving herself away. Her boyfriend, no doubt. On time. He pushes hard on the other end, asking probably why she didn't answer the phone last night. She lies smoothly without a hitch.

"What did all that mean?" I ask her after she's hung up the phone.

"It means that he wants to drop by about four. I told him I'd call him back because I might go shopping with Phyllis."

"In that case, it sounds like he'll be a little early. I guess we'll have to take a raincheck on this afternoon."

"But I don't want you to go. I can tell him I don't feel well or something."

"And have me get it walking out the front door? Uh-uh."

She doesn't push it. I will return to her, maybe, but we will always keep the blinds half-drawn and our ride together will always be overplayed and reserved for off-nights.

Ubangi has returned much earlier. He doesn't want to talk about Phyllis except to say how country she is and how he might drop future trinkets on her. It must have gone badly for him. I thank him for the set-up with Yvette.

"I ain't had nothing to do with it," he says. "You did it all by yourself."

"Something must have happened with Phyllis."

"Her roommate blocked it, man. She was crying about something, then while Phyllis was trying to calm her down and maybe send her off, some food in the stove started burning and smoked up the whole damned place. You know how I felt." He's standing in front of a mirror, watching his face.

"There's always tomorrow. Isn't that what you always tell me? You have nothing to worry about. Anybody could see you had her mind messed up. But why aren't you out on the streets today?"

"I'm taking a break," he says, frowning.

"I didn't know hustlers got days off."

"I'm going to count my money, smartass. Besides, there's a lot of things you don't know. And you almost blew last night, sitting up there grinning at the bitches like you ain't got no cool. If she hadn't been hungrier for action than you was, you'd still be sitting there."

This must be his way of smoothing it over, accounting for my good luck and fun, dummy though I am.

"And talking about me, you ain't touched your horn since we've been up here. Shoot, these niggas up here is good too, Mack. I done heard them. You better get back on it. I'm going to see a contact in a few minutes. He might be able to do something for you. I don't want to get a job for you and have you turn up shaky."

"You know damned well why I haven't had time to play."

"Ain't nobody asked you to get out there like a fool, walking up and down the streets for chump change. I've told you to come on in with me. You can rap smooth when you want to."

He's right. I've touched the horn only once since we've been up here. After he leaves I try it out, going strong until the banging on the walls, the screaming from the other rooms, become too much. Only after the racket dies out can I hear the knocking at the door. Looking like an *Ebony* fashion model, Wendell breezes in. He's been over before to snoop, in a neighborly way. He lives alone across the hall and he has a steady stream of visitors—all men. Late nights you can hear loud music and laughter.

"Don't let those idiots get to you," he says, dropping into a chair, crossing his legs. "Go ahead and play. You're an artist and your horn sounds groovy to me."

He's sat in the same chair before, flicking his cigarette ash as he does now. That time we talked mostly about his acting jobs, our sad isolations. "Everyone has a reason for being in this hotel. I've told you mine. There's simply no work worth my time and there's this one clown who has the monopoly on Othello. It gets so boring, Mack, telling it so much. Anyway, what's your reason?"

"I'm used to this hotel, this room, man. I've been here before. I'm a musician looking for work."

"That's what people get for calling themselves artists! Flophouses and back rooms with no heat. I haven't heard you play on a stand or anything, but you must believe in yourself to take this mess. A friend of mine has suggested that I and others like us, Mack, get rich first and then play around with music or drama."

He has asked about Ubangi and I've told him that he's a salesman. "I don't think he likes me."

"Why do you say that?"

"He just doesn't like me, I can tell."

Once Ubangi walked in while Wendell was sitting there and he woofed about my moving out soon. "Move in with your fag friend if you go that way, but don't bring him over here." He pretends to vomit at the sight of Wendell. The feeling has grown mutual in the five days, though. Wendell stiffening, hissing like a cornered cat when Ubangi passes. He looks relaxed now.

"If you get tired of washing dishes, you can always work construction, you know. I've had many good friends to try it and they say the work is so damned hard, but the pay is outasight. I mean, you're big enough to handle work like that. Me? I'm still waiting tables. I got myself an audition coming up Monday, though. It's one of those little black theaters springing up all over the ghetto. I doubt if the part will be interesting, but it will be something." He jumps up when he hears the phone.

"Well, I just wanted to let you know that little news. I know what you're going through. I'll see you around."

Is it the hotel that does it? Or have all of us brought our weird ways with us? I watch other roomers slide along the walls to their rooms: bleary-eyed old men with aristocratic voices, young hooked women of fading beauty. They say very little to me and I to them. Nothing missed either way. Yet it's these silent ones who are banging away like crazy as I try to play. I stop again, my mind zooming to Yvette, her prom picture.

About now, Yvette's boyfriend will be bursting into her room, looking around, giving her the third degree. With her straight face and laughing eyes, she is lying too. Suddenly I smell the smell of her, ride the rise and fall of her smooth young belly. All the stupid commotion has stopped and I go back to the horn, shooting flat tones into the drab afternoon.

Crackerjack lives on a quiet street where big cars are parked and children play in and out of cool shadows. Yesterday he called to invite me over for dinner. He lets me into his overheated living room where organ–tenor sax music is booming out. The smell of chitterlings has snagged on my brain as he shows me around the apartment. The clear plastic covering on the sofa, the large picture of swans above it, the blond color TV set.

"Nice pad you got here, C. J."

"Ain't no big thing. Come on back here and meet the people." His wife, Bea, and their ten-year-old son smile warmly at me, and together the three of them give a picture of tight-lipped bliss. Crackerjack and I spend most of the time before dinner talking about the job. My hopes are high, however, that his contacts have done me some good.

"Sykes can be tough on you when he want to, but he ain't no really mean peckerwood like some I've worked for. Every half-hour or so he'll come sneaking around, making like he joking and playing when all the time he be checking your work. I just keep busy while he stands there making corny jokes. Then after he leaves, I work my butt off for ten minutes before I slack up to bullshit a little. That's the way I been making it down there for three years. Thad, bring us some more beers."

His son mechanically obeys, sprinting from a side room to the kitchen, opening the beers and bringing them in. He hasn't cracked a smile since the introductions. No sign of spirit. Crackerjack has caught me watching him.

"He's just ten and he's a lot hipper than I was at ten. I'm hipping him young too. Look at him. When I told him you were a musician, he almost floated out the room. See, I got him this trumpet for his birthday and he's been taking these lessons and everything. But I think he's going to be more the business type like me. Hey, Thad, bring your horn out."

"What about those contacts, C. J.?" I ask.

"Everything's cool. Just drop over to the Black Knight next Thursday night and talk to the organ player. He will be expecting you."

"That sounds good to me."

"My man's the best there is too, Mack. He can play the way-out jazz and the gutbucket stuff, so don't let me hear you woofing no more about lame Boston niggas."

His son has whipped out the trumpet, but he has a chance to blow only a couple of notes before Bea calls us to dinner. "He's going to be a bad one, one of these days. A new Clifford

Brown or Diz. Trumpet player or whatever, he'll be bad, just like his daddy."

Dinner is taken care of in record time. Chitterlings, spaghetti, cornbread and Kool-Aid. My mind is on the gig all the while. The first in months. How sweet the thought of it! I can hear the steady, loud applause, the heads working when we really get down, the feet tapping out the pulse when I soar out on a string of fresh runs, returning to find them still with me. Behind me musicians who aren't afraid of themselves and those sounds they've heard and locked away inside.

Crackerjack and his wife are laughing over a report on the latest conversation with his brother, a schoolteacher. He puts on airs, drives a smaller car. He has no style and doesn't know anything about cutting corners. Thad isn't laughing. Though he's tried to take up for his uncle, he's too busy feeding his face. Something strange about him. Though I don't pretend to be anyone's ace family man, my rule has been that the kids can tell you quickest about the health of the home. Thad seems a flower, thirsty for sunlight—life. Before I leave, I've promised to play duets with him on one of my free afternoons. He smiles and I wonder about future sons. My own. What messages will I have for them?

Giving me a lift home, C. J. shows off the speed of his car. Then he turns down a side street and tells me he's going to put me into something.

"I'm sort of in a hurry, C. J. . . . . Slide it on me next time."

"It'll just take a minute. She got some outasight friends, Mack. You ought to see them. If she didn't have my nose open already, I could sure go for one of her friends . . ."

"She who?"

"Marie" is all he says, zooming down narrow streets I don't even recognize. Whoever Marie is, she makes Crackerjack move in a hurry.

When we finally stop, he leads me to a classy apartment building. Explains. Marie is a divorcee he's been seeing off and on for over a year, a woman who knows what she can or cannot expect from men and gives accordingly.

"I met her at the tracks. She's a sucker for the horses like me. The day I met her she was winning big. I said to myself, 'C. J., you got to get next to her.' Plus, she looks good. She been a good bet ever since, heh-heh."

No one returns the ringing. He tries again, but nothing comes. "She probably over at Billie's. I'll call her later and set up something for us."

"Thanks, C. J., but I got a handful now," I lie.

"Just trying to help. One more won't hurt. When I see a good man, I try to help him out, turn him onto things. I can help a good man like a good man can help me."

"What does that mean?"

"Relax, man. I ain't tryin' to hustle you."

As we speed along, I give more thought to the Black Knight gig. What does he expect in return? Beware the grinning backslapper. Have I been pulled into something uncool? The excuse for his wife when he wants to see his Maries more than usual? I'll cool him on that real quick. I was fired once from a steel mill for storing some tools in a locker as a favor to a buddy. When our foreman searched the lockers and found the tools—stolen tools, he said—my buddy kept quiet. I was sent walking from a club gig when the manager's girlfriend latched onto me as I was leaving the place. Hysterical, she said that her man was going to kill her. When the manager caught up with her, she was still pleading with me and I was trying to save my coatsleeve. He decided not to kill her and fired me instead. So I've learned to accept few promises and fewer favors. My life has been a history of holding the bag.

Five

STEEL GIRDERS reach three stories for the sky. Two floors on the building have already been completed and that's where most of the brothers are now, cleaning up, setting up, cutting up. I'm told that it will be an office building with no windows, just peepholes to keep an eye on the natives. Here in the middle of their turf. Battalions of blond secretaries will be bused in and men handcuffed to attaché cases will be shot through the tubes that run clear to their front doors in Never-Nigger Land. If I didn't need the job so bad, I'd help burn it down. Or throw a brick. Or at least picket, like the welfare mother and the nationalist brother behind me. As it has turned out, I didn't look them in their eyes when I came an hour ago. Shame, their eyes must have warned. Is a steak more important than your dignity? When you're down to peanut butter and crackers, dignity is an old souvenir you hock and feel no pain. They watch me even now, hoping I will get hip and break from the little fire, the brooding Puerto Rican, the two Italians and the two brothers who rap to kill the cold.

The idea has been Wendell's more than mine. Later this

morning he'll be auditioning for a part in a play he doesn't like
and he will get the job because he has told me he will. But
then you'd never catch him wearing anybody's hard hat.
We've agreed that I am in bad shape. At least until Thursday
night when I'll play with C. J.'s friends. We've agreed too that
I'm not above robbing or killing to keep from starving. Like
any man. But consider the straight things first. No more
sudbusting in the cafeteria. That must end. The post office is
two weeks of changes just getting hired and the hospitals
aren't hiring now. So I hang around construction sites.
Wendell's friends have told him that construction work will be
about the best and quickest money around for me. My running
buddy Ubangi and his partners have said it's for chumps with
no mind. None of them has told me that it's a risk getting on,
especially in the dead of winter when work is slowest and the
crews are smallest. The work whistle has blown ten minutes
ago and still I'm sitting with no promise of anything. Nothing
except off-the-wall conversation and all the morning air I can
swallow.

"Fire more important, Swine," says the skinny man. "If they
wasn't no fire, you'd be eating meat raw like white folks do
and if they wasn't no fire, you'd be freezing your narrow ass off
right now. And don't try to tell me no different."

The brother called Swine scratches his double chin and
laughs. "My mama told me a long time ago not to ever try to
tell a fool anything. But all this time I done figured you just
half a fool, King. And I say that to say that you might half
understand what I'm saying. If there wasn't no water, you
woulda dried up in your mama's belly and not be here to argue
about which is more important."

"Don't talk about my mama! I don't play that shit."

"Shut up, fool! Ain't nobody studyin' you or your mama

neither. If a bird had your brains, he'd fly backwards, I swear."

King warms his rusty-dusty hands over the fire, then passes on a skin magazine that the Italians have been grinning over. "You got your nerve talking about somebody being dumb when you about as heavy as one of the snowflakes yonder . . ."

Across the street the snow sticks to trash piled high in cans squatting at the curb. Damn all of it. Wendell, the cold, my empty pockets, the hard can I'm sitting on and now the snow. Damn it all. Every musician in this town can't be starving. And I know I'm bad. Quiet as it's kept, I know I'm about the baddest around. I know I'm bad. Even if nobody else knows.

Suddenly the foreman like an ugly hope over us. He looks directly at each of us. Again. His mouth working to shoot out tobacco juice and his eyes settling on the Italians.

"You two, follow me!" And off they go into the bottom floor.

"Damn, whitey a bitch, ain't he? He knew who he was gone pick when he first got over here. Always looking out for number one. More bloods gone have to think that way more often."

"When we get something," says King. "Them's that got keep on gettin'!"

Bent into the wind, junkies nod past. There have been other winds and darker days when I have whistled tunes over the growling in my belly. Columbus, Ohio, for example. Columbus looked a lot like Kansas City to me. Settled and closed. Columbus, where bloods loved their old Buicks and where I hung out afternoons in a pool hall and talked trash and watched foundry workers make it to the liquor store after work. A pimp town because of the popcorn pimps standing on corners going hungry. Then a job in a foundry came my way and I sweated and settled and wondered if I would ever get away. Days I worked alongside dirty-haired hillbillies who left Kentucky to die in the shadow of factories. Nights I looked for work playing my horn.

Two months into town and then came the night I really got going. The eagle had swooped that day and Cecil, a skinny dude with a beard who worked the same shift with me, pulled my coat to the Blue Gardenia Club.

"Bring your ax down tonight, and like, sit in with us. Sometimes we get some sessions with cats coming up and sitting in. But then again we get a lot of cats who come on like a hurricane and go out pooting. You never know." So I bought a box of reeds, a new pair of bell-bottoms and called myself ready.

After two numbers the house was on fire. Drunks paid attention and the waitresses stopped waiting. The best man on the stand was Snooky, the organist, just one year out of Macon, Georgia. He chased me onto another track, a track that led through the secret fires of all those listening. They danced between the tables and at the bar. Between sets, Snooky, shy Snooky, who never looked at you long, said, "In this town you don't hear shit this good every night." We slapped palms and he invited me to a party that he was throwing for his sister that night.

"Run, muthafucka, run!" Two ripoffs in trenchcoats and big hats skid across the street. One of them has a bag of money and coins are running everywhere, down his leg, everywhere. They must have skipped the bills to get the quarters. Cupcakes spill out of inside pockets when they dip to sweep up the change. Quarters as diamonds, cupcakes as gold. On the case, a siren is screaming just a few blocks away.

"Come on, man!" They shoot down the sidewalk, and in full stride, cut a right-angle turn into an alley.

"Look at them jokers fly!" His trash cart parked, an old man has peeped it all. A woman carrying a shopping bag and cane has peeped him peeping. So when the coast looks clear, they get to the coins about the same time, the woman leaning her cane against a fireplug. By the time the cops get there, they have blended back into the scenery. The first mistake the cops make is to pick on a helpless junkie sliding past.

"Get yo hands off me, funky muthafuckas! Pig muthafuckas," screams the junkie, cooling his nod.

A bald man is jumping around the back seat of the cruiser like a monkey trying to sit on a fire. He sticks his head out of the window and yells something at the cops. They yell something back and he pulls his head back in momentarily, moving all the while. The cops are bothering everybody on the block. No one has seen or heard anything. The pickets are especially blind.

"Is you crazy?" the welfare mother asks the cop who has crossed the street. "You gone come over here and ask me what I seen? You must be a fool. I wouldn't tell you bastards if I did know which way they went."

"Look, lady," I can hear him say, "this is important. They have just robbed a delicatessen of twenty dollars and we can take you downtown, you know, for withholding . . ."

And the picket sign is suddenly an axe after the necks of all the sergeants-at-arms who have messed up. It misses. Before you can say "up 'ginst the wall," the cop has drawn his club and is standing his ground, his lips curled like an Irish wolfhound's, tasting battle.

"Y'all just keep fucking with us. Get on back where you belong. Get away from here!" And she charges toward the cop. The little nationalist is a blur. He catches her in front and stops her dead in her tracks. If I didn't see it, I wouldn't have believed it. He's outweighed by at least a hundred pounds and he stops her cold. She's stunned. She backs off a little and listens to the brother. Now is not the time, he is calmly saying. Now is not the time. The cop should thank him or something. After all, that woman might have taken the club and beaten him to a pulp. Then beat the pulp. But the cop just shakes his head and swaggers back to the car.

"See that?" I ask Swine and King, who have stopped running their mouths. "See that?"

"What?"

"That little cat stop that woman? She was about to catch the cop with a sucker punch and you missed it."

"Yeah, but she look like a rough one, don't she?" King chuckles. "A big woman like that don't be shucking if she moving that fast."

"I got one like that at home," says Swine, stroking his belly. "And she definitely ain't nothing to play with. And jealous? Man, you ain't seen nothing. Sometimes I tell her she got that graveyard love because she'd rather see me in the graveyard than with another woman. That's one reason I done stuck so close to home all these years."

"Ugly nigga like you can't pick up much in the street no way. It's best you housebound."

The ripoffs are blocks away now. Maybe they've ducked into a restaurant, and with alibis intact, have begun pouring Alaga syrup over hotcakes. Things on the street are already back to normal; junkies pushing on toward the magic touch, the trash man after his diamonds, and the old woman to a quiet place. Maybe.

"Snooky's sister, man is wow like how can I describe her? She is so fine, like wow what can I say?" The man has been babbling like that ever since we left the club.

They called him Killer Joe, after the song, and he drove a

Cadillac that smelled new. He was a buddy to everyone around the club and bought a lot of drinks for his special friends. The band, of course, was special and we'd get first word on the many parties he'd know about. People were hard on Killer. I always thought it was because he wasn't a hustler or anything they might fear. So they rode him heavy about the jailbait he'd been seen driving around every afternoon.

"You'll see her soon, my man. You'll see her."

Party-party people had packed the place. Some disguised as Indians, others as British lords, but most as the hip captives they were. Popping their fingers or just leaning back into the dark, smoking. Fine black women everywhere. My nose led me to the kitchen, where bookoos liquor bottles sat on the table. After hiding one bottle, I reminded myself to pace the drinking. It had gotten so bad some time before that cats at the foundry had started calling me Cutty Sark.

"There the bitch now!" That hot-breathing Killer Joe, slavering to me.

I moved to the edge of the crowd, trying to avoid Killer Joe. After all, I didn't need him or anyone else to point out Sassie Mae. If she was so bad, I'd know.

I began to wonder if I would leave the party alone and then there she was in front of me. There. I would know her but could not believe her fineness that made the room, the finger-poppers, and the music, nothing. She had just finished a dance and had turned to smile at me.

"You must be Mack. Don't look so surprised. You see, I know everybody else here. Snooky's already told me about you."

"I hope everything he's told you works in my favor."

"Well, that might depend on you."

I couldn't know then that the best thing I could have done after that first dance with her would have been to run to the door. The frown at my questions, the way she held her head—all of it said something that I later called a warning. I wanted to listen, to hold her and listen, but she was soft as doctor's cotton and my feet forgot to move.

Killer Joe like a sudden shadow. "You got the hammer, Mack! You lucky nigga you. You got her!"

Later there were afternoons of heavy snow. Sassie Mae in the window of the record shop where she worked; fly Mae spinning oldies-but-goodies that were blasted over the street while she checked her make-up and her stockings in the mirrors. Knees and thighs on view to Mt. Vernon Street. Mae taking time out to help make time. Her winning the Saturday night Miss Miniskirt contest four times in a row and the prize wig she wore. Her walk wicked in every which way. Me, fumbling and there to stutter and watch her move to the stacks, to the record player, to the cash register. The quick kisses stolen on the sly. She, all four women of Simone, and more.

Boss Mae: "Mack, remember I'm a grown woman and I don't need nobody in this world to take care of me. Nobody. Not even Snooky. Don't start acting funny on me and trying to give me orders. We split the rent, we split the bills. You my man. You been my man for two months now, but don't start acting funny."

(The night she came in drunk after a big night out with the girls, a little club of single and bored schoolteachers she had started running with; I called them the Jive Five.)

Mouthrunning Mae: "And why don't you clean yourself up sometime? Henrietta and Lucy be over here and you just be sitting up in your dirty workclothes belching beer like you don't know better and playing them dumb records over and over."

(Mingus mystified her, though Monk made her smile.)

Sweet Mae: "Do I ever ask you to do what I know no man can do? I've never asked you to pull down the moon and make it my diamond like some women will. I've never asked you to be a king of anything. Just be a man. That's what any woman who calls herself a woman wants. Give only what you can. That's me, sugar. I can't help it. That's me."

High Society Mae: "Look, Mack, I'm giving you slack and you just don't know it. I work. I got some money. I'm not like the others you see, lying up in bed all day, curlers all in their hair. And shit, I don't have to go around looking tacky either, fine as I am."

(A new dress, thumbed to her shoulders and she whirled in the mirror, laughing in my angry face.)

I knew so much then and understood so little. Moving in together was a small decision and she had even begun suggesting marriage. That was too many changes away.

There were days when I walked around with my horn and pretended to look for jam sessions. Those days I ate greasy food and drank wine with strangers. Cold, I would tell myself, so cold she'd throw water on a drowning man. I had gone looking for a woman and come back with a child who mistook kindness for weakness. So we battled hard and long to stay real for one another.

(Bitch, you ain't the Queen of Sheba. I know we got bills to pay, but some nights I just like to lay here in the crib, you know? If your friends don't go for it, let the door catch them on their asses.)

I had been away for two days and suddenly started for the apartment, crashing the sidewalk games of children, running past the conversation of thieves, running back to that big-legged woman of mine, bursting through the door.

"Sassie Mae!"

Mae, curled on the couch, eating an apple and reading *Jet* magazine. Her lips managing to mouth a few last lines before she looked up. "Nigga, you look like you on your last go 'round. Your other woman must not be doing you no good. Go take a bath and get yourself together. And another thing. The next time you make up your mind to go away and stay so long, don't expect me here when you get back."

"My love just came down on me a few minutes ago, over by the park."

"If you got to leave me for two days to get your love to come down, then maybe we ought to hang it up now."

But she was fronting. She had been partying some herself. I could tell. Dirty dishes stacked in the sink and the dust an inch thick. Cigarette butts with lipstick traces, cigars—I could tell. Yeah, Mae, where are you sleeping this cold morning and whose breakfast will you be too sleepy to cook? Where do your sad lovers go to forget?

When the group got the contracts back, it was like smiles from the spirits. Two club dates and two dances around the state. The dances were Snooky's idea. Weird Snooky. Funky American Legion halls in small towns would be soul injections, he claimed. The overhaul we needed.

"Y'all ain't been that long from these get-down dances that y'all done forgot how to get over," he would say. "Mack, you ain't forgot to honk, have you?"

"No, Snook, I ain't. But why should I go back to it?"

"It'll show you how far you've come," he said in his mystic's voice. Cecil believed that the dude was simply homesick. ("That's all. We should chip in and buy him a ticket to Macon and save ourselves all these changes.")

"Snooky, what do we get when we win this so-called Battle

of the Bands?" We had just pulled into the last town and had found the dance hall.

"One hundred and fifty dollars apiece and a pat on the back," he said.

"What if we lose?"

"Just the money." He grinned.

I made up my mind to be so bad that night I'd have the pimps dancing. I might even get so happy I'd sing "I've Got a Woman," the way I did in Cleveland. Biscuit Brown and the Untouchables were our competition. Sisters hung close to the stage in Saturday night Afros and I slow-danced with them while the Untouchables made noise or stood around on the stage looking ugly. The sisters swore they knew Columbus like the steps to the latest dances. Some claimed they had heard me play there and one thought she had two of my albums. I let her believe that and asked her about her boyfriend watching us dance. They all had Mae's voice, if not her hips, if not her perfume, if not her softness.

"I see you gone spend your money buying up all the pussy in this town," said the signifying Snooky.

"The night I have to buy pussy is the night the sun comes out."

Though most of the strays were taken up, I did find one for Snooky. She said she'd mess his mind up and keep him in that town for days.

Both bands were on stage for the last hour of the show. We alternated tunes and on one song I laid a lush line and a student of black music stuck in that town asked if I had ever heard of Gene Ammons. We chased the Untouchables off the stage, blew them into bad health. Any fool could see how close we were that night. I bent notes out of shape and Snooky built stairways right out to the night. We couldn't feel bad about

losing. We knew the game. The locals needed the encourage-
ment. After all, we had liked the crowd and the mommas who
snapped their fingers and shimmied and made us welcome. We
forgot the push and shove of our lives and found ourselves
holding the hands of women whose faces we'd forget in two
days. It was the night that was important, wasn't it? But wasn't
it a mess in that overheated motel room, with those large
thighs wrapped tight around you, when you felt the first
slipping away inside you and you whispered "Mae," and
coughed until you remembered the strange woman's name?

"Uh-huh, yeah," grunts King. "She plenty fine, all right." He
passes the picture on to Swine. After Swine has passed around
his family picture, the least I can do is to show them the
wrinkled snapshot of Sassie Mae I've kept in my wallet.

"A woman that fine can mean trouble," Swine says, passing
the picture to the Puerto Rican. "Was she?"

"Not at all, man."

"That's good," King says. "Bad women is my weakness. If I
had brains for every bad woman I've had, I'd be running this
world . . ."

"And be hard as hell on women."

"And be hard as hell on women. Say, brotherman, how long
you been in this town?"

"One month," I tell him.

"Well, that's one month too long if you ask me. I been here
fifteen years and you see where I'm at, don't you? Bad women,
no money, and rednecks. Them's my downfall."

"Stop crying," complains Swine. He points at me. "This man
here ain't got time to listen to you cry."

On their way to school, kids throw rocks at a three-legged
dog. The patrol car is still circling the block with the
bald-headed monkey in back, scratching his nose. They must

expect the ripoffs to come back for the few coins left on the sidewalk. Instead the kids scoop them up. The pickets laugh, Swine and King laugh, the Puerto Rican laughs. The harshness of this winter in the laughs.

The foreman hasn't looked our way for fifteen minutes. A bad sign, they say. All of us agree to shiver through another fifteen minutes. You never know what might pop up at the last minute.

The Puerto Rican moving away. Then King, then Swine, who stops to come back and shake me. "Look, my man, unless you want to sit here and watch the street all day, you better come along. Man say he ain't got no work today. At least no work for no niggas."

"Who that cracker think he is?" I ask the backs ahead of me. "His shit stink just like mine."

"Sho," says King. "But he on the pot right now and you out in the field with a corncob."

They laugh and mumble to one another about the employment office. The Puerto Rican says nothing to nobody and drops into a subway station. I'm headed inside. I look back to catch the nationalist easing over to warm his hands over the fire. He smiles and gives the fist.

I will sleep for a couple hours, then check out other leads. Wendell won't have that problem today. Ubangi won't either. About now, they're just getting up. More power to them. It'll be my turn one of these days.

A snaggle-toothed ghostman on the corner, whipped without mercy by the wind. His fingers, stiff and ashy, beat the air beneath his mumbling. He is speaking in a tongue only he and his spirits know. Speak on, skinny man, speak on. Just you and the wind out here anyway.

"Watch out, ole crazy muthafucka!" a face shouts at him. Dirty newspapers driven against his legs. Outlast this dirty sun, these helpless folk with your mumbo-jumbo. After all, weird man, there will be those who can explain you. ("The nigga crazy, man. I mean, he ain't got good sense. Would you stand out there when it's cold as hell and talk that silly talk when nobody be listening anyway?")

Important man in the mohair coat, before you climb into the taxi, explain this wild man who speaks in tongues. Start with the openness of his stare. Don't be afraid. Tell it, tell it the way it was before Santa Fe, when you were fourteen. Now Crazy Leon had large gray eyes, cat-eyes we called them on the sly, snickering from a safe distance because you never know what a crazy dude will do. Somehow we grew silent before those eyes accusing.

Explain him, you loud people waiting for the bus to go meet the man. Begin with the empty pop bottles collecting day in the alleyways, bottles worth two cents each and Leon always getting the most until I stole them. Or start with a back room, thick with the rose sachet I sold his mother.

"Was I good to you, honey?" Ernestine, Leon's sister, sixteen and a year older. One month before Santa Fe.

"Is grass green, Ernestine?"

"Why you like to be so cold all the time? You been hanging around with them wild ones, like Tiny and Boo. Uh-huh, that's where you got that from."

"Don't be worrying about who I hang around with. I say myself. I don't be saying other folks. That's the way I'm built."

"Ooo-wee, listen to Mr. Man!"

Her fingers gave me shape those noons. Hot licks of her tongue and I grew hard. "Mack, you think we'll ever get married?"

"Do what?"

"You heard me."

"Do I look like the type to be tied down?" I asked her.

"That ain't the point. You still got other girlfriends?"

"Uh-huh."

She touched me again and I grew harder. Then Leon's bike braked outside the window. He must have found a lot of bottles because it took him a long time to stack them all behind the house. Enough time for me to get all my things and make it out the front door.

You there, woman in the drugstore, dusting off displays, explain him. Just say that once upon a time Reverend Jackson was whispering in the foxy organist's ear as Ernestine and I took our seats at the back of the church. The tall usherette had led us to our seats, whispering to Ernestine, "This is babe bro's day, huh?" Ernestine's sad nod. And we sat and took in the sad church. Old-timers who had put the church down when it had bought an air conditioner and had become too comfortable to pray in, slid into front seats, their fishing trips postponed. This would be better. Leon sitting stiffly in the pulpit, to one side of the altar. He gripped the arms of the straight-back chair and his upturned stare hushed the audience. He sat like that as the choir sang two more numbers and as the announcements were made and the missionary offering taken. He sat like that through a youth choir hymn and a solo by Deenie that floated to the heavens. Coughing and shuffling of feet as Leon arose and moved slowly to the altar. "Let the church say amen." And they amenned when he nodded thanks to Deenie.

"Let the church say amen for this beautiful Sunday morning."

"AMEN!"

"Let the church say amen for Reverend Jackson and the good deacons and deaconesses, all the good people who have steered Tried Stone Baptist through many a storm."

"AMEN!"

"And amen for those who helped the storm along."

"AMEN!"

"Now let everybody say amen for themselves to give thanks
for God's presence as they sit here this morning."

"AMEN!"

The "amens" dying a little each time, the last one unwill-
ingly, almost a question. Leon was not bothered and went on
as if everyone understood.

"I am the truth and the living light. I am the TRUTH and the
living light. I am the truth and the living light. Heh-heh. The
living light, yes sir. That's what we have to be, you know, and
that's why He put us here. To light the way to everlasting
light. Now I know some of you be saying 'Naw, he didn't do no
such thing' and be trying to find something in the Bible that
say different. Some of you won't say it, though you believe it,
that He put us here to drive a fine car and wear fine clothes
and live in a fine home. Oh yes you will. I bet some of you
thinking that this very minute. Heh-heh."

Crazy Leon grinned and shook his head, pounding his fist
into his palm. "Now most folks just believe that the Bible is
only a Sunday kind of book. But I don't agree with that. No,
sir! Folks got to believe in the Bible if they want to get
anywhere with God. You can't fool God, not the almighty
God. Just take them folks who all the time saying they got
charity in they hearts and be just walkin' and talkin' right on
by that beggarman up there on Eighth Avenue. They feels
sorry for him, that's all. But sorry ain't charity. They two
different things. Listen now. Sorry means you just slow down
and shake your head and keep right on past him. Oh, you
might give a dime or a quarter, but that ain't nothing. Charity
means you stop and stay and give a little of yourself. Heh-heh.
Give of yourself.

"Just like faith and trust. Trust will take you part of the way
but faith will carry you the distance. Now you don't trust

everything and everybody. Just because you trust a man when you see him don't mean you got faith in him. You might turn your back, and just as soon as you do, the man do you dirty. But anybody you got faith in can't do you no dirt. Can't. No sir, 'cause faith is from God and you touch that person with your faith and y'all be like one person . . ."

Reverend Jackson ran a handkerchief over his bald head. He had never heard anything like it and never would again. Deacon Wilhite and those critical looks. People turning to glance back at Ernestine. Silent jurors with the law, the Lord's law, in their hands and they don't play. No crazy man would ever again preach in their church as long as they could help it, trial sermon or not. That message was plain on their faces. No nut can ring down heaven. Ernestine ran out, her head down. Leon did not notice her, for by that time his eyes were vacant and looked on the ceiling where he must have seen an angel's face. The organist broke in after an hour and both choirs drowned him out.

"Run it down, jim," cracks a hustler, easing across the street.

Crazy Leon could beat us in basketball, though baseball was his ruin. We waited for his fits whenever he started losing badly and we would dance around him laughing and knock his fast balls into the next block. Him chasing us from a peach tree once and standing in the rain one night with a broom handle and a rusty knife, guarding it. It was Leon who offered Ernestine in his way, not knowing I had been lusting after her ever since I stumbled into an armful of her at the Sunday School picnic. He even talked to her for me. Otherwise it was Chuck Willis or the Drifters on a Victrola and I would tell her to listen close because the music would be me. Crazy Leon stoning crackers who sped through our streets screaming "Niggers! Niggers!" Sometimes we'd catch them and calmly whip their asses. Crazy Leon who loved a girl with bowlegs, and shot baskets alone, for she found a new boyfriend. Crazy Leon who told on Darnell and Itchicoo sipping cough syrup in the church basement, who screamed through the busted lip they gave him that night.

Go on, Crazy Man. I know where you're coming from. Just you and the wind and me. Go on, speak your piece. We're all in this together.

Leon and Sassie Mae, more than most, the two who've made me. I've shot pool for the rest of the day, losing badly. When night has finally come, I've called Yvette and gotten no answer. I've held out that she's felt my need and is headed for my place to cheer me up. I smoke in the dark, listening for her footsteps, remembering her thighs.

The hall phone rings. It's Crackerjack's wife. "I hate to trouble you, but have you seen my husband?"

"No, Mrs. Good . . ."

"Oh . . . he hasn't come in from work yet and I thought he might have stopped off over there. He says you and him usually have a drink together at your place . . ."

I let that go by. "I didn't go to work today, Mrs. Good, but if he drops by I'll . . ."

"Yes, yes. You tell him I called." I sense that she's been crying, the pause is awful. "Tell him to come home."

I go back inside and wait some more. Tomorrow night will be different. Tomorrow night I'll be on the stand, blowing. I'll be complete then, away from sad voices. Then. Tonight I open my third beer and wait.

Six

SOME OF my best friends are the blues. On mornings like this they lay around mean and funky in this overheated room. They don't knock any more, they just come on in, swift as a dream. Flying all around my head, they do battle with the noises I try to make on the horn, a mismatch of a battle, for the blues won't fight fair. You shut your eyes and they'll show you an ashtray full of cigarette butts and another lonely room. You close your cars and hear a woman's voice or the whisper of a Greyhound bus down a dark highway. They'll show you that you can never have enough of nothing, and you'll never be alone.

I put the horn down and go to the window. Street bare except for the unemployeds huddled across the street, slapping palms over some joke. Their grins against the chill. Ubangi is away all morning, fitting on new faces for himself. He won't rest until he has hustled up on a gold mine. My words have no effect on him, like the freezing rain that hit the window all day yesterday. But check it out: the money is in his pockets, not mine.

I watch my spit fly down, just missing a man walking below. He looks up and curses me. I wave and blow a flurry of notes at him, high screeching notes that drive the weirdos from their beds. Ungrateful for the tunes that will liberate their rotting souls, they bang on their pipes, beat their walls with brooms. After I've closed the window, still holding that one high note, I notice a shower of chicken bones past the window. It's always like this. They go on for minutes, pounding and screaming.

"NO PLAYIN', MUTHAFUCKA, CUT THAT SHIT OUT!"

I'm waiting for one of them to knock at the door so I can dent his head with the horn. But they suddenly grow quiet. I put the horn away and let the blues slip back in.

I hear steps in the hall, then a key in the door. Ubangi pushes in.

"Look like you got the simple cats going out they heads this morning. The cracker downstairs on the desk told me to tell you to practice on the roof."

"Tell him to kiss my ass."

"I already did." He takes a carton of juice from the refrigerator and sits on the table. "Been a slow morning, Mack, up until a half-hour ago. I'm standing in Dudley Station and minding my own business, you dig, when this square-looking cat comes up to me. He wants me to take out a subscription to one of his magazines, so I look at him kind of funny and tell him I don't read that much. Then, Mack my man, he commences to go into his act. He tells me about how he needs some cash for college and how I have to take a subscription so that he can stay in school and come out and be a credit to the race. While he's saying all this, I'm seeing you in his place, then I'm seeing me in his place, then I'm seeing both of us out in Milton or Mattapan or jive places like that, running down the same shit to Miss Ann. See what I'm saying?"

Then he sips the juice, and from his grin, I can tell he's

ready for my questions. But who would be stupid enough to fall for that? How can we pass as college students? Even if we did pass, we're still black and therefore suspicious in those quiet streets. I fool him. I make a bologna sandwich and drink the last can of beer.

He's smiling in the mirror now, styling his dark-green drip-dry suit. As usual, he takes my silence for submission. He knows I don't like sitting around construction sites on cold mornings. He knows that the cafeteria job and Sykes will have to go. He knows how this newest idea can stitch some pride back into my pockets.

"We can start soon as you ready, Mack. I can get us ID cards printed up. Phyllis work on campus, you know. You just give your main man the word and we'll start."

"You know I got a club date tonight, 'Bangi. So you'll just have to wait awhile before I'm up for something like that."

"You got time, man. I'm just puttin' it out there for you to think about." He's out the door in a flash, back to the streets he likes so much. Again I try to play, but the winos, like hawks, are back at their perches. I leave the horn on the table and go out to the street.

The morning is gray and looks grayest in the direction of the beauty parlors and "tonsorial marts." I walk toward the deserted end of the street, pushing up the hill toward the forest of buildings. A few of the boards have been ripped from the windows and the walls inside are burned or peeling, show old calendars or lighter spots where pastoral paintings have hung. The crowds who have lived there have been hounded to other parts of the city and their homes will fade to parking lots.

In one empty lot young bloods play King of the Hill on a mountain of rubble. The game is simple: whoever stays on top the longest is the King. One brother is laughing and kicking while his buddies try like hell to push him off. A couple of them watch me out of the sides of their eyes. I am not of this block, a stranger. The boy is pushed off and another, shorter and heavier, wins out. After beating his chest, he jumps off the pile and runs toward an Eldorado parked just down the street. Inside, two hustlers are eating barbecue sandwiches and listening to a loud tape of the Temptations. The King of the Hill asks for money and has to beat his friends to the quarter that one of the hustlers tosses out of the window. Then he cases me as I pass. Screws up his face and shrugs. "Hey Mr. Man, you got a quarter?"

I shake my head and he looks sad for me. I turn the corner and start through a housing project. Shouts from a basketball game bounce from the red fronts of these buildings, spin through the playground, and roll dead at the huddle of high-school cats sipping cough syrup in the parking lot. Their minds tripping them to the moon as they lean. The ones with brighter eyes play ball and call themselves Alcindor, Big O, or Earl the Pearl. All of them hitting their share of the points except for one, a slow, pigeon-toed boy. The ball must belong to him. They show him little mercy, blocking his shots, stealing from him. They look a little relieved when they notice me watching, since they know the slow brother has had enough by now.

"Want to play, mister?" the pigeon-toed boy asks. I nod. "You can take my place. You guardin' Foots, that big badfoot nigga there."

Foots sizes me up, then takes the ball out. The other men on my team nod. Every man on the court can outjump me, though several are shorter. Three, maybe four of them can outshoot me. For a moment, though, I wonder what I'm doing here, and by the time I conclude that I don't know the answer,

Foots has fired off a shot. "Face!" he says as the ball swishes through the net.

My turn. My men feed off to me to see what I have to offer. I one-bounce it to the corner, jump and shoot. Two points. "In yo' eye, Foots!" shouts Slow Boy from the sidelines. "Old man put it in yo' eye!"

And that's how it all started, for if it was just a game a few minutes ago, it has become serious now. Slow Boy agitates like the Signifying Monkey, sitting in a swing. Then I block one of Foots' hook shots and my men whoop it up, slapping my palm. Foots makes the mistake of going for my first fakes and I get around him with ease, driving in for lay-ups. We run away with the first game and Slow Boy is no more good. He runs up to Foots, points a finger in his face and runs off. Foots hasn't cracked smile number one. The payback is coming, I know. I want to tell Slow Boy to keep quiet, to split, but this is his way of getting back at the big boys. The other team huddles during the break, then comes out strong. My first shot is blocked and I can hear Foots snicker. Rebounds that I might have pulled off the boards in the first game are slapped out of the air to their men. Foots again. He has me sweating now. I call on my legs for strength, fearing the death of my reflexes. They win the game with Foots winding up high-point man.

"Best two out three!" they yell.

"We let you win that one," I woof, edging off the court. "I got to get downtown."

"You ain't scared, is you?" Slow Boy asks loudly. I pronounce him a lifetime agitator, doomed to the edges of games, allegiance shifting with the winners.

"No, I'm not scared."

"Then why you running?" Foots asks. "Let's play this one for money."

"I wouldn't feel right taking the money from a jitterbug like you. Save your money for bubble gum or something."

He rubs his hands together. Slow Boy resettles on the monkey bars, and the older boys ease over to check us out through their high. They lean and loudly make plans to cop the welfare checks from the project mailboxes. I wonder whether Slow Boy will be among them in another year or two, by then too hip for basketball.

My legs have failed me this time and I spend most of the last game hitting occasional set shots from the corner. I even manage to block another hook shot that Foots has thrown up, but it does no good. His team is feeling its oats. One of my men tells me that I shouldn't feel bad, that Foots and his men are all starting on the high-school freshmen team. After the game, Slow Boy comes for his ball.

"We be playing out here every day. Why don't you come on back tomorrow and practice up with me before the big dudes come over?"

"Shut up, Slow Boy."

"You don't have to act that way just 'cause you lost, mister." He snickers and runs off with the ball. Before they file off, everybody tells me "good game" except for the cough-syrup sippers, who turn up their collars and harmonize an old Temptations tune.

I cut through the projects, idling toward Humboldt Avenue. Tonight can change all these dreary days; tonight I'm sitting in with Okra and his group at the Black Knight Club. Cracker-jack reminds me every day that they need a good horn man and that I should be thankful to him for this lucky break. Okra's group has steady work in the city, so steady that Okra doesn't even need a day gig. I'll skip the cafeteria again and call in sick, rest and stay cool until the night. Tonight will demand all of me.

An African gift shop leans on a beauty parlor at the corner. Voodoo dolls and tikis beckon through the window. From here I can see the fine woman sitting near the back. She smiles and I cool it inside.

"Those work, sister?" I ask, pointing to the dolls.

"Strictly on white folks and hopeless Uncle Toms," she says sweetly.

"I can dig it. My boss is white folks, you understand, and I need something to whip on him."

She nods, sniffing a cube of incense. "A little black magic can dazzle the Devil, my brother."

We laugh together, though I wonder if the "my brother" bit is standard for the customers. Just then a bearded man, about my height and weight, walks from a back room, humming. He kisses the woman on the forehead and gives the fist sign to two men looking in the window.

"We have other statuettes, brother. Ashanti fertility dolls as well as these carved in Haiti."

"I don't know really that much about either," I confess. Then he introduces himself as Antar and his woman as Malaika, his wife. "Much future in a business like this?"

They trade looks, smiling. "Well, we started off a few years ago in Milwaukee, and the only people who bought any of our carvings were schoolteachers who used them for decoration of their basement bars. Oh, there were a few eccentrics around, old Garveyites and whatnot. But we had to leave there or starve. Now people are waking up to their beauty, so it's been picking up steadily." He continues talking, pointing out how we've been separated for so long from ourselves. His wife nodding as if hearing it for the hundredth time. A man steps silently from the back with a beautifully carved cane. He whispers something to Antar, then ducks behind the curtain.

"Why don't you step back here and rap with us awhile,

brother? You say you're a musician? Good! We're discussing something that you may be interested in."

I follow him in back as a couple walks into the store and Malaika smiles upon them. Behind the curtains sit the man with the cane and a man about my age, heavy-set. After the introductions they continue with the conversation as if there's been no break. Henry is the older man with the gentle face and Omowale is the younger. Henry is the type you see on street corners, passing out leaflets for rallies, the grizzled warrior left to man the mimeo machines.

Antar points out an old chair, then takes a seat on one of the many chairs that clutter the room.

"Where were we?" Henry asks no one in particular. "Yes, legacies. What we have made to give the children? What the young and never-again-meek will inherit. Yeah, that's it!"

"You sharp as a tack, old man," Omowale says. He fishes among the masks on a table and finds one that makes him chuckle. It is a mask with a grin so ugly it could stop time. He puts it to his face and keeps it there until we leave.

"Omowale is the walking-talking spirit of Haiti, Mack," Antar comments. "I took him there on my last trip for carvings and he buried his slave name there and has come back masquerading as the hideous grin of fate." Hearing, Omowale laughs and bows.

Henry's voice like a burning spear. "Andrew Dolphy, also known as Antar, the poet, the dramatist, the dreamer, consider the legacy of your own father. I knew of him when you could count the number of black surgeons in this city on one hand. He was a man dedicated to his craft, as dedicated, as you must know, Antar, as you are to your own. Politics? His job was saving lives and being the best at what he did." Henry pulls a pipe from his pocket and lights it. Looks away.

"That is not enough, Henry. While he was saving lives, my

mother was teaching me to say 'thing,' not 'thang,' teaching me that my only responsibility was to my own future."

"Teaching you to hate niggas, like mine was," says Omowale through the mask.

Henry frowns. "Maybe. Then too, she might have known of other paths to those bridges over the waters she's seen so many fall into. In other words, what was there that could save you while you went about trying to save others? Faith ain't an easy thing to keep long. Movements come and go, but people stay and scuffle. Look, my feelings have been fire too, and those feelings have driven me the way fuel drives a train. They've also come close to burning me up. I've tried to learn to control things a little."

"You should know better," says Antar, "than to think that if everybody just hang loose and do their own thing, the situation will be copacetic. I mean, you dug on the thirties, copped a zoot suit during the Harlem riots, saw Du Bois hounded, thought Little Rock was a big deal. But you're still an idealist, Henry. More than me, you're an idealist."

"Maybe I'm that too, but all of us have our dreams, our gods. Holy Jesus, Allah, Damballah—aren't they all the same? Distrust the man who doesn't dream. He's dead. He'll pull you down in his hole." I notice the buttons on the lapel of his coat—FREEDOM NOW, BLACK POWER, and the eternal red-black-and-green.

"Only the sleeping man dreams. When he is awake, he moves," says Omowale.

Antar considers this, looks at the unopened boxes. Spider webs high in all of the corners of the room. A cash register rings in the next room. "I don't really mean anything like going limp. Look, I went into the South a few years ago, knowing I could change it along with the rest of the people bored with college. All of it was strange to us at first—the pain and poverty there. The packing up and running in the middle of the night. We registered voters to vote for the lesser of two evils then. What did we gain? Open doors for the tourists from the North who could afford those motels and restaurants. There are a few brothers in office down there but any real changes we won't see. Our sons might. I wonder, though, if the blood and the long wait will be worth it."

"But Andrew, what are the alternatives, not only in the South, but anywhere?" Henry asks.

"Remember, I'm from Nashville myself," Omowale says. "I didn't read about hate in a book and I can't wash it away with any chickenshit logic. I do know that everything at our disposal—magic, bullets, the blade—has got to be pressed into service for the liberation of black people. But first he must be spiritually in tune with himself."

Henry's question still hangs heavily and all three recognize it. He points at me with his cane. "Let's take our musician friend here. The musicians I know are among the most apolitical of people. What will your revolution do with him?"

"His music will space out whitey," Omowale says. "Drive the cracker mad with abstractions, put righteous voodoo on his ass. Musicians can control the spirits, remember."

"You and your goddam spirits." The old man laughs, then lights his pipe.

Once I thought my music would pick up where Malcolm's words died. Time and miles have had their effect: I'm not so sure of what I can move. Have I been crazy from the start? Would they understand my short history? Yet, even before fleeing here to this city, I've learned that making up songs against oppressors, against anything, would be a waste of me.

"And your play, Antar?" Henry continues. "A man chooses between two women. For their politics? Bullshit. For his ability to love one as a woman. The other as a hollow symbol of what he thinks is right at the time."

Antar smiles a patient smile, as if collecting a memory. Then he looks at me, expecting me to say something about the music thing, but I keep quiet this time. We're about the same age, this man and I. Maybe someday we'll be able to talk about the different storms we've been in.

"Henry, our methods are what make us," he pronounces. "The point is we must agree on one method before we can move."

"Listen, man, your method makes you a prince, a thoroughly civilized black man. I don't mean that as a curse either. You've had the best schooling this country can offer, have traveled to Europe before you were twelve. Your family knows some important white folk and most of the important black folk. But they couldn't hide it all from you. You peeked out, saw what was really happening in the back streets of this world, and been screaming ever since. But when you stop screaming, I'm just saying that you should accept all that in your past. I'm the savage. I've lived in these streets, I know them. You don't go anywhere without me and I can't go too far without you. To know that, we both have to first know and remember where we're coming from . . ."

Antar shakes his head and stands. He's announcing that it's time for us to split. It must be work time or something. "Mack, by now you can see that we settle the big questions here every afternoon. You have to come back in again."

Omowale has put the mask down and he too shakes my hand. Henry nods and I leave after telling them where I'm playing. I buy incense and a carving out front. Wave good-bye to Henry, who has followed me and has started in the opposite direction. Listening to them has been good for me. Music and spirit and power are what I've tried to talk about with others. I've only got empty stares, but these men seem different, I'll check them out again.

The basketball game and listening to the three men have allowed me to give the slip to the blues. But back on the street I can hear them. Closing in. Their friendship suffocates. I duck into a bar for a quick beer. The empty talk of the midafternoon drifters rattles through the dark room. Figures huddled at tables slowly emerge from the gloom. I put a coin in the jukebox and play Charles Brown's "Please Come Home for Christmas." Then I phone Crackerjack.

"What you into?" he answers, yawning.

"Same ole, same ole. Look, you can tell Sykes to go to hell for me. Tell him I ain't coming in again today. Tell him I don't feel like it."

"Yeah, that's what I'll tell him." Crackerjack chuckles. "But that ain't answered my question. A fox, huh?"

"Yeah," I lie.

"I can dig it." He lowers his voice to a whisper. "Meanwhile, if my ole lady call you, tell her we was playing cards with Okra last night. See what I'm saying?"

"Yeah, C. J."

"Is she fine?"

"Who?" I ask.

"The bitch. You know, the one you missing two days' work for?"

"She's outasight, C. J. Her roommate is sho nuff bad too. I'll run it down to you later."

A few people nod to the music, and I try to finish the beer and run before the gloom resettles in this place. Then a heavy hand drops to my arm, I turn to an unfamiliar face. The man says he recognizes me from the hotel, and it's clear that he wants to talk. He won't be giving out soon either because, looking more closely at him, I can see a hundred stories in his face. He starts in on them one at a time. The time he was drugged and kidnapped from Boston Harbor and woke up on a steamer headed for Morocco. The hash and pussy there. I let him buy me a beer after that one, though still ready to make my getaway. There are more calls to make. One to Yvette, one to Michelle, who has threatened to come up for a week. Then he pulls my coat to the fact that he is a demolitions expert and that he can wire this barroom up in no time and blow it up.

"Really?" I ask.

"Uh-huh. And here's another thing. I always keep my room wired up for the young jitterbug dopeheads who be hanging around that corner all the time. I'm on the first. floor, you know. A naked wire around the windows, yessir, and I wets it three times a day. Any muthafucka stupid enough to be climbing through one of my windows will get a jolt that'll shoot his ass to Kingdom Come."

This is the kind of dude Antar and Omowale will need in their army. Henry is right: don't write off the veterans. Edging from my stool and keeping an eye on him, I try to break. He grabs my wrist. "Have another beer. I didn't never tell you about the broad on the second floor, rear, who be all the time asking about you, did I? I mean, her face ain't nothing to call home about, but her body would make a preacher lay his Bible down."

Pulling away, I nod and make a note of that. My good news for the day? This winter will get colder and an empty bed is often the coldest place on this earth.

"Just going to the john," I tell him. I hole up there for a few minutes, time enough for him to find another ear. I ease out behind them.

When I get back to the room, I give Yvette a try. A man answers the phone. In the background I can hear finger-popping.

"Ain't nobody by the name of Yvette live here," he answers. "Who you?"

"Santa Claus." I drop the phone on him. She doesn't waste time at all. Three days without me and she's got another man eating her omelets, taking her to all the jumping joints on Tremont Street. I lie down to think this one through. I can hear Christmas carols piped from some distant church, the laughter of people below, no doubt with large bags overflowing with gifts. The blues have been laying in wait all the time. Hat up, blues! Find another lonely room!

> *Bells will be ringing the sad, sad tune*
> *O what a Christmas to have the blues.*
> *My baby's gone, I have no friend*
> *To wish me greetings once again.*

At least Crackerjack might have warned me about Hurricane Wanda. He has hipped me to everything else under the sun—Okra's disposition, who the club owner is hitting on, things like that. He should have told me that Wanda and I wouldn't get along. If he were a real buddy, he would've stopped me from drinking—that would only aggravate things between Wanda and me. But instead he will show up late, too late.

Arriving at the club early, I run into Wanda in the kitchen. She has the cook's ear and looks at me as if I have interrupted something heavy. I introduce myself, and after giving me the once-over, she turns back to the cook.

"See my high cheekbones? Kinda high, ain't they? Uh-huh, now check out my nose, just as straight as it want to be."

"That still don't mean you an Indian," the cook says.

"It don't mean I'm pure nigga either."

The cook looks at me, scratching his head. If Hurricane Wanda is an Indian, Geronimo must have been a slave. Even with her long red wig and the red speckled band around her head, she couldn't pass for anybody's Squaw White Dove.

"What tribe you from, Wanda?" I ask. "Blackfoot or Crow?"

That one catches the cook in the belly. He doubles up and drops to the floor. "Hee-hee, Blackfoot or Crow. That's a good one."

"Mind your business, sucker," she says. The cook finally gets up, dries his eyes, but leans against a sink to laugh again.

"Cut that out, you ol' fool. I see this rookie's mouth gone get him in trouble around here. Lots of smart-mouths been thrown off this job before. They best realize who be running this club. Me, Hurricane Wanda." She says all this looking at the cook. For some kind of effect, I guess. I push on.

"Wanda, I bet we could become good friends if . . ."

She wheels on me, hoping to draw blood. "You ain't man enough for me, honey."

"I bet you wouldn't say that behind closed doors."

Patting her thigh and giggling, she goes schoolgirl. "Your eyes may water, your teeth may grit, but none of this fine stuff you'll ever get." She struts her mighty stuff away.

The cook and I laugh over it. We hit it off nicely. I learn that he's a blues guitarist, though he's been working as a short-order cook for the past fifteen years. He's played around Tennessee and upper Alabama and tells me that music is not what it used to be.

"Sometimes I'd pick that guitar so hard and long, my fingers would bleed. And folks in them days wasn't so choicy. You could play anything to them as long as it was blues. Them mean, fonky, get-back-in-the-alley blues."

He slides me a plate of barbecued chicken with three slices of bread. As soon as I finish that, he drops another chicken leg on my plate. "Go ahead, eat!"

I gobble this up too, thank him, then move out to the bar to ready myself for the night.

After the first set I sit with the trio in Okra's old Cadillac. We sip wine and a joint or two goes around. The first set has gone very well, the horn making a natural fit with Okra's mean organ, Bennie Tatum's steady drum, and A. C.'s walking guitar. Okra cuts on the switch to get the heater going again.

"You play a whole lot of horn," says Bennie Tatum. He passes me the half-empty jug of sweet red wine.

"Yeah, sometimes we don't know what we'll get." Okra laughs. "The last cat Crackerjack sent down only knew one note, and it was flat. Remember him, Bennie?"

"Hell yeah. He called us some square niggas for not bein' able to get to that note."

"That don't mean there ain't no badass dudes out here blowin'," says Okra. He nods to two men who have come up to look in the big window of the club. "Both of them mean. One play trumpet and the other play flute. We let them sit in once in a while. As a matter of fact, look like they got their stuff with them tonight. But just sitting in won't help them pay no bills."

A. C. hands back a roach that I pass on to Bennie. I lean back and close my eyes. I've been this way before: Snooky and Columbus and winetime between sets. Buicks and the early ride out to the foundry. Mae too. Fine Mae.

Then the heater stops. "Vacation's over, brothers." Okra puts the jug back in the brown bag and lays it on the floor. The next set belongs to Wanda.

By the time we're back on the stand, we're in good shape. Bennie Tatum is grinning into space while working the bass peddle. Okra runs his hands back and forth across the keyboard, while A. C. goes into the "Shadow of Your Smile." It sounds so smooth that everyone shuts up, including us, and Okra doesn't bother to interrupt it to introduce Wanda. But the crowd still manages to explode when Wanda goes on stage. She takes the mike and coos to the audience for a few minutes, making sure everyone knows that Wanda is on the scene. Her tight pink dress is riding well up her thighs, holes cut in the sides for flesh to peek through. Then Bennie lets his guitar do some heavy walking while she shimmies back and forth across the stand, snapping her head.

She smooths rolls of fat down her sides and breathes something into the mike. The show is on the road. We go into "Respect" with Wanda staying right on top of every note, taking no chances of laying back or jumping ahead. What her voice can't reach, her shimmy does, and the audience loves it all. She turns to the side and whips it on them again. Heads rocking, dudes grin up at her and try to show off their steps.

"Come on, y'all, put your hands together!"

"Sockittomesockittomesockittomesockittome . . ."

I have little chance to open up on the first two numbers, laying until the third, a ballad where I can work my show. "Girls, on this next one I want you to hold that man of yours real tight. He might be your husband, or your boyfriend, or maybe somebody else's husband or boyfriend, but I want you to hold that man real tight on this song. Go on, girls."

It's "Do Right Woman, Do Right Man," and the first bars have the middle-aged women at tables without men screaming, "Sing it! Sing it! Sing your song!" Okra humming along with her. Heads on the shoulders of partners. Arms locked tightly. The cash register rings and I'm the only one to hear it. Then my chorus comes and I do the little bit I know best.

"Play it pretty! Play it pretty!"

Wanda comes back in a half-bar off. She catches up and I begin to snake my way through the last chorus, losing her. All she has to do is keep on singing and I'll be back under her. She starts humming, though, throwing me a nasty look.

"What was wrong, sister?" I ask her later.

"You," she says. "Don't you know anything about keeping time?"

The next number is a getaway tune, played uptempo and guaranteed to wear out the dancers. And Okra hides little, breaking bad from the start. After doing her bit, Wanda moves off to the side, popping her fingers, patting her thighs, frowning at me when I slip a scream or two through the horn.

"Who you say you is? This ain't no kind of jazz place." She really has an attitude now. I swallow it and walk away from her. One monkey won't stop the show this time. Okra, Bennie Tatum and A. C. have spoiled her, supporting her bad singing with long chords. Yes, she's slid a long way on that big behind of hers, but she won't put me out in the cold, job-hunting, if I can help it. I need this job too much. We don't speak another word for the rest of the night, but I know that she will whisper something to Okra the first chance she gets.

The next afternoon, Okra calls me and tells me to lay until he gets back to me. Wanda wants me off and they want me on. The manager is Wanda's boyfriend, but the owner, an aging hustler, is a homeboy of Okra's. Nothing to worry about, he's said. It will only take three or four days. So I spend Christmas Eve on the roof, blowing the blues away.

Seven

I HEAR someone's teeth chattering, and after opening one eye and finding no one around, try to get back to the dream I was into. As usual, I was being chased, this time by headless men in capes. I was losing them too, but the noise has ended it all. I roll over into a blast of cold air from under the window and learn that it's my teeth that have been doing the chattering. My face is ice-cold. How long have I been freezing under this window? Apparently, after raising the window high, Ubangi has rushed into the shower before the other tenants use up all the hot water. The radio and the coffee are on. This is the earliest he's been up since the morning of the Big Hunt on the Cape, the earliest for me since those mornings I've tortured myself at the construction sites. It is four mornings after the night of Hurricane Wanda.

Ubangi comes in from the bathroom, throws the window high again, and beats his chest in the face of the vicious whistling hawk. Like a crazy man, he laughs at my sluggishness. "You look like a million dollars this morning, heh-heh."

I get the tail-end of the hot water, then dress straight—

striped shirt, tie and blazer that 'Bangi has lifted somewhere. The Sledges would certainly be proud if they saw me now. Daddy would smile and remind me how high I can climb if I try. Mack made it, y'all. Mothers pointing me out to their children as a model of good behavior. My legs going to jelly under that kind of weight.

I must admit that if I didn't know myself any better, I'd fall for my own front. Dressing silently, Ubangi approves. He wears the same outfit, but there's something about the scar under his chin, his slack motions, that cancels him out as an undergraduate. He'll have to pass as a weird law student.

At the subway stop, freshly scrubbed chumps almost knock us down as they spring to the supermarkets, slick furniture stores and welfare-office branches that they run in the neighborhood. We cool it inside the train, about to make it to the pads they have just left. Their women back in bed by now. Aside from running down how we're actually doing black folks a big favor by ripping off the man, Ubangi claims that we might even cop some leg on the deal.

"You done heard about how freakish them white bitches is. Train porters, bellhops, trash men—they all got stories. And the way we made up here now, they might snatch us right off the street."

"Ubangi, just one thing."

"What's that?" he asks, overdoing it, pulling out a pipe and packing it.

"The earring. The earring has to go."

"Uh-unh, naw! I might dress up in these funnytime clothes and talk weird, but I ain't taking off my earring." By his look, he's as serious as a heart attack.

"Okay, then. They might not notice it anyway. But if they do, you can play it off like you're a gypsy or something."

"I ain't studying you or the whities. This earring is me."

From the end of the car, domestics eye us suspiciously. They whisper to one another, giggling. I have to put them at ease. Who knows, they might come in handy out here in nowhere. After all, they are the knowers of the juiciest secrets. They know how stupid their masters are. They've seen them let their hair down and they've run from that ugliness on occasion. Yes, they know.

Ubangi bragging a mile a minute, steeling his nerve. "Mack, after today you won't feel so bad for walking off that cafeteria thing. You don't have anything to worry about."

I've put my dishwashing thing in the wind. Yesterday things became nasty and I decided I'd rather make it on hustles for a while. It has been coming to that. Sykes has been a convenient excuse.

"Hello, stranger!" Bettie had shouted. "We thought for a while that one of them fast women down on Tremont Street done kidnapped you or something. We were sho nuff worried about you."

"That's right." Spoon chuckled, coming up behind her with a stack of dirty dishes. "We had the FBI, K.K.K. and Lassie on your trail."

"Never can tell about Mack, y'all," Bettie snapped at my heels. "He be here one day and gone the next."

"A nigga like that don't need no job," added Fuckup, putting in his money's worth.

"Yeah, and a nigga like that ain't gone have no job if he don't straighten up and fly right," cracked the Jack.

He called for a celebration behind my debut the other night. Fuckup broke out a sixpack from the cooler and everyone sat or stood where they were and leaned while Crackerjack told how I set the night on fire with my solos. But our little party busted up when one of the waitresses warned us that Sykes was on his way out to the kitchen. We barely got the beers out of sight before the fool charged in.

"I want to see you!" He was pointing at me. I followed him upstairs to his office. He looked smaller, more helpless, behind the desk. Downstairs he looked the part of the overseer, but behind the desk he was a clown. His game was up, all front. He spoke in the tone of the man confiding in his best slave to get the goods on the others' acting up. Of course, I had my two-day vacation hanging over my head. But he didn't use that. He just told me that someone had been stealing a lot of food from the kitchen.

"It's been going on for three weeks and I want to get to the bottom of it. Everyone knows I'm running a shoestring operation here, yet last week ten steaks got away." His eyes narrowed as he fingered the pen clipped in his shirt pocket. "How long you been working here?"

"Three weeks. You know that."

He thought his silence carried the weight, pointed the finger toward my nose, but I shook him off. He couldn't get anything out of me, even after he tried to scare me about taking the two days off. Then he stooped real low.

"Well, I figure it's you or one of your other good soul brothers. How well you know Good or Johnson?"

"Not too well," I lie.

"You tell me which one did it and I'll forget you didn't show up those two days, and I might even consider moving you up to the front." He winked. "Besides, Johnson been saying you lazy anyway."

I left the office. Then he called up Crackerjack and Fuckup. They came back quiet and frowning and I knew he tried to divide them with lies. They claimed they were cool, but a few minutes later Crackerjack eased up to me. "I told that damn Fuckup to be cool, but you know he don't listen to nothing! He figure he can steal the whole damn restaurant without them knowing. But that cracker ain't dumb. He knows who it is. Mack, he didn't believe a word I told him. He just using this to get back at you for staying off those two days. And he trying to scare me 'cause that little redhead he want been up in my face ever since I been on this job. I'm leaving this motherfucking job in another month. I don't need it no way."

I stayed around for another hour, but it did no good. My mind was made up. I dropped my apron on Sykes' desk, picked up my check and cursed his wasted face. So last night when Ubangi pressed the question of hustling magazines, I was a pushover.

The train rumbles through the quiet blocks. Streets still sleeping. Trees skinny and straight like proud virgins. The domestics get off, one by one, shaking their heads and laughing their best laughs until evening. Ubangi's dozing now. I've asked him more than once if he knows where we're to get off. He's told me to relax and that he's checked everything out.

Ubangi Jones, Ph.D., easing up to the door where the master's woman stands smiling patiently as he runs down the years of hardship, toil and changes that the university, the world, the universe have put him through and how badly he needs her subscription if he is to rise and at least have a fighting chance. Any magazine will be fine as long as its rate is the ten-dollar minimum, and he will have her close to tears by the time he has to rush from the house and the old clothes she tries to press on him, clothes her oldest son has stopped wearing, having gone full-time hippie his senior year in college. He figures this kind of game will bring us eighty dollars apiece by four o'clock.

Me? I have it down pat. I will be Dr. Feelgood. I will be as smooth as Poitier coming to dinner, as cocky and quick as

Muhammad Ali chasing bears around the ring. I will dazzle the master's old lady with my knowledge of anthropology should she be up to asking about such things, and I will just generally pimp myself like nobody's business. If Ubangi can pull eighty, then I can pull a hundred. I've got a rainbow tied around my shoulders and my pockets bulge with lucky charms; a stiff rabbit's foot my Daddy slipped me when I left home, a yellow mojo tooth identical to the one Ubangi carries, and a pouch of goober dust that Ubangi claims will cover our tracks if we have to move in a hurry. The dust can turn any posse to crippled bloodhounds with nose trouble.

We get off with the last domestic and Ubangi shakes my hand. "Mack, I'll see you here at four. Remember, if we cross paths, I don't know you." We check our maps, my area shaded in red, his in blue. He slaps me on the back and leaves.

The first house is a pushover. The only questions the woman asks are where does she sign and if I can take a personal check.

"Just cash, ma'am. Contest rule."

I have walked away from that one with a crisp twenty-dollar bill in my pocket. In the next house a dog is barking and somehow I feel that the whole neighborhood is now on its toes, peeking under the blinds this very minute. The niggas are here! The niggas are here! It will be enough to send this wild mob after us with TV guides and their husbands' golf clubs. I tighten the grip on my attaché case. The fangs on that dog are for tearing. But now he's suddenly yanked out of sight and the barking fades. After that scare I have a mind to hoodoo this house good.

A boy of about twenty, with bangs, stands in the door. "Yes?"

"Hello, is your mother home?" He gives me the once-over and leaves me in the door. After calling upstairs, he stands in the large room watching me, his bare foot playing over the thick rug. The seriousness about him promises trouble. His mother is a fussy, nervous woman who never stops moving. My act is as smooth as it has been the first time, though.

The pest wants to see the phony list. He looks it over and asks to see my ID. Of course he won't find a thing wrong there. Ubangi's friend has done a good job.

"How much did you say it would cost?" the woman asks.

"That depends. Most of them will run between ten and fifteen a year."

Her son watches me while I sign her up for the sports magazines. "Tony's just wild about sports, aren't you, hon?" He winces and walks to the other side of the room.

"I'm sure you'll like to know that the choice you've just made entitles you to a free bonus choice. Any one of the ten on the green sheet." My voice is a carnival hawker's, the salesman's in the clothing store who beats the poor out of their paychecks.

"What year are you in at the university?" the boy asks.

"My last. I'm completing my thesis on the Missing Link."

"I was in Poli Sci myself when I was there."

"Tony was also a bad boy when he was there," his mother puts in, looking around for her purse. They trade stares.

"My mother needed me home," he tells me, venom beginning to drip from his jaws.

"I'm sure you have self-respect," she counters, smiling at me and taking her time about the money. I stand, hoping she'll take the hint. They don't even look at one another now. They've probably waited all morning in different parts of the house to get someone in the middle like this. They'll use you as a rug and leave the mud of their problems on your head. I know better than to take sides. I just want the bread. When she gives it to me, I leave them watching me as if I'm their last hope.

I don't like walking right into their lives like that. It's like walking into a bathroom and catching someone in there looking guilty. I'll make a point to stay out of traps like that for the rest of the day. The lawns on this street are carefully kept, though brown, like those in Santa Fe, where on days much warmer than today, the air floated gentle noises that went with the homes, that met you with each note distinct. Indians or Mexicans as gardeners, and I would come into a street to knock their hustle with my lawn mower and a can of gasoline, my sneakers, and my dungarees rolled unevenly. The lazy, balding men watched you from side patios and widows smiled from front windows. Junior Cook and I would go out together those afternoons and he could have them believing their sidewalks needed cutting. There were some who were nice enough to bring a pitcher of lemonade and leave it in the dark cool of the garage with a sandwich or two. I'd eat quickly and go back under the blazing noon to trim the walks and watch the sports cars with dudes of my age with nothing to do those afternoons, not even swimming or tennis, but just simply back and forth in those sports cars, waiting for something to happen. They'd look at me and some might even try to make conversation, wanting to eventually work the talk around to "colored girls" I might turn them on to, but never getting that far and therefore saving some teeth. Then I'd pick my money up at the side of the house, three dollars lying next to the chaise lounge where the wife-daughter-sister lay on her stomach, tanning the hell out of her back, and they'd say you did a great job, not even turning over, just scratching the backs of their necks, and I'd move on with three dollars and thoughts of three new 45's or a shirt. I'd get to another house, knock on the door, and ready my line.

In her white uniform, the sister blinks at me. She looks interrupted as hell. "What you want?"

"Haven't I seen you someplace before?" I ask.

"Uh-uh, naw, man. You ain't seen me before." Though I have seen her at the club "out with the girls," she fails to recognize me. She's been the one dancing alone in the aisles, having a ball.

"Sorry. Look here, I'm selling these magazine subscriptions and working my way through school. Dig it?"

She shows a gold tooth. "Sure enough? Well, the lady who live here can't read a lick, just between you and me. Right now she probably upstairs watching a quiz show or trying to fool me looking at some damn Ellery Queen book."

"Well, why don't you be a mellow sister and call her down so I can run my thing and be on my way?"

She throws back her head and laughs. "Boy, come on in. You about as crazy as you look."

I follow her to the pantry. She introduces herself as Della, then reaches into a cabinet and pours me half a glass of Scotch. "They won't miss it. I call it my breakfast cocktail." She adds milk, stirs it and hands it to me. Her drink is on the table, already made. "You was on the train this morning, wasn't you?"

"Yes."

"I said to myself, 'Della, them two dudes is up to no good out here. They got as much business out here as a man on the moon.' "

"You got us wrong, sister . . . I'm in school . . ."

"If you in school, then biddy got lips," she says.

She can blow the cover off the whole thing and there's no real use in trying to fool her. But how far can I trust her? I have to get past her to get to the money.

"How do you know Boss Lady won't sneak down here and catch us rapping?" I ask.

"You just take it easy, greasy, 'cause you got a long way to slide." She drops her heavy self onto a stool. I bet she's a hard, fast liver from the old school, this Della. Partying until two and three in the morning, up and on the job by eight. She laughs. "She won't bit more sneak down here on me than her man will do right. She trusts me. I ain't here to scrub and cook like you think I am, young blood. Me and Devera talk all the time like you and me be talking now. If she came down here now, I'd just make her a drink and listen to her cuss that skirt-chasing husband of hers who got more money than my man got lies."

"Sounds like you got a good thing going, then."

"You better believe it! Della ain't nobody's fool. Say, how y'all find out about this gold mine out here?"

I put it all on Ubangi—his idea, his pushing, his everything. I'm still cautious. Classical harpsichord music seeps into the room, and Della frowns.

"There she goes with the music of hers. You had breakfast yet? It ain't good to drink all that liquor if you ain't. I should have asked."

"That's okay, Della, I'm in good shape." I check my watch. I should be walking out the door now with more bills in my pocket. And Della looks like she's not through yet. The music sweeps through once more.

"Some B. B. King would be nice about now, wouldn't it?" Then she hands me a brown case from under the sink. "These people so wasteful, honey. You just don't know."

Inside is a flute, practically new. "They throwing this away?" I ask.

"Uh-huh. If you can play it, you can have it. A gift from Della. But let me hear you play it first, because if you can't, I can take it home to my nephew and let him fool around with it."

I remind her that I'm in a hurry, but she won't take that as an excuse. I put the flute together and blend the notes with the music slipping from upstairs. Della is impressed. "You pretty good on that thing. Look, finish your drink now 'cause she'll be down directly for some coffee. I'll tell her you just walked in."

I'll have to tell Ubangi about Della. We might form a dynamite trio and really raise hell out here. Della could wheel and deal from the inside, keep an ear to the gossip. It could work. But now she's on a crying line about some no-good man who has just done her wrong. She talks on and on. I could have finished two houses by now.

". . . and they always coming to me crying Della this and Della that. They don't know I got worries of my own. I can't sit still all the time trying to solve all they problems. Shit, I know enough about them already to start my own college on white folks. And, young blood, don't come talking about the boss of the house either. I'm the lady of this house. Don't nobody else in this castle know what's happening but me."

"I can dig that, Della. Since you such a down sister and have pulled my coat to so much, why don't you drop by the club some night? I'll fix it up so you can get in free, and uh, won't have to worry about paying nothing for nothing."

She likes the sound of that. She goes to the foot of the stairs and calls down the tenant who lives upstairs. She is a very blond woman with a cheerleader's muscular walk. By the time I finish running down my game, her face has grown sad, showing wrinkles that the make-up can't hide. I don't think she's heard a word I've said, however, even though her eyes have been glued to my lips from the start. Della grumbling as she moves to get the woman's purse.

"Thank you, ma'am." Della shakes her head while I slip the bills into my wallet. I make a note of the address and wave again to Della peeking through the window.

My shades go on. I feel that everyone has gotten the word by now. They'll finger me in line-ups as the one who robbed them blind. I'll be good for nothing but playing in a prison band. These games can mess with your confidence. Imagine anyone giving bread to an arrogant beggar, though. The one who licks the boots carries off the prize every time. Della knows it. Ubangi knows it. The world knows it. Even out here they know it, these bleary-eyed women and their husbands who are ex-second-string football players, top-dog managers of the planet.

I knock off two more houses before noon. Guerrilla swipes. I have left one man in the door stuttering. He has thought I look like a busboy he knew in Hot Springs, Arkansas, and swears that I must know Eddie Lee from Arkansas. I have taken his money, unproud that I didn't swing at him or say something about his mama.

From a corner I can see Ubangi two blocks down. He cuts a step in the middle of the quiet street and lets his laughter roll like happy thunder. Otherwise there is nothing moving, no sound. He disappears and I find a little park where I can try out the flute.

On another street the women are older, with loose flesh hanging from their arms. In one house the maid serves me tea and I try to get her to open up, but she won't. She just runs from me, hissing "Hush up." Only one Della to a suburb, I guess. They turn me back on the street empty-handed. Then I run into Della on the street, a coat thrown over her shoulders. Puffing. "Y'all better hat up."

"Do what?"

"Somebody has called the cops. They just called to tell Devera. It must have been one of them gossipy heifers on this block. They just want the cops to check you out."

"How much time we got?" I ask.

She pulls me by the wrist. "That's what I'm trying to tell

you. You ain't got no time. Come on! I'm parked around the corner."

To my surprise, Ubangi is sitting inside looking bothered. He just shrugs when he sees me. "Della, how'd you get the car?"

"I'm supposed to be out getting groceries," she says, mostly to herself, as we peel rubber from the curb. We get to the subway station as a squad car speeds past us. I toss my ID card out the window and push a few bills into Della's hand.

Ubangi still looks as if he's in a state of shock. "A train will be along any minute," says Della. "Hurry and be careful from now on. Mack, I'm gone follow up on that invitation."

I pull Ubangi from the car with me and Della roars away into the noon. Dust and paper settle to the street behind her and all goes quiet again. No sign of the train as yet.

"How much?" I ask him.

"Seventy-five. How about you?"

"Sixty."

"Just when it was getting good, too." He throws his pipe far into the high grass across the tracks.

"Good woman, that Della."

"Yeah," he says. "Mack, I run into a dude the other day who just swooped back in from Montreal. He says bloods got it made up there. They got good jobs plus the bitches go crazy over them. That might be some place for us to think about. I know I'd get over up there."

"You bring me out here and we almost get busted. Now you talking about Canada? What are you going to be next, an Eskimo? You're slipping, man. If you ain't, then grits ain't grocery."

He mutters something I can't catch, and when the train comes, he takes a seat far from me. But this time we're the only ones on the train, hightailing it off the frontier with only a few ambushes to our credit.

Eight

UP, BLACKMAN, up. Important roofs are collapsing around your head. It is no time to sleep, only dreams come to the sleeper. Feel sorry for yourself later, retired from the beat of the streets when you can rock away your last years on woodplank porches and talk baseball with yourself. Right on time, you left home and blood and you flew. Thought that music could have a social good, could reveal unity among the group. Too early you have left town after town when the suns missed your front door. To hell with it all, you told yourself, when you hocked your horn and for weeks made it on great northern beans and cornbread—breakfast, lunch and dinner in one easy sitting. And you have sat and waited and hoped—no, not in the settled hope that old folks fix on their faces, but in the panic prayer that the next wind might bring something new, a smell worth following maybe—anything to keep you out of the hell which is you. The time you walked off the stand when a teenager with a flat-top haircut, thick glasses and floodwater pants matched you phrase for phrase on "Four," yeah, before you got it together and blew him out of the room, silencing him. Make it easy on yourself, bend like a wise willow. Winds do change and you can help them change. Those old rockers on the front porches can only catch the hope-to-die breath of rotting dreams and forever spit short at the passing world.

Up, up. Breathe the close stink of others, finger the texture of their shadows and take them for friends. Check closely the breath of the world misting the window. I wonder why I must keep telling myself in these off-the-wall ways that I must feel and keep feeling, see and keep seeing? But do this I must, or grow stale in cold rooms, in dim cafés with others without homes. Easing down waterfronts with weird solos on my mind and breaking off to listen to hidden laughter, cries. Coloring the wind the palest shade of gray and wandering, wondering. No damn future in that, jim, you'd best be believing.

I should know that. I, Mack, son of a dreamer who knew no place, or at best contrived it, sawed and nailed it together, made it holy with his lone drunken laughter, late nights, before Mama's scolding faded and their duets, cackling and whispering, brought up the sun. I, Mack, who declared the spirit of Coltrane and Rollins just a few dues away from hearing "Spiritual" and "Blue Seven," sixteen then, and repeating them run for run through that winter. I should know that music counts for as much on rooftops as it does above the noises of drunks in anonymous rooms. I, who have seen the genius bared on black streets, singing "See-Line Woman" while shaking out bargain-basement rugs, doing the barefoot boogaloo to the rhythms against coffee-can bottoms, high nodding and snapping fingers to the way-out pulse of the traffic, quoting from "Revelations" and dipping, spitting snuff that browns empty beer cans behind the stoop, playing hopscotch with two braids trailing, sneaking past gang members making plans for ripoffs, past snaggle-toothed laughs in those littered afternoons. I, who have witnessed but have never found the place to tell the tale, to make it live. Keep it whole. To be open to those melodies is the best thing you can do. To play riffs off their joy and pain, even in loneliness, you can do. You are them and they are you and God will tip down for that communion and snap his fingers; will then better understand your need to lie late in bed and rap to yourself. God will then be your runnin' buddy, the way he's wanted to be all along, but you were running too fast.

Yesterday they carried a body from the brick building down the street. It is a dormitory for students at the Bible institute. Two carriers—one white, one black—worked quickly in the cold, cursing their way through a sluggish sidewalk crowd. A third attendant had pulled back the doors to the ambulance and was blowing into his fists, waiting. Looks of surrender blessed the stretcher, the body of the skinny man, unmarked, it was told by some, except for a few stripes above the thick bandages on his wrists. His lips dried to gray. The near-dead man must have known the work of razors, must have known Saturday nights when dudes sprinted out of alleyways, with "I'm gone get you muthafuckas!" thrown over their shoulders, over broken trails of blood and cool assassins making it in the opposite direction. Almost dead, he had to notice blood in the early morning's slush, blood unseen by churchly crowds with eyes glued to the rewards in the next world, blood aging to purple, to black, then forgotten under the next layer of dirty ice. And yet it was the razor that filled his hands with warm blood, that darkened the mattress, the floor at the side of the bed, with the only witnesses a Bible, a stack of worn mimeos, a picture of a girlfriend and snapshots of them at a summer Baptist camp. The hospital contacted his father in West Virginia. Later that afternoon I tried to practice, but I couldn't. I called Yvette but she never picked up the phone. That was New Year's Eve.

New Year's Day has sparkled patches of ice on Warren Avenue and two bent winos arguing over wine. One has smashed the bottle to the street, then stepped back, a little amazed at himself. Threads of mist shooting from his mouth as he has pointed to the redness growing along the gutter. Stranding the argument, finally. From the window, I've guessed that it must have been very serious business. A wino doesn't throw away his grapes. It's much like a blind man strangling his seeing-eye dog. Such an action can only guarantee him many cold days. His peace of mind will be slick truces hustled off by grinning Italians, who have squatted on corners next to all the grocery stores, who will know his first name and watch him smile toothless smiles and slowmotion to a park bench where he can knock out his bottle in peace. To an alley below the shouted gossip of large women in windows. To a hallway between crowded lives teasing madness. The back room of a pool hall or barbershop where crap games float and no one notices him copping a sip or agitating steel workers into near-fights and harmless dozens contests, while they clench dollars in their fists. To his room where he will stomp roaches and sleep with a loaded pistol beneath his pillow.

Let him be Antonio, slight, with wrinkled shoes, squinting into the wind on Mt. Vernon Street. "This used to be a city, friend!" His words tugged hard at the lapels of my coat and I nodded stupidly. I had stopped to give him a light. "Now what the hell you call it? You tell me, huh? Whores by the trainload, sorry-assed hillbillies, and niggas doped up." He spat brown into the light. Antonio, war veteran, proud of the six languages he knew, father of a son who managed to find him every payday. Exile from Hell he called his life, later his book, ten years in progress. Eyes red that would soon take the dullness of jelly. He blew smoke quickly, wanting to make his points while the scream in his words held me there. He had been busted once, he said, for just being cool and carrying around Mill's On Utilitarianism. The cop thought him an undesirable alien. Get to that.

Meeting one week into sudden spring, Antonio and I sat in the rest room of a motel popular among rich playboy ministers. Spring has its smell, its song. That year it was lilac and the tune was James Brown's "I've Got the Feeling." Antonio hawked and spat into the toilet. In another room silent marches were being planned. King was dead.

"They kill him, they'll kill anybody," he said, booting a shoeshine box across the floor. "Anybody! Even they mamas, they sons and daughters, to keep what they think they got." Then as if he understood my every thought, he nodded at my prophecies of doom.

"I could teach you a lot, Mack." Then he fisted out his fury, our fury, the fury of earth and ages, upon the lazy sun-filled street below.

"All of them must be killed," I said. "All of them. With razors at close range, poison, with voodoo—anything, but they must die. The halitosis of their history is fucking everything up. Let their white-eyes roll back in their heads. Blood and money are the only things that shake and move their world, the only things they respect. Spill their blood to remind them they are human too."

"So many watchdogs they have," Antonio said. "Po' crackers and store managers. They would drop their bombs on their own heads before they'd give up this nightmare palmed off by hustlers with no style, this America."

"Are you suggesting we wait on their sanity? Ha, Antonio, my man, it seems you're running out of answers."

He shook his head and passed the wine. Applause thundered

in the next room and someone with a good voice started "We Shall Overcome" and was joined by others. The effect, though, was that of a scratched record.

"Answers?" he asked. "I don't know, maybe I am slowing down. Even I get tired of sounding wise." He dropped his head when I smashed an empty bottle against the wall and the applause kept coming.

"This morning I heard the man tell the world that the group was going to keep working in the tradition of King's philosophy. He told the people to stop burning and told the militants to shut up because they had the wrong attitude. As if niggas pulled that trigger. Are people losing their minds?"

"I don't know, man. He sounds like he was just as confused as everybody else and he was going to take a stand. It's too bad the man said what he did 'cause he looking the wrong way. Mack, you and me ain't no kind of saints, and to stay men we got to keep our eyes open. We got to keep a good jab in the white folks' faces and the knockout punch always ready in our stash."

I had smiled then and considered his words the delusions of all ancient men in shiny-seated pants. I wondered if the wine would take care of his confidence, erase my instant plans of "revolution," doing-good-for-the-race ideas, living other lives. King was dead and I was no fighter. We shook hands and I promised to check him out again. Antonio would read me a chapter from his book, teach me to shoot an automatic. Outside a couple standing straight and patient in front of the bus station. They were dressed for a season of quiet Sundays. The woman was worrying her husband about the bus to Atlanta, already fifteen minutes late. And King was dead and the man frowned when she said that it was a nice day, that spring should be for always because she didn't care nothing for winter no way. He cursed her when she admired too long a dress a

white woman wore. And she fished in her purse while her face
groped for the right expression. She smoothed her dress across
her stomach and a pigeon swooped from the gloom of the
buildings and waddled past them. Her man leaned against his
shadow on the wall and closed his eyes . . .

"Who is it?" Bearded in shaving cream, Ubangi is moving
toward the door. It seems I've been dozing off and on for
years. I slide out of bed and ease for the sink.

"It's me. Miss Mary," drills the voice from the hall. "Who
you think it is?"

"Miss Mary, you know you ain't got no business here first
thing New Year's morning!" Miss Mary is a numbers runner,
one of the best. Ten years she's been on the case, ten years
without a pinch. She will tell you that the direct approach is
the best way to keep people from crowding you. For instance,
she will limp up to a rookie cop and tell him that she runs
numbers. He will laugh and nudge his partner. And later they
will wave when she passes and smile the smiles they reserve
for spry grandmothers. Everyone knows her, helps her along
when she accepts help. But what does she want at this hour?

"You done messed up once, Ubangi Jones. Yesterday
evening I came here to pay you off and ain't nobody around.
Y'all niggas must not like money."

"How much I hit for?" Ubangi asks, leaning closer to the
door.

"A quarter," she richly says. That's not a bad sign for New
Year's Day and just our second time playing. A dime of that
quarter is mine too. Sixty dollars! The number was 201 from a
dream in which I was kidnapped to a foreign war and stranded
on a plain with two hundred men and their leader. They
started for me and I climbed a tree, a huge cypress which
stood alone on the plain. I woke up at that point and told it to

Ubangi. He played it, since he knew his dreams on such matters were good for nothing but the trash man.

He's grinning now and stroking his chin. "Let her in," I tell him. "Are you losing what little is left of your mind?"

"You in a hurry, Miss Mary?" he asks, turning back to the door.

"You damn right I'm in a hurry. What's wrong with you, nigga? You know how many folks I got to see by noon? About fifty-leven of y'all hit that number yesterday and damned near broke the bank."

This is getting silly. He's pacing around in front of the door. He's nailed to a superstition my grandfather nodded to. To ensure a year of good luck, the first person to cross your threshold on New Year's Day must be male. If female, expect hard times ahead. It said nothing about an old woman bringing money.

"Slip it under the door, Miss Mary."

"I ain't slippin' nothin'. MacDuffy say to pay off face-to-face with everybody and that's what I do. And I don't be paying off in no hallways either. It's dark as hell out here anyway. Ain't y'all got no lights in this fonky hotel? Somebody might hem me up out here and bump me on the head and take all this money."

"Get the money," I tell him. "Some of it's mine, you know."

He shakes his head and starts to pull on a shirt. "Well, just a minute, Miss Mary, while I get some clothes on." But she doesn't wait. I can hear her steps on the stairs. Ubangi looks at me as if he's just done in Lady Luck. He's out the door in two strides and down the stairs in a single leap.

When he gets back, we'll have to have a long talk about his superstitions. Now, I believe in a few lucky charms myself, but there is a limit. Last week he was screaming I would face certain death for drinking milk after a large order of shrimp.

"Fish and milk will knock your dickstring loose," he claimed. "Watch." Then it was watermelon and beer and other choice combinations he's kept under his hat from North Carolina.

Ubangi in nothing but thin clothes and house shoes, in the whistling wind. Miss Mary walking away from him, waving her hand. She's making him pay for his backward ways.

Wendell peeks in. "Is it safe?"

"Ubangi's outside now if that's what you mean."

Laughing his dignified laugh, he makes himself at home in a hurry. He's heard the whole thing. "What do you plan to do about your homely friend and his superstitions?"

"I'll probably just leave him alone," I tell him.

"Well, maybe that's best." He looks into the large pot on the stove where Ubangi left the black-eyed peas to soak overnight. "With ham hocks, right? Y'all really gone get into it this year. Good luck for days."

"Ubangi's doing the cooking today, not me."

He takes stock of the room as he always does, pacing its measurements, though he already knows its possibility as a stage. Cool, he is, since Ubangi still regards him as he would a snake. Stones him whenever he can. I remember Claude, who had no talent that we knew of and watched us box in the streets. Who became a head drum major later and high-stepped to his glory, despite our snickers. Claude, the meek one, who stayed among the gossiping girls. Wendell is much more sure of himself. Offers his ass for kicking sometime.

Watching Ubangi and Miss Mary on the street below, I try to shoo him away. I tell him Ubangi's coming up, but he simply comes to the window to see what I see.

"Mack, you won't believe it, but I've found a job."

"What are you using for luck?"

"Connections," he says, laughing. "It's one of those neighborhood theater things. They're opening with a couple of short plays next month. I doubt that I'll be with them long, but at least they seem better than those silly people downtown who are always putting on those horrid musicals. You just won't believe this play. I'll be doing one of those anguished revolutionary routines, a man torn between two women. One is a beautiful creature, tainted with bourgeois ideas—you know, car, steady allowance, European vacations. The other is a solid sister who is a leader among the underground group that he belongs to."

"You as a guerrilla?"

"We can be what we choose to be, Mack." He laughs again, flicking an imaginary ash from his lap.

Then suddenly he's stolen my face. Gloom far beyond our years. A style of hope. "I wanted to tell you about this funeral I've just come from. My rich uncle in Springfield died last week and his funeral was yesterday. I think I've told you about him. He was the one who could never understand why I didn't go out for football."

"Uh-huh, you've mentioned him. It must have been sudden."

"It was. I didn't go down until the morning of the funeral. I could have gone earlier, but there are too many people in our family that I simply cannot stand. Anyway, when I got down there I learned that he had left me a lot of money. That scares me."

"Money scares you?" I ask. He hasn't always been an easy one to figure out.

"My uncle's money does. He never liked me. He always wanted my aunt, his sister, to turn me over to him so he could whip me into something like him. But he hated the rest of the kinfolks more than he hated me and that's how most of his money came to me. When those fakers heard that, they all lined up to hustle me. They reminded me of every bullshit favor they've ever done for me. Man, they remembered everything and all of them standing around his grave, trying to make tears."

It was a strange moment because I felt close to him, not that I even liked him much before, but—in that moment—I knew him in a small way. "Funerals are for the guilty, Wendell. The living guilty." One day I'll make it as a confessor with pay. Reasonable rates, half-price in the mornings. Everything else will be cut loose—cafeterias, night clubs and so on. I'll listen to everyone's troubles, keep my own under guard, and send them away with the cure. "You'd better split now. 'Bangi is coming up."

"I'm not afraid of him, you know. Besides, I'm not over here talking to him anyway . . ."

He has started to speak again, but is cut short. I turn to see Ubangi in the door, his frown sucking up the room. He slams the door behind him and stomps to the stove, not looking at Wendell. "What is this shit, Mack? I keep Miss Mary out of here, almost losing all that money for us, and I come back and find this punk sitting up in here like Elizabeth Taylor or something."

"Kiss my Elizabeth Taylor ass!" Wendell suggests hysterically.

"Tiss my tizbeth taylor ass!" Ubangi shakes his head, turning to count out dollar bills. "And you call yourself an actor. You can't even get mad right."

The most painful stab, that is. Wendell is on his feet. He's belching smoke, staring bullets into Ubangi's back. But I see the claws of a cat shredding the air before the large dog snaps off its head.

"Mack, first it's Miss Mary. At least she's a whole woman. But you let this sissy slide in here. A half-woman the same as a whole woman as far as this thing go." He puts my share of the take on the table. "There's nothing like knowing who your friends are."

"Stop talking silly, man."

"I'm as much a man as you are!" Wendell snaps, hands to his hips.

Ubangi looks at him as if he's seen a mountain move. "A hot piece of pussy and a Tootsie Roll would knock you dead on your ass."

I'm between them now. Wendell is going on and on, woofing like a champ, though he's easing toward the door all the time. He's no fool after all. He knows what a couple of blows from Ubangi's fists might do for him.

"Well, I'll be damned," Ubangi says. "It looks like my ole partner Mack is taking up for a punk." He's squeezing two ham hocks like they're rubber balls. With no dignity at all, Wendell flees, slams his door and bolts it. Next time I'll let him pay for what his mouth gets him into. At least he might have waited out the storm of Ubangi's anger as any sensible man would have done. But no, he wanted to act.

"The way you're starting off this year, you won't last, 'Bangi." He's turned the fire on under the pot of peas. He's putting on his coat now.

"You might be right, Mack. This shit is too much for me, but I ain't going back to the Cape or North Carolina with my tail hanging down between my legs. I'll be back in a couple hours or so in case anybody calls."

"I may be out too."

He doesn't answer. We wear the lies of our lives like old tight coats, our wrists showing. We can spot another bad fit a mile off and we hate it for being uncool, for being us. We avoid it and look away. There is the so forth and the so on of the Avenue, for example. The Creole twins, Rose Anna and Anna Rose, are working this end of the block. In the cold, with all their lovers dead or inside and warm. The twins stand absolutely still as long as they can, hoping, perhaps, that Love's spirit will track them down. While they wait, the Noah's Ark of Roxbury rocks to a stop at the light. Creatures from a gone world blink at freedmen they assume diseased. Lost. Their powdered faces pressed to the windows, mouths slack to the little girl doing the James Brown on a corner while she waits for the light to change. They judge before they understand this. In the cold, the awful cold of this season. Were they sharper, they might notice Cain and Abel in Stetsons, finishing a roach in front of the fish'n chips joint. Or the high priest of somebody's tribe rapping long and loud in a doorway down the block. Or, in his tight coat, the hatless giant, fast disappearing around a corner, blowing into his fists and cursing ghosts.

Two days later I move out. The decision has quietly been working itself out for days. I didn't expect Ubangi to understand. He's preferred to drop the weight on the Wendell incident, although I try to tell him it's more than that. I need some time away. I need a different part of the city. I need a place where the heat is better. I have told him a hundred things, but he has dodged all of them.

"You pissed off at me for something else, then? The magazine thing?"

"No, no, man. It's not as if I'm leaving the city or anything."

"Mack, you my main man, even if you don't get no smarter. You know that." He's given me the beat-up stereo he won in a tonk game.

The apartment is a large room with a spitting radiator, a closet for a bedroom, a stand-up bathroom, and a kitchen with three roaches—all of them swift as thieves in the night. It once belonged to a friend of Bennie Tatum's who had to leave in a hurry for the West Coast. Some of the furniture will go to Bennie by agreement, but I'll have the necessities. I even have a telephone. I have lived in tighter spots, so I'm not hung up on the size. I just hope I can be left alone by the neighbors, with none of that beating on the pipes mess. I unpack my bag and go out for breakfast.

Jamaica Plains. Two young Puerto Ricans hold down a corner and see me as a stranger. Bilingual signs in store windows. I slip into the first restaurant I find, order a bowl of chili, and go toward the back where I can watch the street. Looking like hard times, Fuckup is slouched in a booth dunking a doughnut.

"Fuckup, what you doing here?" I ask.

"Eating my breakfast like you is," he says, nodding for me to sit. The gray of the day in his face.

"Look like somebody has just copped your clothes, your ride and your woman."

"Close to it. I got fired from the restaurant yesterday. Compliments of your buddy, Crackerjack."

"What are you talking about?" Fuckup's jokes have usually been jokes on himself, the kind that show him off as a man with his guard down. Of course, everyone has leaped to help out, kicking him in the side when they can. But to claim that Crackerjack is so cold? That's something else.

"Well, Mack, there's a lot about the dude you just don't know. He's the jivest nigga in the world, if you ask me. About a month before you came on, another dude was fired for stealing steaks. Now all of us copped something while we was down there. On what we make you have to. But Rufus, this man who got fired, stole forty-'leven steaks. So Sykes put the pressure on and C. J. cracked. He put the finger on Rufus to keep his little funky hustle. I should have cooled it then, knowing if anything happened it would be his ass or mine, and Sykes don't like me no way. He didn't like Crackerjack either, but I'm at the top of his shit list, you dig? And then there was a little fox who used to work there and me and C. J. bumped heads going after her. Crackerjack remembered all that too. So you see, Mack, I was a sitting duck." He licks his fingers and studies the street. Fuckup, the grinning blank, isn't grinning now.

I finish my chili in silence. This thing about Crackerjack is coming out in the open. Even though I've kept my nose clean, what surprises is he holding for me? Outside a man blows on his fingertips and politely pushes a *Muhammad Speaks* toward an elderly woman. She shakes her head and hurries on.

"That's a drag. I didn't know he'd pull something like that."

"Like I say, Mack, you don't know him. He'll do you a favor and expect you to pay it back double someday. If you don't, he'll put some shit in the game. Watch him, man. I shoulda wasted him."

I try to turn the talk to lighter things, though it is not easy. Fuckup is on parole for something and he's afraid of what his parole officer will say about his losing the job. It turns out too that he's been a musician and played a flute with various groups that have sprouted up and died in the city. A world of musicians doing anything to get in out of the cold.

"You didn't think I was just another nigga sudbuster, did you?" he asks.

"Uh-uh, but what leads you working on now?"

"My brother-in-law thinks he can get me on at the Post Office. I guess I'll try that for a while." He tries to smile, but it does no good: his face doesn't brighten.

"Drop down to the club some night," I tell him. "Bring the flute and maybe we can get into a thing." He waves and goes back to dunking his doughnuts.

I haven't heard from C. J. in three days. If he's as evil as Fuckup claims, he might be on my case this very moment, jabbing needles in a doll with my face. His wife called again last night. Her voice coming weakly over the phone and those gaps of silence when I couldn't answer all her questions. It turned out that I could only cover Crackerjack for one night, and this time he's been gone for three.

The phone rings as I come up the hall. "Is this the number I dial for good loving?" comes the voice, chilling in its familiarity. I drop the phone like it's a snake dipped in cowshit. I go to the window and raise it. The phone rings again, but I let it go on for minutes. The voice has been Michelle's, or a damned close copy. Ubangi up to his tricks? He's good at imitating voices. I remember one of the many times he's got me, imitating the desk clerk over the phone and telling me my mama was on her way to the room to take me back home. Yes, Ubangi. When the phone rings again, I'm on it.

"Come right over, you fine thing you," I sweet-talk into it.

"I plan to do that. Mack, this is Michelle."

Before I can recover, she's told me that she has taken me up on my invitation to come to the city, and that she's in town. Of course I can't tell her that I've been just kidding about those invitations, that our affair is over and done with. Ashes to ashes to ashes. I can't tell her anything, and instead stutter into the phone. I've heard her say she will be right over and she's hung up before I can stall her off to get myself together.

I straighten up the room and rush out to buy a bottle of rum with the little money I have left. When I get back to the apartment, she's standing in front of my door with the patience of a beautiful cat waiting for the gentle stroke of its master's hand. But when she sees me, it's something else again. When we break from the clinch there's a tear in her eye.

"I didn't think I'd ever see you again."

"Don't be silly, baby. You knew that time was the only thing separating us."

"It was the time that was so terrible." Her bag is heavy. She's planning to stay quite a little while, I see.

"You're losing a few pounds," she says, dimples going off all over as she pinches my side. "Your women must not be taking good care of you."

"There's nothing they can do for me. I need a for-real woman to take care of my needs. But I won't lie about them coming around, Michelle. You know my daddy did not raise a monk and you took a chance rushing over here unannounced."

"I gave you a full fifteen minutes to clean house. Then if I caught any bitch here, I'd scratch her eyes out."

I look at her closely. Is this a new woman? No signs of hard living. No new tough wisdom in her eyes. She's coming on like a sweet-smelling heat wave and I'm a man dying alone in the funky cold.

We settle quickly after she's approved of the apartment. She confesses that Ubangi gave her the address and that he sounded a little down over the phone. I shrug, remembering. I'll have to tell her how many circles Ubangi and I have run in since coming to Boston.

The first day is the ride in the blazing whirlwind, calm at the wind's eye, thrown out, rocked on the edges, then plunging down, down, the smell, driven to the core of memory. Calm again near evening as the snow begins and the muted voices float past the sweating windows until the whisper of our breathing drowns them out.

"It looks like I've just beat the snow," she says, coming back to bed after palming out a peephole in the window. Her walk, a dance to the snow. "You know, you haven't lost your touch. I can't believe what you tell me about spending most of your time hiding from these women up here."

"Straight up, Michelle. They don't really appreciate me."

And we walk in the snow later. She finds something rich and

strong in the neighborhood and the dimly lit faces of Puerto Ricans. I didn't spot it this morning when I went out. But she's funny that way—one minute wanting to know the whole world, the next wanting nothing but to be left alone. Quick too with halos for the new.

"I'm back at the club now and I've written a song for you. I wanted it to be sort of a surprise, but I'm not that good at keeping secrets from you. I've been working on it for weeks and tonight we'll blow your mind with it."

She just smiles. "I know it will be better than your letters. Anybody ever tell you about your letters? They're like limp cold hands."

"Thanks."

"Oh, look at Mack, sad Mack. I didn't mean to sound so bad. I just meant that, well, there I am down in that hell, expecting some help, you know, and I get your letters that really aren't you. It's like a stranger who'd rather not be bothered."

"I'll make up for it tonight," I tell her. And I will. The song has a thread so tender that it scares me. It's been moving around through my head for days, snaking slowly around a simple clean rhythm. It has been dedicated to no one, no memory I can finger. It has been just something tender in me that exploded, that I wanted to control because I am ashamed of it. It's better, perhaps, that I blame it on Michelle.

At the club she sits with Okra's girlfriend. They hit it off very well. Meanwhile, I get the group's nerve up. We've only practiced the song once and even that rehearsal was cut short.

"We can't do it, man," Okra says, shaking his head. He likes all songs down pat, run through at least a dozen times.

"But my old lady is here. I've sort of made a promise, you know?"

"But it ain't gone sound like nothing."

"Remember when the owner came in and requested James Brown that night and we slid it on him? And how you put down those bad chords on 'Round Midnight,' when that trumpet player eased into the club? You bad, Okra. Just be bad now, that's all."

Behind that he has no choice. Wanda is out with laryngitis tonight. We get to it on the second set, but right away I know the song's in trouble. While Okra is laying down the first melody, a drunk sitting next to Michelle knocks over his glass. Getting up, he knocks her glass over too. Then I'm into my solo, watching her help him pick up the pieces. It's a solo that can make a rock cry. But by the time they get things straight, I've finished and Bennie has taken off, his fingers catwalking the strings. I catch Michelle's eye and she shrugs helplessly. Okra's girlfriend is tugging at her. If it's not one thing, it's another. About new dresses downtown probably or dingy historic sights. She presses on and on and will not be denied. The song ends. Behind that tune, happy types are crying in their beer and new lovers are a foot higher off the ground. I feel drained, all those beautiful things still in the air, unheard as far as I'm concerned because Michelle couldn't hear.

I try to cheer her up, but just manage to drink a lot of wine. She tries to cheer me up, but misses with her words.

On the second day she lets me know that she's running from her mother. My balloon of pride goes limp. She needs someone to take her in, that's all.

"Does your mother miss me, by the way?"

"She misses you like she misses poison."

We're walking again. Most of the snow has melted and run black streams through the gutters. This time we're caught in the flow of downtown crowds. She walks the city with the wonder of a child walking her first circus. Still she claims she's seen Harlem, pulled along in her Girl Scout suit by her aunt, the sister of her sailor father. Harlem, that she didn't like. She's noticed only the winos and the lonely people there, just like the ones she noticed last night at the club.

Then she pulls me into a shop to buy her a bright-red scarf. She wants it not to wear, but to trail at her side. "My mother has picked out a man for me," she says, not looking at me as we head toward the Commons.

"What kind of freak she pull out of her hat this time?"

"Awful," she says, "you can be awful sometimes. Besides, he happens to be a very nice man. He's a doctor and he lives in Providence."

We duck into the Commons, scattering pigeons. Panhandlers line the walks a short distance from the entrance. They take one look at me and pull their hands back in.

"My mother's getting worse. Every day now she rants and raves. She's just broken up with another man, you see. A white man, a timid accountant in town. Each time she breaks up with a man, there's a week of screaming about my father and by the end of the week she's found a new man for me. The doctor has a little Portuguese in him. He's the first one she's found who does."

"Are you planning to marry him?"

She doesn't want to answer this one. We stop near the pond, unable to see our reflections in the dirty water. An older couple argue near us, and she's dropped my hand to check them out. The man cuffs his woman gently upside the head. Then the woman spots Michelle gaping and she walks away, her man trailing close, woofing up a storm.

"Why have you been so afraid of me?" Michelle asks me suddenly. Like a fool I break into a hundred cowardly pieces. I kiss her quickly and pull her from the dirty pond, back to the crowds on the street.

By the third day she's an old maid brooding over her tea.

We've had lunch with Ubangi, who's had to split to make another appointment. His parting words: "Give Ivone my love. Tell her to hold on just a little bit longer, because I'm sho coming back for her."

"That poor girl is in bad shape over that man," she says. "He never writes, you know. And has only called her once or twice since he's been up here. Always that 'hold on' stuff. Every time I run into her she looks very low. But she's a lot stronger than me. She has a lot of faith in that man."

"Don't you have faith in me, sugar?"

"Uh-huh."

"You don't sound too sure."

"How can I be? Everything has to be spelled out in front of me. Like us being here now. I have faith in the present. But when I'm down there alone . . . it's hard then, Mack."

"You think it'll be easier here? Loneliness settles like the snow outside the damn window. It's not as if you can run from the snow, Michelle. I used to think that I could outrun it or there'd be that special place of the unlonely . . ."

She nods. "Maybe we were better together when you were telling me all those crazy things about us getting together. Sometimes those lies keep things sweet and simple."

"What I feel now is no lie, but it's not enough for me to make any long promises. We don't need the games. Look, you need to get things straight with your mother."

She sips her tea and makes a face. "Well, anyway, I had already decided to leave tonight. I have the funny feeling that I'm pushing. Maybe you're right about everything. I don't know."

"Going? What the hell are you saying? I told you to stay as long as you wanted. I just mentioned your mother be-cause . . ."

"No," she says, eyes closed, shaking her head quickly now.

We take a subway home, not saying a word. The motion of the train relaxes us. When we first got on she kept edging from me when I tried to get next to her. People have looked curiously from under their newspapers with screaming headlines.

In silence she packs quickly and we only have time for a last cup of wine before we're in a taxi headed for the bus station. We get there as the last call goes out for her bus.

The door closes and the bus pulls off. It disappears around a corner and I'm left standing there next to a girl crying after a soldier. She looks at me and shakes her head. I follow her back inside, humming that beautiful song that Michelle never got to, and I know that she has gone from me forever. Back to her mother.

It's Sunday now, jam session time, and I've gotten myself together since Michelle has left. Ubangi has made it a point to get to the Eldorado Lounge, where I've been jamming the past three Sundays. Something is weighing heavy on his mind today. When we stop outside after the session, he's rubbing his hands together, and it's not because of the cold.

"Not a bad session, main man. You actually tried to get loose for once. I didn't know you had it in you."

"I'm the baddest you'll ever want to hear. Remember that."

The session has been a holy communion. The heat went off as we were beginning, but no one left. The stand was crowded: ex-musicians with names around town, some of them looking bad from scuffles with scag or cheap wine; schoolteachers who endured their jobs to eat, and a white dude who eased in from nowhere with a handlebar mustache and played like Mingus until he broke the bridge on his bass. And we've cooked and cooked this afternoon. Then word has got out that Hightower, the legend of Roxbury, is on his way down with charts for a heavy piece he's been working on for months. People have been known to catch him woodshedding in alleyways, spittle at the corner of his mouth, working his trombone slide into a blur. Or in the back of a poolroom—he doesn't care. For him, space is where you make it. So a few of us laid out with our horns while the stream of rhythm sections dribbled to mediocre players.

When he finally burst in, his fans edged closer to the stand. Bringing their drinks with them, they pulled up their collars and blew into their fists. There were six of us up on the stand and we made room for him. Not speaking, just grunting and nodding, he dropped his heavy coat on a chair and leafed through the charts. We were a little disappointed when he handed them out. It wasn't the long piece yet, simply a Monk type blues, which showed, though, that he knew a hell of a lot about music.   ·

Within minutes the big dude had blown himself into a sweat. Whenever he went through a nice run, his fans would go wild, slap each other's palms and claim him as their man. But no one expected him to stretch his solo twenty minutes. I was at the bar myself, rapping with Ubangi, when a cheer went up. The heat was back on. Of course, everyone claimed that Hightower's solo had done it. He finished during that applause, nodded, and stepped back, resting his horn at his side.

He walks on ahead of us now, adjusting his fez, fitting on his dark 1956-style bebop glasses. "Shoo-bee-doo-wopwop—bedoo." A few dudes fall in step with him and we follow them to the bus stop.

"What's new?" I ask Ubangi.

"There's a boss party coming up next week I want to pull your coat to. But let's go get some food first."

Sunday evenings are the sluggishness in things. Snipers,

plumbers and priests slip through the wet streets. He steers me into a restaurant that stands crooked on a side street. Its windows steamed. A soft song by Smokey welcomes us.

An albino cook in a chef's hat is dropping dimes into the box. "What y'all want me to play next?" he asks, flashing his yellow teeth at us, at the street, at a booth filled with four women.

"Some Ray Charles and some James Brown would go right with this sweet potato pie," one of them yells.

"Coming up." The albino boogaloos back to the kitchen when the song comes on.

Then a waitress, hairnetted and ungirdled, moves up to our table. "Can I help you gentlemens?" she asks, nodding at the handwritten menu in front of us. She goes on in a monotone. "We out of roast beef and the corn muffins will take another fifteen minutes, but we got plenty of everything else on there." Cottonfields in her voice. A frown to tell us she's stuck here and would rather be at least ten other places.

As she leaves with our order, our eyes follow the bounce of her heavy hips, their unbothered bounce to a humming bass line off the jukebox.

Ubangi shakes his head. "Must be jelly, Mack, 'cause jam don't shake that way! Look here, what I wanted to tell you about was a pimp's convention some dude told me about a few days ago."

"A pimp's convention?"

"No shit. They gone have it out at a motel somewhere outside of town and the dude says I can be his guest."

"You crazy?" I ask.

"You damn right! I ain't stupid enough to sit around in the cold trying to get me a construction job. Besides, you always claiming something is stupid. You said the same damn thing about the magazines."

"And what happened? Tell me, why ain't we out there running them damn magazines?"

He shakes toothpicks out of the hot-sauce bottle and hands me one. "It'll be just like a party, Mack. That's all. I just wanted you to meet some of the most influential dudes in Roxbury. Most of them run the clubs and shit. Look at it this way, it's just ole Ubangi trying to look out for his good friend. Now, if you don't want to go, that's that. Nothing to bust a gut over."

"Well, a pimp's convention just ain't my shot."

The waitress is back to place our silverware, napkins and glasses of water. "Sugar Mama, what you doing later tonight?" he asks. She smiles dryly and walks away.

Then his eyes narrow in seriousness. "Mack, you think I could make it as a pimp?"

He's told me not to bust a gut, but that one really gets to me. When I come up for air, he's still looking stone serious. "What you laughing at? I mean it. The dude I was telling you about say I got a good future. Say he might even loan me one of his to get started."

"Well, it sounds like to me you better watch this dude. He might be setting you up for something and it won't be easy street." Certainly I don't have the heart to tell him he would starve in a day if he had to rely on his rapping power with women. A love man he's not, at least in the way he wants to be. Basically, he's a strong arm.

" 'Bangi, a pimp has to be cold enough to sell his mama."

He prefers to drop the subject over the plate of steaming ribs. This time the waitress grins a warm-blooded grin at both of us. The room is now in perfect pitch. Jitterbugs have tipped in from the cold to get warm and stand in front of the jukebox popping their fingers. The booth of women is rocking to the beat, one of them throwing up her hands and rolling her shoulders as they get up. "Tell it, tell it!"

We start to work on the food and don't bother to look up until a shadow darkens our plates. It's a pleasant surprise to look into Della's face. Dressed to kill, she's a different woman. "Well, well, what are two college boys like you doing in a joint like this?" Her three friends stand beside her smiling.

"How you been doing, foxy?" I say.

"Don't you be foxy-ing me. Y'all almost got me fired from my job."

"Do what?"

"Fired, man. You can hear. But I smoothed it over."

"Wow, I'm glad to hear that," I tell her. "When you coming down to the club, Della?"

She laughs. "Y'all something else. Always trying to push somebody off the track. I tell you about me almost losing my job and you come asking me about some nightclub. I'll be down, honey. But meet my friends." She introduces them and I miss all the names, though the face of one of them I won't forget. To say "pretty" might cheapen it with glitter. She looks as good as Aretha sounds. Her face speaks only to me, while everyone and everything has checked out to leave us there. Alone. Then she looks off, smiling. I must be staring too hard.

When they leave, the room has gone flat. The jukebox annoys, the jitterbugs are in the way, and the waitress becomes a loud-laughing country girl.

"What was her name, 'Bangi?"

"Who?" he asks. "The waitress? Her name is Anne, same as my sainted mama's."

"No. The one with Della. The one in blue."

"Man, I don't know nothing about no names, but she sure look good." He's busy sopping the last of the sauce with a ball of bread. "Just call Della. She know. But you better hurry 'cause I might beat you to it."

Tomorrow I must talk to that woman and ask for a little time. Tomorrow can be a new beginning.

Nine

HER NAME is Novella Turner and she's lived in Boston for six years. For most of those years she's been married. After that soured, she and her daughter, nicknamed Little Precious, have made it alone. They live in a new apartment building only four blocks from my place. Since Novella is from Charlotte, North Carolina, I've kidded Ubangi about having known her. ("Shoot, Mack, just because she from Charlotte and I used to run women in Charlotte, that don't mean I know her.") Yet he might have seen her picture in the newspapers when she had to duck eggs and spit from a welcoming committee, since that was the morning when she and two of her friends, the smartest students from an all-black high school, walked to the front door of the white high school to enroll as seniors. He certainly must have missed the story and the action when the city was shook up by three little girls and how Novella's father stayed off work the next day and put a .38 revolver in his hip pocket, a move which quieted the mob and closed the school while teachers and preachers gathered to skirt issues.

Last night, our first night together, she led me to Crumbly Rock Baptist where she's the lead singer in the choir. I confess I was proud of her, standing up front, soloing her heart out. Arms outstretched, head back, eyes closed as she went into her song, she made even me feel the spirit. I hadn't been to church since I had left New Mexico, although I could never forget the fire of our little church. The smiles among the congregation at Crumbly Rock warmly welcomed me as a lost son come home. By the second chorus, I was moving on time with them. One deaconess shot up, freezing, with her arms held high, her head knocked back by the force of the spirit. Another was helped out by two attendants. All this before the sermon. By the time the choir had started on a clap-happy gospel number, Reverend C. E. (cross-eyed? chicken eating?) Fuller, who doubled as choir director, had gotten away. I had been paying no more attention to him than the faded mural of "Jesus at Gethsemane" behind the pulpit. Both were expected scenery. But he began to stab and sweep at the singers as if he held torches that would frighten away any evil spirits in their souls. I mean, he naturally performed. Skipped, tripped around the altar, holding the lapels of his coat. Then down to the floor he danced, letting his feet riff meanly to the music. Up one aisle to the back and down another. Next to me, a woman sent up a scream that knifed into my head, her tiny fist catching me in the chest when she threw back her arms. In seconds, two usherettes scooped her up and carried her out just as she began to kick and twist as if going down in deep water. When the screams started, I stood as a man stands in his home not hearing the sounds, not smelling the smell of fire. He may only get wind of it when he begins to pay some attention to the crowd pointing wildly from the street. The grip I had on myself was far more than I could guess, because when the next round of screams exploded, I pulled loose the coat buttons I was pinching. Halfway up the aisle, one of the usherettes had been burned too, and the three of them hit the floor. No one budged at the sight of the women. "Jesus, I'm here! Take me, Jesus!" Reverend Fuller danced over them like a cruel juju man. Then a choir member slumped to her seat and I began to clap my hands, for the quick slide into the hot hands of salvation might have come for me at any moment. But the song soon ended and I was blessed with a smile from Novella. Later she introduced me to Reverend Fuller, who invited us to dinner tonight.

We're on our way to his place now, and she puts her hand in mine as we cross the street. In front of the liquor store they're doing the Friday evening dance, hustling into the store, wearing work clothes—coveralls, three-piece bankers' suits, nurses' uniforms—then back outside, sidestepping the women who take Salvation Army donations or sell *Watchtower*. I have beat the rush, tucking home my brown bag hours ago.

"Novella, what do you think he wants with me?"

"I have no idea. I think they just want to be sociable. They're nice people, so there's no use coming in with your guard up."

"As long as he doesn't try to twist my arm to get me back into the church, then we'll be straight."

"Come back into the church?" she asks, flooding me, the street, the planet with the thousand lights of her smile. "Come back into the church, Mack? I thought I was reason enough for you to be there each and every Sunday. If I can't do it, I'm sure no man sixty years old can."

"Well, go on with your bad self." Don't tell me my woman ain't together.

Plainclothesmen cruise past in unmarked cars, trying to

frighten the citizens with their frowns. Behind pool-hall windows, young brothers are draped in ugly purples and floating on cloud nine. From an alley comes a wind carrying Coltrane.

In front of the three-story building two little girls with ashy legs stare into a Lincoln Continental. "A mark of the trade," I tell Novella.

Bad words on her preacher seem to be the greatest sin. She must know better, though. I've told her you can't make gods of others, that any gods she can conjure will disappoint her, that anything on a pedestal becomes, in the end, a target for birdshit.

Reverend Fuller meets us in the hall. Without his suitcoat he looks trimmer. "Novella. Mack. God bless you both. Come on in and have a seat. I was just doing a little reading here while I was waiting."

His wife steps out of the kitchen, drying her hands on her apron. She's a plump woman with a smooth baby face. A former usherette, Novella has told me. "How you two getting along?" she asks, watching my face, then Novella's.

"Just fine, Otha," Novella says. "Need any help in there?" They go off together to the kitchen.

Preacherman and me sitting and making small talk. "Santa Fe, huh? You must know of Reverend J. D. Rogers out there. Good young preacher, that Rogers boy is."

"I knew him very well. We graduated from high school together."

"This ole world is a small one, I do declare."

I nod with Reverend Fuller. "Yes, sir, it is." J. D. a guard getting no glory, and I a halfback, loving my name in print each week. We hounded trim together and copied off each other in geometry class. Harmonized "In the Still of the Night" on street corners and hung around the older cats, hoping to curse like them someday. "Eskimo" Rogers we called him too, because he wore wools and corduroys most of the year. Then he sold Chevies before the days he began seeing devils in the sky. They've been watching him closely ever since, placed him at the head of the church to keep a closer watch over him.

"Call me C. E., Mack. That 'sir' mess makes me feel so old, and you know I'm young enough to do most of what y'all do." He winks the wink of aging woman-handlers and we've become instant buddies.

His bad eye bothers me, though, especially when he smiles. I can't tell whether he's smiling at me or with me. His wife brings me a beer and he turns down the football game while I tell him about places I've been over the last five years.

"You been around some, ain't you? Most people I know that has done that much traveling either chased or chasing. Which one you doing?"

"Chasing, mostly. I started out wanting to find a place where I could play the music I wanted to play and be at peace. I haven't found that place yet."

Chuckling, he lights a pipe. "Then too, maybe you've been called for something."

"My mama has said that too. I don't know. Five years is a long time to look for something that you've been called for."

C. E. is skeptical. He won't have none of that aimless stumbling in the dark. There is a direction in all things. Study the winds. Seek the master plan. "People been called in all sorts of ways. Some gets the word in bars, baseball games, picture shows, and other places you might guess. See, you never know exactly when and where the Lord's call gone come and why it has to be you. And it don't do no good to ask 'why

me?' or try to stall, like some do. Believe me, Mack. I've tried
it. Just accept the Word and do. Don't hem and haw, just do.
But you got to be born in the spirit and the love of God."

I keep silent as he works himself up. Sermon time, it must
be.

"That's it, son. Pure and simple. Being born again is what
the word is all about and when you misunderstand that, you be
'bout ready to cuss yourself out for missing out so long. Now,
he fixed my feet thirty-five years ago down in Georgia. I was
twenty-four then, with a good job in the paper factory and
couldn't nobody tell me nothin' about nothin'. Kept me a
pocketful of money and dressed as good as they come. Yeah, I
was a mannish fool. I had so many women I didn't even know
all their names. Fact is, I had been tending to one of them that
very day, back up in the shade by a creek. Sweet, and ripe as a
Georgia peach in June. Martha was her name, sweet Martha,
and we was leaving them woods and coming back to the road.

"From around the bend I heard this coughing, sounds of
men puking, and it wasn't long before I seen these eleven men
chained together at their necks and legs. Before we knew it,
they was on us and Martha jumped back to keep from getting
stomped on. A white man on a white horse cussed us when he
went by. His face was scarred deeply and it seemed like years
while he sat on his horse just staring down at us. All you could
hear was the slow heavy feet of those men and their chains.

" 'Do not look with shame on them. Ha, you playful nigras
can't understand what you see. I could break both of you like
dry twigs before you even tried to understand. But I'll leave
you to wrestle in the bushes. You're just lucky you're of a
different time. Get out of my way!' His whip whistled just over
our heads and he was so close by then I could see the
blood-red of his eyes, the foam in the horse's mouth. Martha,
she fell, and I picked her up. I don't know to this day what got

into her but she just started whooping and hollering and ran up to that man and spit on him. He just looked at her with a sick look, his eyes, Mack, the eyes of one hundred devils burning into your head. Then I was between them and watching the whip coming down and I stood as it wrapped around me like a snake that is hot everywhere it touches. I grabbed and pulled with all my might. The man barely moved and he laughed and cut me again with the whip. I grabbed and pulled him again and this time he fell to the ground, his lips curled back and his teeth showing. And those men, when they saw this, ran back and broke their chains across his body, not saying a word, just sweating and grunting and breaking those chains as fast as they could."

"Breaking their chains, C. E.?"

"Breaking their chains, son." He shakes out his pipe then and starts to refill it. I'm glad I have something to sip on. The old preacher has wound up and is moving now, his bad eye working uncontrollably.

"It was a bad sight, an ugly sight, but those men wanted to be free to be away from that man and that place. And I turned to get Martha away from there 'cause a woman got no business seeing all that blood. The next thing I knew she was fanning me.

" 'Carl, honey, you'll be all right. Just take your time, take your time. I'm sorry if I overworked you.' Well, I started pushing her away because I knew from her teasing that that woman didn't know, couldn't know, would never know what I had just seen with my own eyes—the good one and the bad one—and she was sitting there talking all that junk. I had rolled all around in that red clay in one of my best suits and she talking like that. I just got on up and ran off to see Mr. Amos, the hoojoo man. He asked straight off what I had ate, what I had dreamed the night before, if I had some special enemies that he could call by name for a bigger fee—all them questions he asked me. Still and all he didn't know what it was, said he had been in the hoojoo business thirty years and still hadn't heard of anything like I done seen. Said he had heard of white devils plenty of times, but none on a white horse with a whip. And Martha still tagging along, talking that crazy talk of hers, and laughing. 'Ahmo have to get me a younger man,' she kept saying, grinning and pulling on my ear.

"Then I went to the palm-reading lady, but she just ducked her head and said nothing. It was Martha who suggested it, and it was Martha who hit the nail right on the head when she said that maybe I had been called. Of course I didn't know how she could fix her mouth to say something like that, since she didn't have nary church bone in her body. I had to scratch my head after that. It's just like when somebody tell you something about yourself they ain't supposed to know and you don't want to believe it, but you know deep down that it is true. Most of the time you glad they said it, though you don't know if you should thank the person or not."

He studies me for a moment. Novella and his wife are having a ball laughing in the kitchen. Whatever it is they're laughing about keeps them going on and on. Old Fuller sounds like a real sport in his younger days. Most of these old dudes have been. Still are. Novella tells me that he still raps to the young usherettes. No sense being old, I guess, if you can't raise hell.

"What happened to Martha?" I ask him.

"Well, I stayed away from her for about a week until I could get some kind of peace of mind on the thing. Course my decision was that my arms were too short to box with the Lord, like the old poem says, and I've been preaching ever since. Martha wanted to keep up that foolishness just like nothing happened. I tell you, Mack, she was a real temptation when she wanted to be and it was rough on me, starting out like I was, just to stay strong. My legs was just getting ready to run the Lord's race and I didn't want to fall the first thing out. So I prayed long and kept running from Martha."

"She never caught you?" I ask.

He looks toward the kitchen, grinning slyly. "She did. That's what I'm trying to say. She caught me a year later, when there was no place to run, no place to hide. After that time, she kept on coming to church and became one of the best women in the auxiliary. But all that was before I was married."

"Food's on the table!" his wife calls. "You men can get back to all your important talk after you eat."

C. E. is quiet over dinner, only bothering now and then to ask for the gravy. The women have taken over. They gossip about a good church sister's dress that did her no favors, about the choir's trip to Philadelphia coming up in two weeks. I catch Novella watching me from time to time. It's easy to tell she knows something about this whole evening that I don't know.

"Eat some more," C. E. says after I've refused more greens. "You young people ain't eating right no more. Your belly too flat. My daddy always said a man ain't ate right if his belly ain't poking out when he gets up from the table."

"You don't have any choice." His wife laughs.

"Quiet, honey. While y'all women were in the back dishing dirt, Mack and me have had a very good talk. I've told him we need more young men like him in the church, strong young men, not no runny-nose excuses for men, tipping around, beating and cussing out their elders. Besides, he got a good eye and he know the prettiest womens be in the church."

Novella and I have to excuse ourselves early, since I have to get over to the club. By the time we are ready to split, though, my idea of the preacherman has gone through many changes.

He's lived his life and is still going strong, with no regrets. A quick jivetime hustler he's not and you can't shoot him down because he has a different style. I mean, he's no fool, and I look forward to seeing him again. Novella smiles when I tell her this on the way home. She won't say anything. Just smiles and hums, making mellow the early movements of this night.

The early crowd is the sad one. Islands of sad thoughts, they sit rattling the ice in their glasses and scouring the dark for someone to talk to. I've gotten to the club a little earlier than I expected and I wish I haven't. A musty shroud catches me at the door and bothers me as I look for a seat alone.

Goofy, the regular hotman, is pushing albums. "Looka here, brotherman, you can get one for three dollars and two for five. You couldn't beat this deal with a billy club." And pushers slip through the gloom as kingfish glide in murky river water. Sweet-smelling women, who once got constant play, now must sit in twos and show plenty of their heavy thighs. With their blues, they wait, gut-grabbing blues that are pulling me down into their holes.

In the john a dude in a pink jumpsuit wants to press a nickel bag on me. "You the cat who play the tenor, ain't you? Well, look here, I'm about to get you into some reefer. This some boss shit here, jim. Let me lay just a wee tiny bit on you. Yessir, fire this shit up and you'll be walking in space and I know you can dig that."

I slip away from my instant buddy. He might easily be a cop hunting bounty, collecting a couple hundred off my head. I've seen the type, all teeth, the glad hand, the pat on the back. Then too, he might have been straight, but I prefer to play straight this night, and I spend the rest of the time before the set standing out front counting Cadillacs.

When we finally go on, it's just like old times. Okra, A. C.

and Bennie Tatum hit the road for a week, gigging in New Haven. The contract had been signed before I joined the group and the club owners wouldn't back down. So I stayed behind and worried whether a group's sound could change in a week. But nothing has been lost. As usual, no one speaks while setting up. A. C. grunts across his guitar after a few chords. Bennie Tatum nodding over his drums and Okra, head thrown back, cheeks ballooned, then throwing himself at the organ. We get it on. It takes two sets for Okra's organ to cut away and destroy goodfashion all the evil spirits. A. C.'s solos clean up after him and the victory is complete. Mean, mean. Unity music. By the end of the set, two conga drummers have eased in off the street and they have cooked and cooked like nobody's business. They go for themselves after the set has ended.

A fan buys me a drink during the break. He's been broken into a dozen pieces by the two sets. Only a drink can put him together again. I've seen him there, ignoring his woman, teeth gritted, fist at his ears, veins popping as the scales go higher, higher. He's like the diehard fight fan who bobs and weaves in his seat at the matches. He slaps me on the back.

"I used to play trumpet, my man. I bet you didn't know that." First Fuckup, now him, hundreds of others. Everyone has played at one time or another, it seems. I'll never use that line when I retire. I want to be carried out during a solo, or in bed with a woman. But not broken, telling people what I used to do.

His woman's face as beautiful and as sad as that of Billie Holiday. I smile at her and she smiles back. Her smile is a whisper song of Billie's "My Man": *It's cost me a lot, but there's one thing I've got. It's my man.* The stories in most eyes begin as lies about pain. Her eyes don't bother fronting.

Goofy doubles as club photographer. He's missed me on the

albums, so he zeroes in on where we're sitting. "How about a nice picture of everybody? One for the pretty lady to take home?" The fan falls for it. The picture he takes shows me grinning, dry-lipped, a worried look on my face despite it all. The fan looks half as drunk as he really is. His woman looks like she doesn't know what time it is, what club this is, and doesn't really give a damn either way.

Okra, wiping his neck, rescues me. "Mack, like I was saying, that trip was good for us, but really, we've grown to lean on that horn, man. There was a big hole in our sound and all of us could tell it. Next time, all four of us will go, or nobody goes."

"That's good, Okra. The only thing for me to get into while not playing is bad luck. I've lost a couple day jobs and even a woman."

"Let me help you with that woman thing, man, I mean, I have one I can loan you."

"What's wrong with her?" I ask. "Blind, crippled or crazy?"

"Naw, naw. You know me, Mack. You be knowing the company I keep."

"That's what has me worried." Okra's taste in women runs from bad to worse. I hate to run it down front like that on him, but it's true. The faces of his women hurt my feelings. One they call Running Bear. "That's cool, Okra, but anyway there's something I'm working on now. If it doesn't work out, then I'll have to borrow your black book."

The management is sponsoring a skinnyleg contest, so we get an extra-long break. I try to call Novella, but her line is busy. When I get back to my seat, my fan wants to talk some more. If there's a party going down, he'll know about it. He's where the action is, he tells me. He is the action. I nod, my mind back on that busy signal. Is there another man? She's said there has been nothing big in her life since the divorce, and the marriage dead at least a year before that. No man she's taken seriously in four years, she's told me. And I have believed her. She will be here tomorrow night. I warned her that I will convert her to a new church, the gospel of a different sound. She has laughed at the warning and said, "Maybe."

A hand heavy as doom is dropped on my shoulder. "Mack, you jivetime Negro. What you into?" It's Ubangi, wearing a grin as slick as new money. It's the grin he flashes on chumps, the grin I don't like now. (He says "Negro" when he has something to run on you.)

"What the hell you so happy about? You don't even look like yourself. You go out and find a girlfriend or something?"

"Ha-ha, still the same ole crazy Mack. I see on top of being crazy, you drunk tonight." When he takes off his coat I have to stare. Ubangi is wearing a white silk dashiki trimmed in a rich red. A gold ankh dangles at his chest. He snaps his finger at the bartender. "Order yourself another taste. I'm buying tonight." Then he smooths the dashiki in my gaping face. "Stop bucking your eyes, my man. How would your militant friends dig this?" The original hoochiecoochie man, he is.

"Ubangi, they'd take you for an undercover man right off the bat. Your shoes. They're suede. They don't walk around wearing that kind of suede no more." He shrugs.

"And don't tell me you've gone and joined an organization."

He shrugs again. "I've joined the baddest group of jive-talkers, moneymakers, heartbreakers and soulshakers. That's what I'm here to tell you about. Man, you really blew it when you missed that pimp's convention. First there's somebody I want you to meet."

He waves toward a dark corner and a blond-wigged woman emerges and starts our way. Wanting no one to miss her, she takes her time. And no one can. Her legs, thin and bowed like a scatback's. In fact, all of her is on the muscular side, she would use lye on her man if she caught him up to no good. A hard, scarred woman.

"Mack, this is a friend of mine," Ubangi says, his voice filled with pride. "Her name is Ova Easy."

The whore's whisper is husky. Her lips, close up, are brutal, her wig a stiff joke. "Ubangi has told me a lot about you," she says.

I look into my drink for answers to a hundred questions. Where did Ubangi get this one from? She's ages ahead of him. I know he didn't pull her from a laundromat or a bus station or those other weird places he claims he's always copping women. Oh no, and if he did he must have strong-armed her and if he did that he would have a scar or two. But his face is smooth. So what's the joke? Then he whispers something to her and she shimmies her way back toward her corner.

"Why she leave so soon? You act like you don't trust me around your women."

"I don't," he says, beginning to pop his fingers to the jukebox.

"Why?"

"You say crazy things—you know how you talk."

"Like how did you hook her to hook for you?" I ask.

"Uh-huh."

"And how you don't know what the hell you doing?"

"Yeah, you all the time saying that stuff that sound like it come from home. You ain't my daddy, Mack. Let's see what your smart mouth gone say when she drop this yard on me tonight. Meanwhile, I got some things to tell you, some folks for you to meet, and some sights for you to see. Go up there and play some. I'll wait."

At the night's end, I'm waiting outside for him. In the past twenty minutes every small-time hustler and pimp in the place has slid up to Ubangi and hit on him for some money, running it down smoothly, out the side of their mouths. He's come out alone. Then hunches his shoulder and leads me toward an after-hours joint.

"I ain't gone keep you out all night," he says as a starter. "I know you've got some warm trim waiting for you at home. I do too. You asked about Ova Easy. She's hustling for me right now. A buddy of mine turned me on to her. She works downtown as a gogo dancer in one of them strip places them freakish whities go to. I just laid my line down and the next thing I know she's bringing me suits and shoes and shit. I ain't even had time to screw her."

I don't answer. I just follow him. Talking won't do much good. He's past that, so far past it he hasn't asked himself how he can catch a seasoned hooker in his first time out. I see him under the jail. I see him selling ice cream to the kiddies in the Common, or pushing peanuts at the basketball games after this. I see him sweeping streets.

On a back street we slow up in front of a two-story house. The first-floor windows have been blackened and no sound comes from inside. Ubangi walks up, raps three times on the door and waits. A red eye fills the Judas hole, blinks, shifts. The door swings open and the space is filled by a slick dude who rubs his hands together.

"Evenin', Mr. Jones," the man says, taking the five-dollar bill Ubangi offers. Then he pats us down and grins. Ubangi pulls me to the packed basement. We scratch, push and kick our way to the bar. The couples are jammed close, barely moving to the music. The Staple Singers on the box. Smells drift to funk. The eye-burning smoke, its dry fingers in my nostrils. By the time we get to the bar, I'm ready for another meal.

"Where's that fish, Ubangi? I hope it tastes as good as it smell."

"Bettie fry the best fish in the world, jim. But wait a minute. Business before fish. I want you to meet somebody."

After stretching his neck, he's found his man. A heavy-set cat who wears a red banlon under his sharkskin suit. Next to him a sister looks at me and 'Bangi like we're raggedy-assed cutthroats.

"Mack, this is Big June. June, this is Mack, my ace nigga. Remember I been tellin' you about him? His stuff so heavy now it loses the average chump. He drove a strong man crazy tonight by just hitting this one high note."

"That's a handicap," the fat man says, chewing his toothpick in the manner of movie gangsters.

Ubangi shakes his head. "It's a handicap for dummies, yeah. But me and you know talent when we hear it, don't we?"

The fat man looks me over as if he's going to ship me to the slave auction in the morning. "I want to hear him first, not that I don't trust your judgment, Ubangi. It's just that I can decide better if I hear him. You know how our crowds are. They ain't too cool with that way-out stuff. They like their music like their liquor—hard and straight."

"That ain't nothing but a word, June. Mack, when you want to slide a few bars on June? He just a country nigga like me, except he hide it a little better."

"Sunday night is okay," I tell him.

"See there, June? It's a deal, then. Sunday. I'll call you early and we'll get the details straight." June nods and turns back to the fox.

"Who is he?" I ask after Ubangi's pulled me into line for the fish sandwiches.

"Dude just bought a new club he'll be opening in a few

weeks. Looks like you get first shot. Don't pay no mind to what he be talking. Between you and me, you're as good as in if you want it. You'll have your own group. Don't say 'Bangi ever held grudges."

He goes on to introduce me to other big-time operators with colder styles than Big June, smaller men with thin mustaches. Then before we leave, he tells me that he has to put in an appearance upstairs. No one up there bothers to look up from the poker game.

Outside the cold wipes out the smells and noises of the joint as if they never were. "Ubangi, where's your hog? I thought every hustler worth his rap has a hog."

"It's being special-ordered, smartass. I might even let you ride along with me sometime if you be cool."

"Tell me about the convention," I say. "You make all your contacts there?"

"Some of them, not all of them. You forget I done been here six weeks. That's enough for me to go through Roxbury and see what's going down. Most of the big shots was at the convention, though. Fact is, everybody and his mama was there. And we partied back, man. I know you ain't seen nothing like that. Champagne running on the floor like water. First dude I ran into was decked out in red—red suit, red hat, red socks, red suedes, red drawers, probably. His name was Red Dog and he was from New Haven. Then there was a cat from Hartford who was chauffeured up in his Eldorado with the green velvet top, but he spent most of the time in the car watching television. I later saw the same dude inside and he had whores from all the continents, Mack—a blonde, a Chinese, a Mexican, a high-yellow, and a woman with skin so smooth and pretty and black she was a black pearl and I definitely wanted to get next to her. And all these stallions wore minks, hear me? By this time, my eyes were bugging out they sockets. You ain't seen no women until you seen what I seen that night."

He looks again at his watch and steps up the pace. Across the street a skinny woman flags at a car. Cold and luckless is her look when she gets no attention. Her friend stands on the opposite corner and they crack jokes and laugh to keep warm.

"That's all?" I ask. "They just parade their women around?"

"You would say that, not knowing any better and still being a youngblood and all. But you know that whenever big niggas get together they goin' to start rappin' and cappin' on each other. They no different from jitterbugs. Maybe that's why at this motel all the guns was checked in just like the hats. They had a man working in there alongside the girl and he'd take your piece, put a ticket on it, then give you the matching ticket. So I was standing in line when I ran into Sweet Skeet. I done told you about him, I know. The dummy from New Bedford who called himself a hustler. Always trying to be more than he was. I almost choked when I saw him there. The first thing he showed me was the little roscoe he had hidden down his back. 'No tellin' what kind of shit might break loose,' he said. 'You can't trust nobody.' Of course, if Skeet could do it, anybody could. I was thinking that everybody in the place still had a gun on him or had his old lady carrying one for him, so Skeet wasn't putting nothing special down. Judging by the suit he was wearing, he wasn't doing too good, and somebody would be sure to cap on him before the night was over. He just sticks out that way, like he had a sign on his chest, 'Pick on me.' "

A car shoots past and honks. 'Bangi throws up his hand, not even turning to see who it was. I pull up my collar. Ubangi, pressing on, eyes watering.

"After we ate, we got down to business. Everybody started

testifying about how good they was doing. It was like church, man. Then they paraded their women some more and they showed off their fur coats and diamond rings. But the dude from Albany took the cake. He shut everybody up. When it was his turn, he called his twelve whoas to the front. Then he asked each of them what they got for Christmas. They said the minks they was wearing, the diamonds on their fingers, and the cars they was driving. You could hear a fly poot. Everybody was trying to be cool until it came down on them and then they went wild, stomping and clapping.

"And that's when somebody started joogin' at Sweet Skeet and his two excuses for whores. They told him he was the only pimp they knew on welfare, stuff like that. They gave that poor boy no slack, Mack. He's nervous too, you know. The next thing I know he standing up, almost crying, talking about he don't want to kill no nigga but he gone have to. People disappeared, man. Under tables, out the door—they was gone! The dude took off running too, and Skeet fired at him three times and missed all three. But the dude fell on the floor twitching, not sure yet whether he had been hit. 'Goddammit, goddammit, he got me.' Some kind of mess like that. Of course Sweet Skeet left his whores there and ran. They got a posse together in Eldorados and the last I heard they was hot on his trail someplace in Canada."

Our laughter ends on a brighter street. At a corner we stop at an all-night filling station. Ubangi buys cigarettes while I go around to the john. When I get back, Ubangi is leaning against the machine looking down the street. He motions for me to move out of his way. All of this without a word, fire growing in his eyes, small coals. The attendant comes in to the cash register. He and Ubangi trade looks and he shrugs his shoulder and moves back outside. The mystery thickens. I take a seat and wonder if I will talk with Novella this night. How have I gotten steered away from the warm words that put everything right? I must be a fool. I try to call her, but the line is still busy. The phone is off the hook. She's not gossiping at two-thirty in the morning, that's for sure. She's angry, that's all. I'll smooth it over, just as soon as I do 'Bangi the favor and see what I'm to see.

"Ready to go, man?" I ask. He says nothing.

Then: "I'm gone break that bitch's neck. It's been over twenty minutes."

Then I open my eyes. Carloads of white men clutter the streets. Convention types in rented Chevrolets, waving fistfuls of dollars and screaming at anything black and wearing a skirt. At wives coming home from work, at grandmothers on midnight vigils walked home by daughters. The dittybops walk past, unseeing, though the cars keep moving and don't stop for long.

A man steps out of the building and stops to smooth his hair. His white socks and hushpuppies mark him as a department-store detective or suburban high-school principal. At any rate, his wife is tucked in and he's over here chasing skirts. He rushes for his car just as Ova Easy steps out.

Ubangi cruises right through the door and across the street, like a runaway fullback.

"Why you stay in there so long, whoa?" He commences to put her through those changes, slapping her across the face, shoving her. He doesn't hear the john peeling rubber from the curb and almost colliding head on with another john pulling up. A whore jumps out and runs, her eyes popping in fear.

Ova Easy's knees buckle after a slap upside the head. Ubangi is showing his true colors. He stalks her, shakes her by the shoulders.

"What I tell you, bitch?"

"HEY MAN, DON'T BE BEATING ON THAT WOMAN LIKE THAT!"

The voice shooting from a dark window overhead. Heads fill other windows, some going up and letting music rush out to the street.

I feel a little sorry for Ova Easy. She's getting a real ass-kicking, and I have a weak stomach for it. "Ubangi, lighten up on her!"

He has her head in the vise of his hands. I push him away, and as he stumbles, the wig goes with him. He goes limp. I need the fireplug for support. Under the wig is a quo vadis haircut and a scar running behind the ears. Her head is as smooth as marble. Ova Easy is a dude!

"Muthafucka, you've really blown this time!" the freak shrieks, fishing for a razor or something.

There is a flurry of laughter in the windows and someone points. A patrol car has just roared into the block, its red light flashing. Ubangi is still staring from the wig to Ova Easy's head, then back again. He has her by the arm now and she's still squirming to get away, the other hand digging between the phony breasts. In my surprise I've felt this whole scene slipping away, as a child in his sleep, knowing he will piss on himself, but there's nothing he can do.

"Cool it, 'Bangi. The fuzz!" From Falmouth, from North Carolina, they've come. These two hard faces. Their eyes blaze when they see 'Bangi shake the freak so hard its teeth rattle and a razor drops to the pavement from under its dress. Ova Easy drops to the pavement in a sitting position, dazed. Blood colors Ubangi's eyes. It will take an army to stop him now, and I won't be in it.

The door slams and a cop moves slowly toward me, the billy club drawn. "Okay, let's be smart and nobody will get hurt." But all the while he's raising the club higher and I think of my scalp split and blood spurting. My blood on the pavement. With a forearm I block the cop's blow and catch him on the chin. The blow leaves him cross-eyed. Ubangi is standing over the freak, debating whether or not to finish him right then with a mighty left, or to let him cry first. But the other cop is coming to the rescue at top speed.

"Watch out!" Ubangi slams the sneaky muthafucka in the gut and the gas of sausage pizza is belched on the night air.

My man has bounced back to his feet. I crowd him close, tense that a billy club or .38 slug will find my brain. He will go for his gun now. But he surprises me and goes for the stick again. He charges me and catches me nicely in the ribs. But I'm into the Ali Shuffle and I beat a mean riff on his jaw as his momentum brings him in close. He drops again. Out the side of my eye I catch Ubangi working over the other cop. The freak cheers for the cops. "Kill 'em, kill 'em!"

A nearby streetlight goes out suddenly and in the next moment I can hear the air whistling from one of the tires on the patrol car. A dude in a big hat melts back into the night and I thank him. Then silence and just the heavy breathing of desperate men. I kick the stick out of the cop's hand and set him up for a combination. The sirens are on us now and two cars take the corner on two wheels.

"Watch out, Mack!" Ducking, I spin, but not fast enough. Stars explode from the back of my head and, reeling, I can see the cop's gritted teeth and the pavement coming up fast. A shot. Brakes squealing, sound of running, running from everywhere, coming, coming to end the battle. A kick in the side brings me around. They throw me up against a paddy wagon and pat me down. Ubangi has been pushed inside. People are shouting from the windows, and the cops, ducking a few beer cans, hurry to get us out of there. The freak has its wig back on and is talking to a cop. Before they get me in the wagon, one of the cops gets in three solid punches to the back of my neck. The door clicks as loudly and as finally as the lid on a casket. The patrol cars tear off after we're bolted in, but the driver and his partner in the wagon are holding a regular convention up front.

"I hope they throw your ass in jail," the freak manages to hiss through the back window. Ubangi's parting shot is a gob of spit that slides harmlessly down the bars. Suddenly we roll around the corner, where an older man is thrown in with us, and they claim that he's drunk, but he looks okay to me. His woman stands helpless on the sidewalk, then bends to get the keys he's managed to throw her.

We're moving again. Ubangi staring at the dark buildings. We know we may never reach the jailhouse alive. The other man looks nervously around. He is a graying man of about forty. His lips are moving but nothing comes out. He tells us later that he's recording the streets in his head.

"We ain't going to no jailhouse," he says. "The jailhouse was only three blocks from where we was."

A nerve goes wild under my eyes and those stars, though duller now, explode once more in my head. It seems days ago that the preacher has been talking to me, boasting about a safer, quieter life. Days ago it seems that I left Novella's apartment, promising her I'd be back fifteen minutes after the last set.

"What did they do with the horn, 'Bangi?"

He looks at me strangely, laughs, then speaks to the streets. "You almost got your head knocked off and you gone sit there and ask me about some horn?"

"If it's back there on the sidewalk, then it's gone by now. If I left it in the service station, no, I remember sitting it next to that fireplug." The stars explode again and I rest against the cold metal seat.

The stranger shakes his head. "From what y'all say, I figure the only thing that saved y'all was because of the folks back there been mad for days. The cops shot a ten-year-old boy last month. For nothing, said it was a mistake. They probably didn't want to risk anything tonight. But I know they still want to get y'all. They might try to take us someplace and beat us like they do."

"The hell they will," Ubangi says. "I ain't taking no beating."

"Well, they got the shotgun and the shotgun don't give a damn what you don't take." Skidding to a stop, the wagon throws us forward. We're at the end of an alley, idling now. The light is on in the cab of the wagon and the driver and his partner are talking some more. The nearest lights are a mile away.

"Yeah, that's what they gone do, all right," the man says. "Beat us and leave us out here."

"Shut up!" I tell him. "My head is killing me and I don't feel like hearing all this mess."

The beeps over their radio and the breathy metallic voices. A few things have come clear by now. The cops have been pimping Ova Easy. Ubangi was just a cover to keep the bigger pimps from stealing him. Did the cops know what he was? She might have approached them for protection after they approached her for a quickie, maybe. Or they might have known all the time and kept her out there under the threat of a blackmail sentence of sixty days for freakishness.

"It's a simple game, Mack. I should have listened to you. No, I get my hard-headed self back in trouble. All for a freak. They'll lock us up and throw away the key."

We conclude that the freak would take the johns to a prearranged spot. The cops would come on the set like gangbusters. Meanwhile, Ova Easy has got the john to pay her in the car. Before they're out of the car, the cops are on them.

Ova Easy breaks away, the john gets scared and takes off. Then the cops and Ova Easy later split the take right down the middle. The next day the john would have a tale for the boys at the office. Once in a while the freak would take one upstairs for show. After all, other whores would see all this and talk.

"Somebody told me something like this a long time ago, but I got so excited about this idea of pimping I forgot all the common sense I ever had."

"One thing I'll never understand, 'Bangi. What did they do with the freak when they went upstairs?"

"Anything and everything. You know how freakish them whities is. But they ain't in this wagon, neither is Ova Easy. It's your ass and my ass they got."

"And your pimp friend, the one who set you up in the first place, was he in on it too?"

He doesn't answer, keeps his head turned. Our leader gives us mean looks. "While you fools are talking about some whore, these crackers about to do us in."

We've rolled to another part of town and they've thrown in a big Irishman who's bleeding heavily from the nose. Then a seedy couple. The woman sits up front on the other side of a screen divider. I have a feeling the danger zone may be behind us now.

"Hey, you fruits can't lock me up!" the woman starts screaming at the cops. "I'm crazy. I belong back in the nut house. We were only celebrating tonight. I'm crazy. Harry, please tell 'em something."

Her man just moans and groans. She tries again. "I'm crazy! I'm crazy, you bastards! I just got out of the nut house last week. Take me back. Not to jail, you shitheads."

Her man tries to calm her, but she'll have none of that. He shrugs and turns to us. "Got a cigarette, guv'nuh?"

Our leader hands him a pack. "Ask like a man, goddammit! These cops ain't stole your balls yet. Take one, but be a man and speak like one."

This rattles the old man slightly, has him shaking after he's lit his cigarette. Our man snatches his pack. "Be a man, goddammit! I didn't say you could have them."

The wagon stops at a light, and beside us a brother is rocking behind his wheel to the music coming loud and clear off the radio. In a cafeteria they look curiously at the zoo on wheels. On the next street they throw in a mousy man for sprinting bareheaded after dark: suspicious character. Then up empty streets we rocket. The city in the last long round of waiting for the dawn. Be a man. Berserk Pair Arrested after Attempted Ambush on Policemen. "I'm a man." Our leader is on his feet now, falling on me as we take a corner on two wheels. Then he steadies himself. "I'm a man, goddammit! I'm a man! I'm a man!"

I'm nodding with him before I find my own voice. "I'm a man!" But it's all cut short when the wagon stops and he's thrown hard against me, knocking the wind out me. Suffolk County Jail.

Ten

THE SCREW looks like death sucking a lemon. Tonight he and his friends are running a red-hot shuttle between the cell block and the large pen where we've been fingerprinted and our names filed on IBM cards. "Lock 'em up!" are the sergeant's last words as he gums the hell out of his tobacco. Like puppies wagging their tails, the lackeys jingle their keys in joy. One of them comes for me and I make sure he doesn't touch me as he leads me through a narrow passageway. I get a spic-and-span closet of a cell painted hospital-green. Ubangi gets the one next to mine.

"What about my phone call?" I ask. Thanks to the Leader, I know this much about my rights.

"Hold your horses, pal. You'll get your turn soon enough. By the way, what you in for?" I don't answer. He keeps it up with the keys after he's locked me in.

"Well, at least you ain't spouting off one of those long stories you people always got. Everybody's innocent, nobody's done nothing. That's all you hear around here. You blacked out—right?—and the next thing you know you're running down an alley with some broad's purse or punching some guy in the face. The stories I get you wouldn't believe . . ."

He backs off a little when I grip the bars as if I want to break one off to beat him with. "I'll bring you a band-aid," he says. "That cut looks bad."

I haven't noticed the blood that has rimmed the top of my coat collar. The billy club must have opened that cut up, unless one of those sissies has been scratching. ·

Others are led past us in assembly-line monotony. College students drunk from fraternity parties, shifty-eyed idlers in wrinkled pants, slick-faced cats with someone else's blood on their shirts. When the next crop is marched in, the noise of the place shoots into high gear—screams, moans, belches. Some of this, I suppose, to greet the new arrivals. Other noises as stiff tongues at the screws who seem to enjoy their work too much. I wonder if they're getting a commission from this business.

The Leader has been led away and strait-jacketed. They have pronounced him eternally insane and taken him to a room where he can hear his own voice, alone. He must be crazy, they've decided. No nigga can come into this jailhouse like he owns it and scream "I'm a man!" in the sergeant's face and get away with it. No sir, a nigga like that, you don't know what he'll think of next. They'll cure him and release him to talk to himself and make people think it's just the wine that's made him that way. His woman, I hope she will understand. The screw hands me a band-aid through the bars and hustles off.

"Ubangi?" He's been quiet on the other side of the wall. "Ubangi?"

"Huh? Speak up, man. I can't hear a goddam thing for all this noise in here."

"Do you think that captain will come through?" I ask.

"How do I know? I don't know what the hell will come through tonight."

Big June has told him that if he ever gets into trouble, to tell any screw to get word to the captain. When Ubangi tried it on the dope who fingerprinted us, the guy just shrugged his shoulders and smiled a dry screw smile.

"You need to have a talk with Big June when we get out of here, Ubangi. I mean, Ova Easy and now this captain . . . June's supposed to have him in his back pocket."

"Shut the hell up, will you, Mack? I'm thinking."

A man is escorted from his cell to take a piss in the trough that runs the length of the cell block. The screw eyes him as if he might try to make a break for it. The man looks sixty. A belch goes off from one of the end cages and the screw returns it with the finger.

"What's that?" comes the whining reply. "Your age or your IQ?" Even the old man taking the piss has to laugh, almost stepping into the trough.

But it's three-thirty now and where should I be? A thousand places other than here. Ubangi has asked if it's my first time in jail, and I've lied and told him it's number three. He might have lied, though, when he's told me it's number nine for him. But it's useless to question. No matter if it's a hundred, it's still new each time. Any moment you might find yourself screaming like crazy. Or, if you're cool, you sit collected on your little bench and feel the nerve under your eye do riffs.

"Ubangi, when you get a chance to make your call, who are you going to ring?"

"I don't know, man. You the only friend I got in this town."

The noise flares up again and dies down just as quickly. In front of the cell on the other side of me stands the sergeant with four screws, two black and two white. They're quizzing a college boy.

"They say you hit a little girl in the face at that party, that right?"

Mumbles. The screws nudge one another.

"What does your daddy do?" the cop asks, getting right to the point.

Mumbles again is all I can catch. There is another pause as the sergeant nods. "Okay. I'm going to let you off now, and you can make your call." The cop says something to one of the white screws, who leaps to unlock the cell door. The red-faced boy follows him out.

"When do I get my call?" I scream at them as they pass. The sergeant looks through me without slowing. Ubangi gets the same treatment, the bootlickers not even turning their heads as they pass on to the next one.

I slump to the bench. We should have packed a lunch for this one. Another day? A week? A workhouse where we'd make license plates or build roads? Where hope would be an extra pack of cigarettes? Then I think about the horn that I've lost. Certainly it won't be waiting back on that street. I'll have to borrow some money to cop one at a pawn shop, or find a junkie with an extra tenor in his stash.

"Say, brother." It's one of the screws, shifting nervously. "What you in for?"

I tell him. He nods, understanding. A philosopher. "Cold world, ain't it? I heard them talking about taking y'all downstairs for a little head whippin'. But looka here, I think I can get you out of this mess. Know what I mean? I might not be able to get you both out, probably just one. But like I expect a little something, you know, for my efforts." His head swivels back and forth. I can't see the sergeant with the other lackeys, but our man is letting us know that he's risking something to be here talking.

"Just get us out, man," I tell him.

He winks, then joins up with his boys. I relax.

"Ubangi, whoever gets out first will get the other one out by morning, okay?" Who could I hit on for money? Crackerjack will be good for fifty, Okra for thirty and I have twenty in a drawer at the apartment. If bail is more than that, we're lost. Maybe our friend is working on the money problem too.

"Okay, Mack, you go. You might do better than me gettin' some money." Not a happy confession for him. I can hear him whistling "Sweet Georgia Brown." Our friend is back in a half-hour or so, grinning.

"Which one?" he asks.

"Take my man over there," Ubangi says.

The man still looks over his shoulder like he's springing me from San Quentin, Hollywood-style. He unlocks the door to the cell and I follow him down a long hall. At the end is a set of steel double doors. We stop in front of them and his palm shoots out.

"I talked them out of giving y'all a head whippin', and I got everything set up. You just go through these doors and they'll check you out. Now, can you do anything for me?"

I empty my pockets in record time, turn them inside out for the cat. All I have is $1.21, plus a stick of gum, two toothpicks and my Afro comb.

"Look, man, this is all the bread I have, really. But give me your name and address and I'll slide something on you first chance I get. You smoke, don't you?"

"Do shit stink?" he asks, taking the money.

"Well, I can get you some choice stuff too."

"When you get it, just come on back down here. But like I prefer money. I'm on six nights a week. Ask for Jesse Dawkins at the desk. If they can't reach me, just leave the money in an envelope."

We shake hands and he dashes back to his gig and I split to

freedom. But two steps inside those doors, I freeze. Sitting behind a screened-in desk, a cop is handing Novella a pink slip and counting money. Her eyes meet mine and tell me it's all going to be all right.

I spin to catch the screw, but a sentry at the door blocks me. "Where you think you're going?"

"I left something back there," I tell him, picturing Jesse Dawkins with my last piece of change, slapping himself on the back now and chuckling. He hadn't figured on my catching Novella posting my bond.

"Whatever you left, we can call down for," says the big cop on the door. He looks like forty miles of bad road. I turn away. Jesse, you're an imitation of a faggot with no style. Your mama is a man and your daddy's on his period. You're a lump of shit steaming at dawn in a back alley. Jesse, you're the champion ass-kisser, an ugly spasm. May you be coated in maggots, shit and pigeon feathers and be hounded for the rest of your life by the stones children will throw at you, by the piss of aging junkies, by the many boots already in your butt while you kiss the rosary of your key. May the slime forever ooze from your jive grin, may your blood harden past pus to jellied snot. And if I catch you on the streets, I will make it a point to whip your ass.

Novella starts to speak, but I pull her by the wrist and we hurry outside.

"Are you hurt, honey? The blood . . . what did they do?"

"Nothing, nothing. How did you find out I was here?"

"A member of the choir, Mack. Every night Emma sits up waiting for her son to come in. She remembered you from the night you came to church and she called me as soon as she saw them take you away, and said she was scared to call before that because she didn't know whether they would try to shoot y'all or something. But the crowd, Emma said, the crowd got too close for that. She said they beat you hard with their sticks. Mack, what did those crackers want?"

I give her the story from start to finish, but though she's seen a few things herself, she can't believe it's been one big ripoff from start to finish. "Sad, sad," is all she says, all that can be said for the mess we've gotten into.

"Where did you get the money?" I ask her.

"Don't worry about it. You just be in court for the trial next week. Mack, you sure they didn't hurt you?"

"I'm sure, baby. We have to get Ubangi out now. Think I can raise a hundred by noon today?"

"Reverend Fuller will help if I ask him, and I know a few more people . . ."

"I have some contacts too. I'll work those first and see what happens. It's been a fucked-up night."

It's five now and the traffic on Warren Avenue has thinned to cabs and trucks dropping off the morning editions.

"You need some sleep," she says. "Come to my place and I'll fix you breakfast. Then we can start to work on Ubangi's bail and get a lawyer."

"I bet you didn't bargain on all this when you started seeing me, huh?"

"Bargain? What was I supposed to do, go back to sleep when I got the news? Give me credit, Mack. I'm even trying to work myself into your corner if you let me."

My woman walks beside me, makes memories limp shadows. The jail is behind us, though I'm far from fully free. I bet she still thinks the only gift I can bring her is pain. And the evidence is against me tonight. I will grow to bring her more. All praise is due my lady.

It takes two days to get the bread together. Reverend Fuller has kicked in fifty dollars. Crackerjack has stalled at first, but has come through with thirty. Big June has only promised to pull some strings, but I haven't heard from him in the last twenty-four hours.

I've tried to see Ubangi, but last night they claimed I arrived too late for visiting hours. Tonight I'm on time. The cop on the desk thumbs through papers when I tell him I've come to post bail. He frowns, then gives me news that catches me square in the face.

"He's no longer here. He's in New Bedford jail. Seems they've been after him for months now, for an assault with intent to kill charge. Charges here were dropped anyway last night."

I slump to the bench. Now what? They don't waste time there, they might have him strung up by now. If the Falmouth and Army people find out he's around, the mess will really fly. Maybe the cops got their heads together with Ova Easy and decided it was the best way to keep their cover. Or has it been Big June again? It's a move from the skillet to the fire, though, and all because of the dumb son of a solid citizen whom he's slapped around down there. They'll try to put him under the jail for this one.

Novella takes the news calmly, as she's taken everything the last few days. She pours me a cup of wine after I break the news and hands the cup to me with steady hands.

"I guess you'll be going," she says. "When are you leaving?"

"Tomorrow morning, I guess. We can call down first, but I know they're going to put him through some changes real quick."

Marsh gas hovers over the outlying suburbs. Separated by patches of sickly forest, these villages are showcased as museums. Signs near bars and motels: General Bradford Drank an Ale Here; Miles Standish Bunked Here for the Night— things like that. At the heart of these places are benches in front of courthouses where old-timers smoke their pipes in the shadows of statues. The early silence of graveyards. Hypnotized by the deadness in it, all six of us have suffered quietly through the first hour of the trip to New Bedford. The overheated bus has us sweating, and clothing is peeled left and right. No one has bothered to notice two soldiers who have flagged down the bus in this quiet village named after a defunct Indian tribe. And no one stirs until they have taken their seats and one of them has turned on a portable.

"Got a match, bub?" asks the pock-faced man sitting nearest me. He lights his cigarette and is eager to talk, but I pretend to be interested in the passing scenery. He gets better treatment from one of the soldiers and soon they're going at it like old friends.

In forty minutes they will open the doors to Filene's and Novella will have to weather the first wave of women at the basement sale. These are the mornings she needs her strength most, she says. But this is a morning that neither of us has slept. We've attacked this day strong from much loving, though the breakfast she's fixed has helped a little. The memory of the night, though, will be the choicest food. As I left this morning, she asked me to check her front and I almost stayed. She looked that fine! Yes, by now she's caught the first bus and has walked Precious to school. She's on the second bus bringing her downtown, remembering, surely she's remembering.

I close my eyes against the scene—we are between villages again. Gray. What is the sound of gray? Dry and raspy without the deeper sadness and class of blue? The motor coughs as we climb a hill, its sound rising, then returning to that steady drone when we reach level ground. I wonder if we can make New Bedford in this thing.

When we made the trip up, the Sledges' old Ford broke

down every five miles. The first time we panicked, thinking the cavalry on our tails, but when we heard no sirens, saw no flashing lights, we knew we had given them the slip. One time we waited inside the car after calling a tow truck and drank beer and pulled in John R. from Nashville on Ubangi's six-band portable. Suppose a tricky patriot had erased the road and painted one that led us to another city? Like say, Buffalo, New York. Would it be any different? Would it be any sweeter? Would there have been another Novella there to grow so large so suddenly in my life? The bus has stopped. I open my eyes on two village workers in sneakers who are hosing down statues. A dumpy woman has gotten off the bus and been replaced by two large girls, sisters they must be, who waste no time and pride eyeballing the soldiers. Then the engine coughs and we're on our way again.

I'll write home when I get back to Boston. I sent off a letter after the first week in the city. The folks sent a worried letter back. My mother sending along the bad news about friends who never got away from Santa Fe, epidemics, and finally asking whether everything is all right where I am. I'll thank them for keeping my room the way I've had it, the trophies dusted, the room aired out. I'll thank them for keeping the faith.

Dear Folks,

In your last letter you made it sound like the plague had swooped into Santa Fe. Anyway, I hope that everyone has recovered by now. People here are too cold for flus. Those tough germs down there would just shrivel up on the noses and die here (laugh).

It's not really that bad, though. I'm still living and breathing and trying to make it. I know a few people, not all of them "friends" and I'm working at a big night club. The money I make is not the greatest, but I still plan to move both of you into a big house and get you a little Cadillac on the side.

The world gets smaller every day, so small that I don't even get surprised any more when I run into homeboys up here. My girlfriend and I were sitting in a restaurant the other night and I noticed two men staring at us. After a while one of them came over. I didn't know whether or not he wanted to fight, so I stood up. He turned out to be Emerson Jenkins and the other man was his cousin, Bubbie Clements. Remember them. They went off to the Navy eight years ago and haven't been back home since. So you see, I'm not the only one out here on the road. And I think I've mentioned that time in Newark when I ran into Dr. Jackson's son waiting tables. He was supposed to be the smart one. I never found out what ever happened to his brother, who was supposed to be dumb.

What did Sister Baby and Harold name their little boy?

Yes, I've heard of Pharaoh Sanders and I hope you like his album that the record club sent you by mistake . . .

Would she understand this trip to a strange town to keep a friend from being lynched? Or would she understand the ass-kissing behind "trying to make it"? Yes, she would. They both would. My father's been trying to get out from under that yoke for years with those wild inventions of his. Anything but that clock-punching routine under corny bosses. Everything's fine at this end, except I know more lies than I've known before.

By the time we make the rest stop, one of the soldiers has eased up to sit with one of the pale girls. Her sister has given up on soldier number one and has begun to look my way. I've noticed the women down this way have no style to their hunting, as open as the sea. Soldier number two fumbles with the portable and curses his backward ways. I wonder if they know Fastback and the crew at the base. Probably not, they look too easy to con. If there is time, maybe I can look him up on the way back.

I'm off the bus, into the john and back in a flash. I have no time to waste ducking conversations. But a band of hippies suddenly fill the sidewalk, dragging picket signs with them. The Master's Children, the boys with beards against their fathers.

"What's happenin', man?" one of them comes on.

"Nothing much."

"Got a smoke?" He lights up, then leans next to me. His friends try to get the bus driver to talk. He hates them, apparently, and moves away from them, muttering something about people who don't work being the scum of the earth. Shouts at the fragile girl who speaks so softly to him, then sniffs her daffodil. The boy is laughing. I laugh too.

"What do people do in this town?" I ask him.

"Waste away in silence, man. I mean, like, no shit, that's what they do." To the sound of snow, no less. He reads the obvious question. "We're just passing through, know what I mean? On our way to the rock festival on Long Island. But like we can't split until we get this kid out of jail. He's hitched down from Vermont with us and when we get here they lock him up for disturbing the peace. Like he's grooving, know what I mean?"

"Uh-huh. Any luck so far?"

"You kiddin' me? They'd like to see him stay there. His folks can send down the bread if he calls them, but he hates his old man."

I nod, tell him good-bye and board the bus. There's nothing I can do. It's bad all over, boss. Strange sad solidarities. His people gather round him just before a carload of local losers speeds past, yelling at them. The fragile girl gives the fading car the finger.

Next stop: New Bedford. By the time I get there, Novella will have finished her lunch break and endured the gossip of the other sales clerks. I wonder how many times I've crossed her mind this morning.

New Bedford turns out to be the parade of industrial faces in industrial streets. A few blocks of neat cottages with neat lawns. It seems, though, that most of the men are out to sea. Stabbing whales, maybe, or netting cod or running down Flying Dutchmen. At any rate, I only hear the shrill laughter of women as I get off the bus. When I arrive at the courthouse, I'm told that the court has recessed and that Ubangi's case is on the docket for one o'clock, not at three as they said over the phone. As I've suspected, they don't plan to waste any time.

I get coffee in a nearby cafeteria and sit in the window to size the town up. Idling past, a brother throws up a fist. Suppose I had in hand a slick plan to rescue Ubangi? The type of trick you might pick up in a fake western. Okay, folks, up against the wall 'cause my man goes free. Riding off under high noon with no posse until those boats come in.

The oppressive sky. All in all it's a dismal place, more dismal than most places I've seen this morning. A place that needs someone like Ubangi to keep it alive. A place where the Stranger is the Devil. In town to rip off the bank or the Wells Fargo truck. From the courthouse walks a plump woman flanked by two cops. She's wearing a white turban and heavy high heels in 1950's style. She must be the judge's wife, there's something about her that is more final than final. Under her gaze, the room goes to ice.

She says nothing to the cops, dropping her hands to her lap and turning a bored face on the street. One of the cops tries to make conversation, forcing his flat voice to go proper, as many men do when they address those who claim to have seen books. He sounds ridiculous. A young long-haired couple skip past the window and she looks long after them. The cop, who has waited for an answer, slurps his coffee in defeat.

Maybe I can put in a good word for Ubangi here. There's enough time for her to pull her old man's coat: This Jones man is as innocent as a lost lamb, she can tell him. He was provoked. Free him, darling. You can do it, free him. No doubt the big girl could swing it. But I need a pitch. I can't just go over out of the blue, like that.

She's watching me now and when I return her look, she's in no hurry to shift her eyes. Another couple skip past, hand in hand, and she watches them until they're out of sight. She's probably thinking like the bus driver. If any one of them stumbled into her court under arrest, they'd be here awhile. The penalty for looking carefree.

She catches me staring at the rock on her finger, but thinks I'm looking at her legs. She pulls them swiftly beneath her and crosses them at the ankles. But she likes the attention and lets the room melt a little. After ten minutes the woman is in a state, laughing with the cops, at the passing couples. Peeking across at me. I've figured that I'm either adding more days to Ubangi's sentence or getting him off. It's still hard to tell and I haven't thought of a pitch yet. Letting the game continue, I'm reminded of the dudes who hang out around the club and trade the stories about screwing rich old ladies for fat fees. Could this be my in?

As they leave, I sprint for the door. A man steps between me and the woman. "What the hell you want?" ask his clouded eyes.

"I wanted some information on the trial of Ubangi Jones. What time will it begin?"

"That's where we're going now," he says. "And we're in a hurry too. The judge has to get back on the bench." She smiles as if she's known all along about my square plots.

The door nearly smashes my nose, swinging back. My man is doomed. A she-judge and she's all steamed up now to do him in! I follow them to the courthouse, whipping myself. They'll put him in stocks in the middle of town and throw rocks at him, or trade him to a Georgia chain gang for a prisoner who can ride the whales. Doomed.

The logical is often too logical. A woman judge fits this town, fits Ubangi's case too, I'm afraid. I sit in the hall to get myself together. The court rats jabber next to me.

"Which one you sitting in on this afternoon, Gus?" asks the one with the cane.

"Ain't much choice, is it?" says his friend. "The biggest trial this year in this courthouse and you going to ask me which one? All they got around the corner is a poor boy who stole some hubcaps. But this militant from Boston is supposed to be wanted in thirty states. They say he tried to kill Dr. Everett's son."

"Somebody needed to do something to that useless boy. But I guess it's going to be a big one. What do you think Judge Becky will do to him?"

"She'll give him ten years just being here. After that, who knows?" He blows his nose on a dirty rag, then wipes what he's missed on a ragged sleeve. They hobble away and I follow. They get front-row seats with some of their friends. Nothing else to do on a dreary afternoon, I guess, but watch Judge Becky in action. I settle in my seat, then I'm told by an attendant to stand as the judge enters from the rear. She throws a look my way, a brief glazed look that one turns on the sea, remembering what is worth remembering.

Then Ubangi is ushered in. He sees me, flashes a grin, and

walks with his lawyer to a small table. He's wearing the clothes I've seen him last in and they're wrinkled and soiled as if he's done battle with forty-leven cops between here and Boston. His lawyer pats him on the back and moves back to the bench to say something to Judge Becky.

A weird silence then settles over the courtroom, broken only by the rattling coughs of the court rats. The lawyers pace back and forth in front of the bench. Ubangi's lawyer points to his watch and the judge nods solemnly. It's a sluggish pantomime and I'm not the first spectator to get uneasy. The court rats are stamping their canes now.

A man enters from the rear and runs up to Judge Becky. He appears out of breath, red-faced, stepping back as she calls the lawyers together and the four of them huddle. Ubangi looks back at me and shrugs. The next thing I know, everyone is shaking hands and Judge Becky is ushered off the bench. The court is adjourned.

Ubangi thanking his lawyer, then rushing back to me. "Come on!"

"What happened?" I ask.

"The hell if I know. The charges have been dropped. The dude didn't even have the guts to show up. He sent some bullshit in about he was sorry for inconveniencing everybody. The lady ought to sentence the muthafucka to gargling razor blades or something. Let's get out of here."

"Damn," I hear myself saying softly, "a false alarm. What do you think happened, man? I mean, to the dude?"

"I couldn't care less. Here I am a free man. What I look like worrying why I ain't got hung? Come on, I owe the world a lot of money already. Shoot, I feel like taking on all the mutha-fuckas today, now! I'd fight all ten of them in a telephone booth!" The court rats are disappointed. They watch us out of the corners of their eyes. They'll have to wait some time, probably, for that next big one.

"The next bus leaves at four, 'Bangi."

"Where that bus going, Mack?"

"Boston. Where else you think it's going?"

"Shoot, you think I be this close to Ivone and not stop over? Man, you crazy. We just stay a few hours, man. I know you got business back up the way, Mack, and I have too. But I got to see her."

A bus is leaving for Falmouth in twenty minutes. While we wait, he tells me how they've tried to rough him up, but he held his own. He's told me about the trip down, chained hand and foot as if he'd knocked over the biggest bank in the state.

"One thing for sure, Mack," he says. "They'll damn sure fuck over you if they can. They bring me all the way down here just to let me go. I've kicked a lot of ass for less than that."

Eleven

WE SIT on Ivone's porch and knock out fish'n chips and beer. After the half-hearted rain, after she has got the jaws with her mother and put us through more changes for not telling her about the bust and the trial, the day has settled to quiet afternoon. The voice of Johnny Ace from the stereo, a liquid juju voice that stirs the grass awake and allows nothing more sudden than a child's laugh to threaten its spell. The album has been part of a sackful of security Ubangi left behind the first time.

Ivone's mother cracks the door. "You come inside or you catch cold, I tell you. It get cold again." In a flash she'd ducked back inside. She's the shyest person in the world.

"Ivone, don't your mama know that bad niggas like me and Mack don't get sick?" Ubangi catches the crumbs that drop from her lips, and comfortably, in a childtone, she giggles.

It must be the weather, the warm sloppy kiss of this wind. All I can think of is trim—churning, grinding, rocking trim. Here it's Michelle, who hasn't answered the phone yet. The two of us in bed, I can see, with the shades up to let in the fading beauty of the day, and her mother, without warning, always it's her sudden mother, storming through the front door and me butt-naked, as they say, sprinting out the back with my clothes under my arm. Trim that yawns, closes, tightly pulls. Trim with a mind of its own. In the swing I turn over on my stomach and close my nose to the smell of incense, my ears to the soft song of bedsprings, my thoughts to a season of change. Even though Novella and I have grown so close in the last week, I'm still weak enough to play with dead dreams. At least, once. Yes, blame it on the weather.

"Where's Michelle?" I ask Ivone. I really haven't wanted to bother her with that question. As she sits there on Ubangi's lap, her look of love is the face of a serene pool, with depths alive beyond believing.

"I haven't seen her in days," she says.

"Well, the last time I saw her, she told me she had another man."

She stretches her eyes as if she doesn't know what I'm talking about. She's no pro at playing dumb. "Really?"

"Baby, don't let this cat fool you," Ubangi says. "Mack ain't hardly worried about that woman. He got his nose open over a real woman up in Boston and she waiting for him now. He just down here now because he a helluva friend."

She shifts in his lap, turning back to him. "Am I a real woman?"

"Damn sho is. Let me run it down to you, you sweet thing you." For an hour they've gone on like this while I've filled myself with beer. I'm a crowd of one. Then she pulls him up by the wrist.

"Come on, you two. We still have a few more things to pick up for dinner."

"You two go ahead. I'm going to look for Michelle."

"Be back for dinner," Ivone warns. She lets Ubangi drive,

draping herself around him, her lips to his ear. She thinks to wave.

Drawn shades welcome me to Michelle's house. I hear no sound from inside and no one answers the door. Has her mother dragged her off to another meeting? Is her doctor boyfriend showing her around a boat show? I can answer none of the questions buzzing around in my head as I walk away. There is only one thing for sure: I'll never darken her front door again.

I walk to the edge of town after deciding to thumb to the base. The first car coming up the road stops. A pale couple. "Going to the base?" the woman asks from her side. They are the type who are always hungry to show off their town, driving me to yawns with reports on cider festivals and school-bond issues. But I stick it out, this beats that five-mile walk. It will be good to see Fastback, G. A. and the rest of them. Fastback will be rolling in money, beating chumps out of their short Army pay. They've probably been to Boston, but since we haven't kept in touch, there has been no way for all of us to connect. Then the voices of the couple break their blend with the motor's hum.

". . . You see, it's not often that the big-timers try to feed off our fair town. But these two had the cockeyed idea of trying to operate a still here and selling rotgut to the poor Army boys. Around town the word was that they were doing okay too. We and the military police chased them out. I'm on the citizen patrol, you see."

"Did you find the still?" I ask.

"Never did."

His wife pushes him on, excited by the tales of the juicy crime. "Apparently they caught the men later."

"That's right. They got them up in New Hampshire one morning trying to steal chickens from a poor man's farm."

Both of them laugh their asses off. I chuckle, suddenly tasting the good wine, picturing Old Man Sledge taking his weekly trip to the bank to deposit his money, the villain's smile caught on his lips. We laugh and laugh at the two big-time crooks caught red-handed in New Hampshire and stuck with every crime committed in a two-hundred-mile radius.

"Where are they now?" I ask.

"Hee-hee. Don't worry about them," the man says, gasping for air, "they're where they won't be selling any bad wine for a long, long time."

We've reached the gate and the guard, a brother, starts to salute the car. Seeing no sticker, but spotting me in back, he gives the fist. I admit that takes me a little by surprise. They let me out in front of the barracks, where two brothers are tossing horseshoes, tikis around their necks. Inside, a brother walks away from a hillbilly, no time for his simple jokes. Something new is in the air.

The second floor pops under a thick haze of smoke. A dozen captives stand around a tonk game. G. A. is talking shit. He has hardly been shipped off to any jive wars.

"Yeah, you funky New York niggas think y'all know something about cards. Well, G. A. ain't giving up nothing, and I'm going to send y'all back to your mamas. Get down!" He slams down his cards, two aces, leans back and fingers his toothpick. "Any more chumps want to play me?"

When he sees me, his jaw drops. "Goddam, Mack! What's happening? What you doing here?" He introduces me around. "This the nigga I been telling y'all about. He up in Boston doing it. Mack, these is the craziest dudes you ever want to see in whitey's uniform. Cornell, take my place while I go rap to my main nigga."

In his room down the hall, he breaks out a bottle of special-occasion whiskey. I tell him about the trial, and after he pulls himself off the floor laughing, he wipes his eyes. "Trouble seem to follow y'all, huh?"

"Troubles are our only friend, G. A. Where's Fastback?"

"Aw man, talk about some weird shit. Wait until I tell you about this. After you and 'Bangi got away, they figured they'd string up one of us as a lesson, you understand, for running with civilians and shit. So they kept quiet and waited for an excuse and any fool knows they don't have to wait very long to get something on us around here. They think up things on us every day. Anyway, we was all at the gym watching Freddie and Saddlehead and them whip some peckerwoods in basketball. The game was almost over when this cat whips out a Confederate flag and starts waving it. Now, he from this base and supposed to be rooting for us, our team, you dig it? With all five of the starters being boots."

"Was he crazy?" I ask, remembering Fastback's temper.

"What you say! Fastback wasted his ass right quick, before every pattie boy in the place jump bad behind it. So we just naturally kicked ass and took names, my man. A couple of us got restricted to the base for a couple of weeks. I guess the white boys just got cussed for losing the fight, because none of them drew a day. We went along with that because we knew what was going down. Only we didn't know how far they wanted to take it. Y'all messed up their minds, Mack. You and 'Bangi. They been out to get every brother here. Things was cool until one of our Friday-night dances. All the gray girls came in this night and ran for the brothers like they usually do. The broads ain't got no time for the okeydoke conversations the white boys be running down, belching in their faces and stuff. They don't know what's happenin'. So one dude gets brave on a bunch of beers and picks a fight with Fastback and the shit is on again."

No one enjoys his stories more than G. A. himself, stringing a listener out to the very end. After he's poured another drink, he strokes his chin, pretending he's lost the thread of the story.

"Y'all were kicking ass at the dance," I offer.

"Yeah, yeah. You know how I can never run from a fight, Mack. Well, anyway, the next day I see a couple of dudes with their bags packed and they say they're being shipped to Maine. Two days after that, two brothers say they just got their papers for Arizona. Next thing I know, Fastback—the blood who ran this place and pulled all our coats—got his orders saying South Dakota. Now, you know no blood ain't excited about South Dakota. Before he left, he had a regular press conference right out in front of the barracks. Dude talked about patties like dogs, man. They shipped so many out of here after that, it wasn't even funny."

"How many they leave, G. A.?"

"That's the killing part, Mack. They left six of us and we don't know to this day why that was. We was in those fights like everyone else. They must have thought we was just pulled in, but that deep down we was on whitey's side. Then they start bringing in all these quiet-looking cats, thinking they were toms. These cats didn't talk loud, and they found out that these new bloods just looked dead in their faces and told them their Army wasn't shit. I mean, I didn't even have to hip them. They had peeped the whole card. Now they running the local bitches silly and smoking so much dope it's coming out their ears, turning on the generals' girlfriends. This place ain't cooled down at all, Mack."

Laughter crackles across the hall, and G. A. sits up on his bed. "There was a day when a boot would be grateful to the service for taking him away from trouble and aggravation at home, and mess his mind up, but no more days like that. We the hook in the catfish's belly now."

It's a new G. A. I'm seeing. A tiny nationalist flag sticks out from a beer can on the window sill. The fist at the gate, the bearded brothers out front, the dittybop mopping downstairs who has claimed he never heard of Fastback—it all falls into place. I pour myself another drink and wonder if I've been the only one standing still these past months.

"You ain't in no hurry, are you?" he asks. "Cop a squat, then, while I play a few more hands. Then we can cut out to Captain Blackwell's for food and trip back for the dance tonight."

My mistake is to follow him across the hall. If I had any real sense, I might have walked to the gate to thumb back to town. I might have remembered that as far as Ivone is concerned I have two strikes against me and to miss the dinner is to put our friendship on the line. Certainly she will then begin to whisper to 'Bangi about that no-good, unreliable Mack. Yes, it's been a mistake—the drinks, sucking the rich smoke from the big pipe that's going around. Getting higher than a leap-jeep.

I manage to reach Novella by phone. "Where are you?" Over the line I can hear her catch her breath. "What happened at the trial?"

"He got off. I told you that before I left, didn't I?"

"What happened? What did you do?"

"I'll tell you when I get back. Right now I want to talk about you."

"Why don't you come back now? Ubangi's a big boy. He can take care of himself, can't he?"

"I'm looking up some old friends. Remember that old couple I told you about?"

"And all the old girlfriends?" she says, taking deadly aim. "Get your lie straight, now."

"Ain't no other women for me and you know that. I wanted

to know if the feeling is still there for me. I mean I've been away a whole day and that's time enough to test the feeling, huh?"

"Why don't you come back home and find out?" She pauses. "Emma got your horn back for you. She knows the man who carried it off the other night and called him before he could sell it."

"Just hold on, sugar. I'll be there in the morning on the first thing smokin'."

By the time we get to the captain's house, the picnic is in full swing. We've had to stop along the way to dance to James Brown, G. A. leaving the car in the middle of the highway while we did it up. Cars creep around us, speed off. Those crazy niggas at it again. Then the captain's lawn and the fading afternoon and the touch-football game. Brothers easing from the house with paper plates piled high with food, crouching along the driveway. Scotch in paper cups. Captain Blackwell greets us at the door. He comes from Quitman, Georgia, and tells me he's known G. A. ever since Fastback was chased off the base. In no time he's jammed a drink in my hand and has introduced his wide wife and the ribs.

"It be like this mostly every Friday, Mack," he says. "We do it big around here." This must be the home-away-from-home. I didn't get to know Blackwell the first time around. He's been one of the six left behind.

I find a bed and flop across the jackets left there. Sleep closes in.

. . . *I am standing in the middle of a crowded street as blind people mill around, hitting, bouncing off one another. They scream out, "Help, help!" their voices rising as the voices of animals, long wounded, knowing death is near. I run among them, hearing my own wild screams, "Me! Me! Me!" They pick up the chant and surround me, imitating my gestures, their*

*faces relieved of pain. Then they toss me to their shoulders and
march me to a burned-out building where chairs have been set
inside. I speak to them of freedom and an old gray-haired man
stands and asks how, and I tell them to join hands. He asks me
how again and I whip out maps of libraries, recording studios,
homes of rich white folks, rifle ranges, back rooms of juju men.
He asks me when and before I can answer, he's up on me,
shaking me wildly, his eyes crazed, his breath hot on my face.
Before I know it, he's stolen my voice and is screaming his own
name. The crowd has followed him off, but not all have
deserted me. A few mold a statue around me . . .*

G. A. shaking me. "Listen, we got to split. I got to get clean
for the dance. Ahmo whip some heavy loving on some lucky
mother's daughter tonight." G. A.'s also known in these parts
as Midnight Mover.

We leave a couple men at the poker game in the captain's
basement. Those men with little luck with the local women
will hang there most of the night, then stagger into the dance
and turn it out.

The dance, I discover, I have never left. My face is
half-numb by the end of the second set. Cool Eddie hasn't
changed the routine one bit: the same corny jokes to the few
soldiers leaning on the bar and the early women who show
through the doors wearing too much make-up. I sit alone
wondering whether to sit in with the band. I can use the tenor
man's horn. I'm sure he'll have another mouthpiece around.
After he's recognized me, he keeps offering the horn to me as a
man offers his last cigarette to a long-gone friend. At the crap
game in back, G. A. is winning money like ninety goin North.

"Say, babycakes, why are you sitting by yourself laughing?"
Ivone. His dashiki washed and pressed, Ubangi trails her.
Because she's giggling, I know she's high and into that tender
world of hers. I play it off to avoid getting on the dinner I've

missed, all of the other cop-outs she will try to pin on me. Of course I did both of them a favor not telling her about the trial. She would have screamed in the judge's face, getting her man ninety years and a day.

"You two boogaloo like an old married couple," I tell them after they've danced stiffly for a few minutes.

"Okay, let's see you work your show," Ubangi says, looking a little hurt.

I find a partner and work up a sweat with ease, making up weird steps as I go along. By the time I've finished, however, Ivone is clapping alone for me at the table. Ubangi has smelled the crap game in back and has taken off.

"I see you didn't find Michelle," she says, almost evilly.

"I think she's hiding from me. You agree?"

She looks in her drink. "Be serious. You haven't heard from her since she left Boston?"

"Uh-uh."

"Mack, she must have told you, she had to! She's married now and living in Providence. Her dear mother planned it down to the color of the living-room drapes and she's practically moved in with them. But she's miserable, baby-cakes, I know. I've seen her in town a couple of times. I can tell."

Then I pull her up to dance. She dances her strange birdlike dance, head high, arms whirling like that night on the beach. This night only her hips moving in time. Many a night Ubangi has told the world that he'd walk swamp bottoms for this woman, that he'd drink muddy water and spit nickels for her tender touch. Though he still messes around, there's no doubting the nose job he has over her. I wonder if she and Novella would have much to say to one another. Different styles, similar substance.

I catch her looking at me several times. I suppose she's waiting for me to break up over Michelle. "Ivone, it's not as if

I were still snapping behind her. What little we had dried up before I left."

"I know that," she says. "You look too lonely sometimes. I hope you've found a good woman. I really do."

Ubangi's back and immediately they're making ready to split. No doubt they're camped at a motel, though Ivone will have to be home before dawn or her mother will turn her into a pumpkin and Ubangi into a scarecrow to haunt the backyard, into things that can never escape this town.

"You think we make a nice couple, Mack?" Ivone asks suddenly.

"Of course. You two thinking over marriage?"

"Mind your own business," Ubangi says. "The cemetery is full of niggas who done dipped in other folks' business."

"I was just trying to make conversation . . ." He looks at me as if I've smeared salt on his open wounds. She takes his hand. I don't know why I said it. The sudden feel of emptiness in things, maybe. I need my woman now. With me. I mumble a good-bye to them and slip into the soft swallow of night. A chill wind is blowing, and miles away on the highway I can hear the diesel trucks rumbling. To flag one down on its way to Boston would be the most sensible thing to do. A nightjet overhead, red eye at its belly, gliding ahead of its sound with Boston fifteen minutes away. To lassoo it down, walk aboard and ride the quick miles to my lady soul. Someone inside a dark car raps on the window. G. A., with a large girl on his lap, a hand working her thigh, the other flicking the ash of a cigar. Teeth.

The sun is directly overhead when I get to the Sledges' house. Reba must have finished early in her garden, though it's not yet fully spring and nothing has broken through the ground to light. She's probably just returned from town, since she's wearing her dress hat, sitting on the porch and fanning imaginary flies as she watches the street. She smells of jasmine.

"What do you think of all this good weather we having down here? I declare, you must have brought it with you, Mack."

"Course now, that don't say too much about that groundhog that came out a few weeks back and seen his shadow. If he had bothered to look around, he might have seen the snow already melting and the robins around. That's what happens to people who put too much trust in something that's afraid of its own shadow."

She cackles and spits snuff juice into a can at her feet. "You know it too? I'm glad you back, son. I knew you'd be back to visit us. I know you used to like it down here a lot. I'm surprised you ain't come on back to stay. Ain't nothing up there in the city, is it? Dupree sho be tickled to see you. And thank you for that pretty Christmas card."

"Ubangi had a little business to take care of in New Bedford, so I thought I'd come down, since I hadn't seen everybody in so long. You look well, Mrs. Sledge."

"Well, thank you. What this world coming to, Ubangi doing business? Umumum. You taking Epson salts for that cold you got?"

"Not yet. It's just a little cough I picked up last night."

Her eyes narrow. "Well, don't let it go too long, now. Look like you losing a little weight, too. Can't your girlfriends up there cook? See if that coffee is ready in back and fix yourself a plate of grits off the stove. I fixed a pan after you called and said you was coming. I remember you used to say grits was your birthmark. Just like they's Dupree's. I got Dupree a plate cooling off now, if he ever get here with his slow self."

Her coffee is strong enough to take the stink out of chitterlings, to bring a full-grown man to tears. One sip and I'm cured of all my colds for the next five years. Volcanoes going off in my belly.

"You know, me and Dupree been kind of lucky this winter. No bad colds to speak of, though Dupree caught him a real bad cough a couple months back. Arthritis don't act up on me like it used to either." She looks at the sky and speaks more to herself now. "It's going to get real cold again before it stay warm. We thinking about taking a vacation and going to Bessemer in the spring. We ain't been down there in I don't know how long." My face is studied. "Overall, you look good, son. Don't look like too much getting you down. You met that boy up there yet?"

"What boy?"

"That boy I told you about who came by our house when we was living down South, Andrew, his name is. We got a card from him at Christmas time. The card had to be forwarded to us from Alabama, since he don't know we done moved up here. He done changed his name to something like Antrain, Ant . . . ?"

"Antar?"

"Yeah, son, something like that," she says. "You met him? How he doing?"

"I have met him, but I didn't know who he was at the time."

"I declare. You give him our address and tell him to write. Tell him we doin' fine too, as fine as old folks can do."

I sip more coffee. The man with his little shop, his quiet wife, selling African masks, writing plays. Yes, the same man who went south looking for something inside him all the time. Our common shelters and needs.

She doesn't want to stay outside too long. I get another plate of grits. I'll have to leave in fifteen minutes, though I want to see Dupree. His plate of grits is cold now and hard, with the edges curling stifflly, the pat of butter fading.

"Mrs. Sledge, what's got your husband walking these days? I see his truck out back."

"Doctor told him to exercise more," she says from another room, where she's looking for the family album. "He usually don't be gone this long. Maybe he stopped to talk a little while. Seen the flowers at the side of the house? Dupree ain't even took time to look at them, he's been so busy. He sho be proud when he see them. You know azaleas is his idea 'cause I ain't crazy about them."

But twenty minutes later he still hasn't come in. I will have to run to catch the bus back and I can't miss this one. "Tell him I'll be down again before too long, and you take care of yourselves, now."

"You too, Mack. And like I say, don't study them mannish women they got running around up there. So much be happenin' these days."

Ubangi and Ivone have beaten me to the station. They hold hands at the gate while the other passengers are boarding. Ubangi sliding off his pinkie ring and giving it to her. Crying, she looks at me as if for help.

"Where you been, man?" Ubangi asks. "We were getting worried about you."

"I just had to talk to Mrs. Sledge. Too bad I couldn't see Dupree, though. There's a lot I wanted to talk to him about."

"It's all so sad," Ivone is saying to no one in particular. Her tragic face. "The things we women have to go through, seeing our men leave us . . ."

"Woman, didn't I say I'll be back down here in two weeks?"

". . . I'll go have a talk with Mrs. Sledge. At least she seems to be holding up after her man's gone. Maybe I can learn from her."

"What did you say about Dupree being gone?" I ask.

She smears a tear. "He died on New Year's Day, Mack. She must have told you . . ."

Twelve

IN ROXBURY and Jamaica Plains we've been made kings of the street. At corners people crowd around to hear us run down our tale of funky screws and Judge Becky. The way they follow us, it's as if we're tossing out free money. It's been this way for a week now. We're pointed at by the crowd that daily shields the liquor store from going broke. Bent, snaggletoothed brothers in long coats call us over for a little taste of their wine, and others in tinted shades drop choice reefers on us. You see, we're the badmen Stagalees who've torn the Devil a new butt. Though few have come to really help us, they've been on the sidelines, cheering, seeing all.

"Ain't you one of the cats who whipped those cops' tails the other week?" asks a man whom I've brushed against crossing the street. "How about a drink on me?"

Since I'm in a hurry to find Ubangi, I have to make like the busy politician. "Yeah, I'm sort of in a hurry now, but I'll catch you later. Is that cool? What's your name?" And as quickly as we've shaken hands and he has repeated his name, I've forgotten it and pushed on.

You never know what will put your name on the lips of strangers, make your story the talk of the bars and pool halls and barshops. Some blow their heads off, dive out of tenth-story windows, or put bank tellers up against the wall in broad daylight. Others preach old and new gospels, kiss ass, or save a life. But most of us have been like milkweed in the wind, not knowing what's happening except that the wind is bound to change. There's nothing special about Ubangi and me, and maybe that's why they carry us on their shoulders. Our story is their story too.

But that extra glide in my stride, that new dip in my hip, they're nothing. After all, I've lost the club gig. The owner claims he can't afford his people getting in trouble with the cops. It costs him enough to keep them happy as it is, he says. Hero or not, I've got my walking papers. I can see Okra going to bat for me again, as he's promised he will, as he must, since our sound has become so mellow that a long layoff might hurt us. He will chain-smoke with the owner and get me back on. "Give me a week," he's said this time. I don't worry when he talks that way. And Hurricane Wanda is in my corner now. She's decided I'm not so bad after all, a result of flattery. So I'll wait for their good news and keep busy looking like I'm busy. As expected, the auditions for Big June never came off.

I tip into a block where big women in sleeveless sweaters hang out of windows, their faces silent comments on the sun-splashed streets. Under them, bongos rap with congas and many people have poured from the red buildings to signify. Nobody's lightweights, four bad drum boys are instigating. It's obvious they've played together many, many times before. A skinny woman, the first in the crowd to get the spirit, shimmies down the sidewalk and starts a train of children behind her. Into the street she goes, bringing a car to a screaming stop.

"Get out and get some soul, man!" she yells, snapping her fingers high over her head. "Some of this jellyroll soul!"

A holy-roller soul has broken out with a tambourine and behind that the street goes up in a righteous black flame. I find a beer can and stick, adding what little I can, waiting for a crack at the drums. Then one of the drummers stands and fishes under his jacket, pulling out a bottle of Richards'. I beat two other dudes to his drum and join the sweet communion of the other drummers, the dances, the stalled traffic, and the universe, if it's hip. Social workers try to get past, thinking we're crazy. The big women in the windows know we're crazy, and rock their heads with us.

"Kumbala-sheeboo!" screams the woman in the fire of the drums.

"Ooobasheboo-debopwop!" comes the answer from a man who leaps into the line. "Shake that thing!" Not even bothering to say how nice my drumming has been, the drummer elbows his way back on the drum. I stand behind him, wiping sweat from my face. Some night he will want to sit in at the club and I'll tell him a few things about himself. I never forget a face.

When they've stopped, groans fill the air like happy-time funk. The drummers back off a little, they'll have to hump more this afternoon. This crowd is hungry. Even now, alone, working out the crazy pattern of our lives, the bony-hipped woman keeps dancing her magic dance.

It's up to Ubangi's new place of business that I've been trying to get this last half-hour. My guess is that he's opened up a record-novelty shop and has recruited ripoffs to stock his place with records, incense, tape decks. It's just a hunch I have, knowing him like I do. I can predict him now. For example, he will look at me strangely when I tell him about the idea Reverend Fuller has given me. Later he will understand the spirit of it, the largeness of it, and will join me.

Last night I went to Novella's for dinner, for her tender touch, for love. But whom did I find there, nursing a large glass of Kool-Aid, but Reverend Fuller. My first impulse was that rage etched in one of the last scenes with Sassie Mae: throwing a chair at the slick young preacher who had started hounding her to seek a church home. I promptly pulled Novella into the kitchen. "What the hell is he doing here?"

She looked confused. "He's waiting for you, Mack. He's been wanting to talk with you for a couple days now, and when he called this evening, I told him you'd be over tonight."

"Tell him he can call me if he wants me."

"I told him, but he said he wanted to see you in person."

"What does he want to talk about? I've paid his money back. We're even again, so what is he doing over here in the way?" She left me there. I hadn't noticed Little Precious and her buddy Amanda wildly coloring their books. Precious must have known something was wrong, however, because she just kissed me on the chin and went back to her book.

The minister's bad eye was steady as I shook his hand. "You know, this is the first opportunity I've had to talk with you. After that incident last week, I want to say that I admire your courage."

Was he putting me on? Novella offered no clue, so I followed him out to the porch. It turned out that no one had told him that Ova Easy was a man, so he thought we had saved a defenseless prostitute from the ravages of a cracker high school principal.

"Course now, the law supposed to be like a saddle, able to fit any horse. But it don't always work that way. I know. Those women used to strut around in front of Crumbly Rock trying to take the young men's minds off the Lord's work. The policemen claimed they could do nothing to get them off the street, so it took some good church sisters to run them Jezebels on 'way from there.

"Mack, like I said the last time we talked, I'm getting older every day. Sure, the Lord called me to deliver the word, but he also gave me sense enough not to be a fool and let the word go feeble and weak. But I wouldn't be worried about resigning if I knew the man to take my place would carry on. People want to see their work carried on, especially if they done put their whole life, their whole soul, their whole might into it. Right now, I don't know if I have that man in my church." I could hear Novella behind us, humming a spiritual. I waited, half wondering where he would take me next.

"My assistant minister, Reverend Hastings—he's a good man, a fine man, gets along well with everybody. But I don't know whether he's smart enough to keep the new choir director and the church secretary from arguing, and whether he be wise enough to keep the young restless ones in the fold. I just don't know. I do know that Deacon Scott and Deacon Jemison got their eyes on it, and they both strong men, but where they'd take the church only the Lord knows. So right now I got one who could cut down on argument, but not lead, and two who could lead, but don't know where. Lately there's been some whispering going around about going outside the church to get a preacher. Some folks kind of liked that man who preached the revival last fall. He's one of them old-time whoopers and calls himself the Original Alabama Prophet. Lot of folks want to see the church stay the way it was a long time ago. Now, don't get me wrong. Ain't nothing wrong with the old times except they be old times. They ain't the new times. Crumbly Rock Baptist needs a modern man, a man who can handle the young ones when their blood gets warm and they want to be out in the streets whooping and hollering with their friends, and a man who can handle the old ones who are strong as oak and set in their ways."

"What you need is a magician," I told him. "A man who wears many coats and who's able to switch them in a flash."

"No, just a man who cares about what he's doing."

"Well, the blind can't lead the blind. I mean, you need somebody who knows the church well, who knows how to preach. A man who leads a band ain't the same as a man who leads the church." That was to keep him from getting those funny ideas of his, and cutting his eyes my way.

He tented his fingers over his belly, puffed on his pipe. "You right about the experience. Things and people move, though. They might not know where sometimes, nobody knows, and sometimes you need a man out in front just to fix how fast they do move until things get clearer."

"You mean a man to make people think they're moving when they're just marking time?"

He was silent for a while. "Sometimes that has to happen too. But I don't want to keep you away from your dinner. I'll wear out my welcome if I stay much longer. I just wanted you to come over to the trial sermons next week and help me out a little. You might even want to preach a little yourself, heh-heh."

"I'm no speaker, Reverend Fuller. And what I might have to say might not get over too well with some of your folks."

He laughed again, getting up to leave.

"Our folks will listen to anybody with something to say."

Can his church be so wide it can accept anything and everything? An idea has grown since last night. I'll let him continue to think I'm the man he needs me to be. Why not music, some sounds, their own sounds at the moaning bench, signified in a sax? At any rate, it would keep him from bothering me with the idea of coming to his church again.

I told Novella about the preacher making plans to turn me into a monk. "Now, baby, you know I'd never let him do something like that." That's all she said, smiling that smile of hers before I got the dinner, the tender touch, and the love I had come for.

But as I walk along now, I think of my mother in her early evening pose: her hands clasped near the bottle of beer in front of her, beef stew bubbling on the stove. If she heard the minister's invitation to a trial sermon, she'd flip. I would be only a half-step from the fulfillment of her prophecy, a preacher. Meant to be a preacher because I questioned trees, took mountains too seriously. And in that pose, Mama smiles. "Go, son," she'd say in her knowing way, "you never know what good thing might happen."

In single file, their laundry stuffed into pillow cases, a family of six troop through the rubble for home. Antar's African Shop still braves this danger zone. What little has been left on the block has been gutted by recent fires. The beauty parlor next door has been closed and boarded up. Under darkening clouds, the shop stands as the last outpost on the ugly street, obvious, and giving a view into strange things. From here I can see Antar's wife patiently arranging jewelry in the window.

"Is Antar around?" I ask.

Her smile is swift, there long before I noticed. This evening's star. "Oh, hi. They're in back. He and Wally have been at it for hours and no telling when they'll quit. You can go back if you like." I decide to linger over the dolls. Otherwise, they will review the entire conversation for me, then argue for my benefit. I'd be hemmed up for an hour at the least. A couple has walked in behind me and Antar's wife is waiting on them now, letting them sniff at incense. Then Omowale comes out first, stretches and loudly announces death to all toms, now and forevermore. The couple look up nervously, not sure where his words have been aimed. They case the exits anyway, just in case push comes to shove.

"If a dude got to hem and haw about helping to do in the Man, then he ain't with us. No bullshit about compromise in our army." When he recognizes me, he collects himself. "Say, brother, what you know good?"

"The only good thing I'll know is when you tell it to me."

"I've been trying to tighten Antar up on the religion of the Yorubas and how it too is a hip alternative for black people seeking help from that Christian mumbo-jumbo Whitey be throwing at you. It is much closer to the black spirit than Islam. What religion are you, brotherman?"

"I'm sort of an exile from the Baptist Church," I answer. "I've been away from it since I was sixteen."

"I can dig it," he says. "We must rap sometimes. I have to slide now, but I'll catch up with you." He moves away on his bad feet, tipping lightly.

Then Antar comes out, smiling. "Was Brother Omowale trying to twist your arm onto his adopted religion? He's their best agent outside of Haiti. That's a fact and a warning." Before I can tell him why I've stopped by, he's showing me the new masks he has on display.

"Straight from the islands, my brother. I got back last week with these beautiful carvings, beautiful! And no one's buying them. No one. We have a rush of trade at Christmas time, but now look at it. You're my first customer today." He frowns and takes me back. He points out the jewelry scattered on a workbench he's put up since last time. He must be expecting a rush come summer.

"Money in those boxes?" I ask him, pointing to the many unopened boxes that are stacked on the floor.

"Money, you ask. Blackness is in those boxes, man! History, artifacts from the homeland and all for a nominal fee that keeps only the most modest foods on the table of my queen, my future son, and myself."

"I didn't know your wife was expecting."

"Next September. Allah has blessed us."

"Now if you could get Him to get the people to spend a little money, your problems would be solved."

"Allah moves in his own way, brother." He lights a stick of incense against the cigarettes I will smoke, pats me on the back. "And what can I sell you this afternoon?"

"This afternoon I'm broke . . ."

"You musicians are all alike, running down that line. No credit here." We laugh the laugh of understanding.

"I think what I have to tell you will surprise you, Antar. Do you remember Reba and Dupree Sledge?"

The way he jumped I would have thought someone tossed cold water on him. "Wow. I could never forget them. You know them too?" On the edge of his seat, he listens. I go through my first stay with them, the hunting trip, their watchful silence.

"Are they well?" he asks. "Are they still getting around okay? I sent them a card at Christmas. Was it forwarded?"

"Dupree died New Year's Day and so far Reba hasn't made up her mind to live with it. She never told me he died and still sets his place for supper. She says one of her daughters is after them—she still says 'them'—to move out to Cleveland with her family."

Tonight we look back on the old couple, touching the jagged edges of their lives, remembering the grit and wit of their ways. But how differently we've seen them.

"Mack, they ever tell you all about the time I spent with them? I called myself looking for my roots while registering voters. My parents came from that part of Alabama. But I guess that in the end I was down there like most everyone else.

I was going to save those people. I was going to straighten out the South when I didn't know the first thing about it. And they didn't budge."

"How did you want them to budge?" I ask.

"Well, I wanted them to get to something different, at least. All that time I was down there, you know, I never did get them to vote." I run down Sledge's one-man war against the military, about his wine seeping through the base.

"That's different," he says. "That's smaller than I was talking about. It doesn't change anything. It might have gotten him some satisfaction, but the power stayed in the same hands."

"I think he was fighting with everything he had to fight with. He was over seventy, man. It might have been different with us, but he was an old man . . ."

"Maybe you're right, Mr. Music Man." He smiles to himself, begins tapping lightly on the head of a conga drum. "Mrs. Sledge wouldn't know me now, though. They knew me then—the Boston boy down South on summer vacation. I think they were gentle with me, or maybe they just didn't understand me. We really didn't understand each other, Mack. But, like I say, I'm not the doctor's spoiled son anymore."

"She'd know. Both of them looked deeply into things. They'd know us a hundred years from now."

"You've got a lot of faith in the old people, Mack."

"They have their ways and make their mistakes like us, but many of them are rocks for us to lean on."

I'd like to see him talking with Mrs. Sledge now. He must have missed a lot the first time around. He would have had to be strong to change them and he was too young to be that strong. Both of us. Even still.

"Who's playing the lead in your play?" I ask, playing a hunch.

"An actor by the name of Wendell Keyes. Brilliant."

He laughs when I tell him that Wendell has been a neighbor. "Brother, you must have been shadowing me most of my life. Wendell's the hero in my new play. He's a mean actor, arrogant as hell, but the best I know." That one was easy, from the earlier conversation about the play with Henry and Omowale. There aren't that many plays in Roxbury this winter.

We laugh together, knowing there is much more to talk about, knowing that even though we took different things from the old couple and went different ways, the path of our hope has crossed countless times. I wonder if he knows Crackerjack, Judge Becky and Jesse Dawkins too. I get up to leave as his wife calls him to the phone.

He drops a pair of earrings into a small bag. "Here. Give these to your lady and read this." He hands me a book. "Let's talk about this next time. Salaam."

Outside, the sky is crying. I have to jog the three blocks to 'Bangi's place to keep my vines from getting soaked. I put the book Antar's given me inside my coat. It's a copy of the Holy Quran. Missionaries on two sides of me now: the Reverend and Antar. In front of Ubangi's building a penny-pitching game has just broken up and the players take refuge in the laundromat next door. The building turns out to be an ordinary apartment building, much like any other in Roxbury. The windows upstairs are boarded up and over the door is a handwritten sign: UBANGI'S UMOJA INSTITUTE OF THE DARKER ARTS. My friend, always on top of things. The odor of disinfectant seeps from the walls, the floor. A riot of sounds rushes out at me. From the closed doors in the hallway some of the noises come clear and prod my memory awake. Suddenly, steps, hollow even steps, before I spot the tall, well-dressed brother. A short chain on his ankle. His eyes are intent on the ham hocks he juggles.

"Yes?" he asks, never taking his eyes from the flying hocks.

"I'm looking for Ubangi Jones." I try to be cool about it. A gold watch chain and many pins in his lapel wink at me.

"The second floor, sir, to your right." He turns on a heel and disappears behind the stairwell, his arms still going. It must be an initiation for something, I decide.

On the second floor, I push through a partially opened door marked "1965." What I see inside turns my legs to jelly. At the front of the large room, about thirty women stand stiffly in rank, all of them necklaced in mink, miniskirts about their blue-veined calves. A man, very black and bearded, shouts order from the dais. He glares at them for a long moment, sneering. Moans start up here and there. They begin to leap up and down, flapping their minks, a few rolling over on the floor in orgasmic fury. Slowly the man fits on fangs and the moans erupt to the hysterical cries of she-lions in heat. Coins, hats, girdles rain to the stage. Some delight in folding blank checks into toy airplanes that zip past the man's head. Bald-headed men in sneakers rush in to haul away those gray women who have fainted and been nearly trampled to death.

"Bitches! Old whores with the moon for souls! Devil women!" He shouts more goodies into their faces and they rush the stage in a flying wedge. His bodyguards are wise enough to hit the leading lady with cross-body blocks and the pack goes flying, leaving a squirming mess for the old men to clean up. One of these men stops near me, sizes me up, and scratches his chin. He introduces himself as Rudy Williams of Morehead College. "Who are you?" he asks.

"I'm looking for Ubangi Jones. Seen him around?"

"Never heard of him myself. You want a pair of fangs or

something? What you really doing here?" He steps closer, squinting.

"Just watching right now, sir."

"Well, you need a Ph.D. to do that. Go 'way and get that."

"But sir, I don't want to cart off dead bodies or do the Atlanta Slide. I just want to watch, then go look up my buddy, but I have a few questions . . ."

His eyes are puddles of suspicion. "Get the master's degree, then, and I'll talk to you. By the way, what sign are you?"

"Sign, sir?"

"Yeah, sign. You know, Leo, Sagittarius—stuff like that."

"Mack," I say.

"I knew we had nothing in common," he snorts. "I just knew it. Be gone when I come back, you hear?" He picks up his stretcher and sprints to the front with his partner. Wasting no time, they toss on a woman and take off again. She looks familiar. I step closer to get a better look as they pass. Her lips twitching and going blue. It's Judge Becky. Bending, I try to catch her last words, risking the old man's bad-mouthing.

"Sacrifice!" I hear her say. "Sacrifice!" Icy fingers race up my spine, grip the back of my neck. What is she talking about?

Up front they've gathered around the man who's become a cadaver, stiff as a board. They stand over him and shout an amazing grace: "We will be friends to the end. We will always help ourselves to what we cannot help. Let us merge and let our commitment nourish future sons."

His stomach is swiftly slit and his innards flung to the mob. They make slurping sounds as they grope for parts of his liver, its juices staining their stubby fingers and dripping to the floor. Someone tries to hotfoot it out of the side door with his heart, but a thick book catches the desperate woman upside her head, knocking her to the floor. The book and the heart bouncing to my feet, the heart still pumping blood everywhere and the grinning face of a neo-tom going purple on the dustjacket. I freeze.

The sound of a coffin lid snapping shut behind me and a key has just clicked in the door. I snatch at the doorknob. Locked in! I race for another door at the rear of the room, but I'm blocked in by three men squatting in a circle, spitting tobacco juice. Two wear coveralls and boots caked in red clay, the other is suited like a banker although he also wears muddy boots. Smells of magnolia and bubbling tar. They are church-bombers who pinch their pimples and wait for the night.

"Shame for them to pick that poor nigra-boy apart likat," says the man in the suit. "Yankees up there just making a mess of things. We know what they're after, eh, Virgil?" Nudging the man next to him, he grabs at his own crotch. They explode in laughter and rebel yells. Three women, their women, straight, plain, pale women in faded dresses, turn away.

I've noticed a deputy's badge on one of the men in coveralls. They talk now of the smart nigra who rode through town the other day and had to leave two hundred dollars behind with the Justice of the Peace, the nigra who skated through their dreams last night, the strutting nigra woman who works out at McBride's place, that crazy nigra who knowed magic, that big buck nigra who raped Aunt Nellie's ghost, the nigra who picked his nose in their faces, the nigra they caught going into the library.

Finally I crash their circle and make it for the door. Dead on my heels is a woman carrying a pair of fangs, behind her Virgil is baying like a hound. I have to skirt an acid-rock group, the Dutch West Indies Company, nearly tripping over a huge amplifier. But I get out just in time, slamming the door behind me. They still bang away from inside, though, so there is no time to waste. I suck in air and hustle off. I can feel a bead of sweat trickling from under my arm, down my side . . . This hall is deathly still. I pause before a mural: a black church, burning through the centuries. Gloom all around . . .

In the first days there was a busy intersection in a large nervous city. Summertime and the living ain't easy. Slow motions in the moist clinging heat. A legless man sits on a corner, chin to chest. A cup with several coins in it next to him. As I pass by, he looks up and frowns.

"Ain't you Petie's boy?"

"Petie?" I ask, dropping a dime in his cup.

"Naw, naw," he says, coming to life. "You ain't no Petie's boy. I can see that now, but at first you did put me in mind of him. I bet you is De . . ."

"De who?"

He chuckles, shaking his cup. "De man who done got my hopes up so damned high. Look here, Daddy Cool, I only need another quarter for me some grapes. You can understand that now, can't you?" His eyes shift to women passing. "Hey there, Skinny Minnie! Go ahead, Red! Shake it, but please don't break it! Lawdy, lawdy, Miss Claudy, you sho look good to me!"

They call him Ole Pluck. They smile back at him or rub his head or listen to his talk for a minute. They are kind to him. But when they leave, he spits. "Don't let them mess you up."

"Who?" I ask, half ready for another punch line.

"Them womens. Shit, between bad womens and white folks, a man just can't know no good."

"Why do they have to be bad?"

"Why do jelly roll? Here you is, supposed to be a cool daddy and thinking everything is good. Nigga, you a fool. You better check yourself before you get sucked in." Guitar chords follow me up the street and I decide that he hasn't meant a word that he's said. I keep walking, my steps too loud. Where do these people belong? What do they have to do with Ubangi? With me . . . ?

A different sun is up, offering a playground in a valley among tenements. I'm sitting on the slide, playing my horn. A boy walks up and stands quietly next to me until I've finished a run that I'm pleased with.

"This some good reefer," I hear him repeat. I turn it down. They call him Booboo and his family lives down the hall.

"Alonzo and Jellybelly say you duked out that big nigga in our building last night. Yeah, the one who rips off the little ladies every time they be picking up their Social Security checks. They say you whipped some Muhammad Ali mess on the cat, say he never even got a chance to go for his blade. I mean, you must be a bad muthafucka to do that. Cain't no slouch do it. Stonehead supposed to be the baddest dude this side of town. I'm glad you wasted him, man, 'cause I don't dig the dude no way."

He sucks in the smoke and holds it. "You making any money playing, man? Think I can learn to play?"

"Nothing but a word. I'll teach you, my man."

He's no more than fourteen but looks an easy twenty-five. I've noticed that he's always somewhere around when I'm practicing. Then his sister Esther comes up. She would be pretty except for that certain coldness under her eyes, at the corners of her mouth. Two abortions have led her to the church and Usher Board meetings on Friday nights. I've made up my mind she's too young for me to hit on.

"Can't you put that horn down to talk?" she asks. Booboo idles toward the monkey bars to finish the roach in peace. "Where you going?"

"I'm going to have a little fun with Amos, if you don't

mind." Amos, an aging paralytic with blue gums. They can stone him because he's superbad in the dozens. They even steal his lines and use them on strangers.

"Mack, you never take me up on my invitations to come to church. You should come this Sunday. We'll be selling hot-plate dinners for a dollar."

"You can count on me this time. I haven't had a good dinner in weeks."

"You won't like Miss Cheatham," Booboo says later. "That's why she wants you to come to church. I know, I hear them talking. Miss Cheatham has a thing for you. She don't give up no leg, man. I can turn you on to more poon tang that run around that church. That is, if you teach me to play the horn."

Beverly Cheatham works late as a waitress to pay for her morning theology courses at the university. Though less cold than Esther's, her face is dull, as if washed that way many, many times. The church-mothers have made themselves busy humming around us. They have watched our faces after we've been introduced—the word must travel fast—and welcomed me more than once. "Ain't no strangers down here at Tried Stone, you hear? Make yourself right at home."

Like an embarrassed daughter on her first date, Beverly Cheatham has to shoo them away. She's old enough to talk to a man. She tells me about the books she's reading and I find I have little to offer, here and there a book on African history. It's obvious that she will go somewhere in this world, and though she's not certain where, it will be far from Tried Stone. You see, her well-ordered thoughts frighten me. Pushing, pushing, she will study and study those books of hers and no doubt will continue to build her pyramids while serving rib dinners, waiting for her break. The way she touches her lips with her napkin, the sweat mustache. She will be alone too, and dragged forever into fumbling introductions. All this in a second, before she asks me what I'm doing tomorrow night.

No matter how hard I try to dress it up, Booboo knows. "I told you," he says, offering me his reefer. "Now, when we gone get on with those lessons?" He's suddenly a man in shades, with his own horn. He waits for my cue . . .

I start again down the hall. Mingus' "Orange Was the Color of Her Dress, Then Blue Silk" dies out. A tattooed white hand reaches suddenly through the wall, just missing me. I hurry away, trying to pick one of the many doors to dive into.

Finally, trusting to luck, I dive through one and catch myself smiling into the irritated faces of aristocratic men puffing on pipes. A speaker on the podium leads a chant.

"We are a community-minded organization. We throw boss parties, gigs, get-togethers, et cetera. Plus, we be so cool . . ."

"Rah! Rah! Rah!"

"Our contributions to the community have been innumerable. The Culture Committee has reported to me that the Big Leg Contests were overwhelming successes and that the dances afterwards were outasight achievements!

"For the new and the curious, and those who continue to sneer at us, let them check our record. Some of the most outstanding leaders and champions of the Cause are members of our august organization."

"ONE MORE TIME!"

"I said . . ." (fingering his fraternity pin).

"THINK ABOUT IT!"

". . . They are members of our blessed organization" (fingering a crucifix).

"AGAIN!"

"Let me repeat . . ." (fingering a tiki).

"DIG IT!"

". . . They be members of our dynamite organization."

Two of them hustle out a shabby wino who has lost his way. It's Ole Pluck! How did he get here? They dust their hands and return to their seats. "Our responsibility is to the moral, spiritual, and intellectual uplifting of the Race. Our duty is to ourselves as members of the Club, our respect for fair play, our nation built with the blood and sweat of our forefathers, some of whom were together enough to belong to our thing."

Missing the point, Ole Pluck brushes me aside and staggers back into the room. He's changed into a suit, though newspaper still pokes from the holes in his shoes. The sergeant at arms catches him with a mighty uppercut. My stomach sinks at the sound of it. From a chair, a fat man manages a flying drop kick. As Pluck tries to rise, a streamer of blood stretches from his mouth to the floor. Saying nothing, he runs his old-man run as they laugh. Courage is a quiet thing.

The leader rattling on without a hitch. ". . . to achieve our goals, we champion steadfastness, courage, humility, patience, love and loyalty to the group, and above all, sacrifice." He tap-dances off to heavy applause.

The audience multiplies to millions—men, women, children. A soft rain is falling on them. On a hilltop, just to the left of the rainbow, many men stand with black boxes marked "The Gospel". Among them are leaders and prophets who have made it by hustling doom. They open their boxes one at a time and allow each other to peek in. None of them is satisfied with what he sees in the others' boxes. They bark at one another, then lock arms, going into a strange dance. Their voices fade, though their lips still move. The crowd is not impressed by the arabesque of arms and they shift restlessly in the rain. The old wino, the creeping man who is everywhere, silent, watching, goes to the hilltop, unlocks their arms and joins their hands. Yes, join our hands so that we can look more closely at each other, see ourselves in the eyes of others . . .

.   .   .

On the way to the third floor, I meet a man calmly spreading goober dust in front of a door, smoothing it out with his fingers, singing . . .

"Take dis hammer
Carry it to de captain
Tell him I'm gone, baby
Tell him I'm gone.

Ef he ax you
Was I running
Tell him how fast, baby,
Tell him how fast.

Ef he ax you
Any mo questions
Tell him you don't know, baby,
You don't know."

"Have you seen Ubangi Jones?" I ask.

"Do what? What he in for—armed robbery? Plenty of us here for that. Cap'n be out soon. Ask him." This isn't the right place.

At the top of the stairs I meet another man, in green fatigues. He's swinging a jack-o'-lantern made from a human skull. He comes on slapping palms. "What's happenin', my man?" I follow him to a room where the walls are frescoes of burning skylines, epitaphs to fallen skyscrapers. Archangels in bulletproof vests check it out from on high. My guide is in a hurry, so I don't have time to appreciate an obscure touch: a woman praying at a church cornerstone.

"You will miss it. Hurry!" Frozen in a circle on the floor are the troopers. A bass clarinet's voice comes, sad and mournful, from overhead speakers. The dance begins. The spectators around the floor provide sound effects, screams that crack the walls, ACKACKACK! But suddenly it stops again. On the wall a huge shadow is creeping, a man limping along. A nervous dude pumps six quick rounds into the shadow. A wiser man throws back a curtain to expose the cowering wino. Pluck again. "Come out!"

They can't get a word out of him except the usual plea: "I . . . I was just trying to get a few shekels together, my man, to cop me a taste."

"Out the way, broken man." He's dropped off at the side and the slow shingaling with the automatic rifles resumes. The clarinet's voice is higher now, screaming, accusing.

"You with us or against us, brother?" The question is for the man shaking next to me. I can hear his knees knocking. They aren't through with him yet.

"I don't understand," he says.

"You will if you don't say something fast," says a guerrilla young in years. "Ain't no middle ground, ole dude." His gun is level with the old man's chest. They're frozen there, unseeing. I inch toward the door. Certainly I'll be next. But suddenly they are talking and the man has taken the gun and is telling the warrior stories. The old convict asks a question that I can hear as I leave. Take a precise stand with your anger, he's saying.

"Are you in and want out of the whale's belly? Or, are you out and want in?" It's a corny question, really, but it's taken the young trooper by surprise.

The man with the lantern avoids my eyes. I have disappointed him in some way I do not understand. Maybe I was to join the dance. I check my watch. It's stopped! No telling how long I've been going in circles in this place. Ubangi might have left.

A woman sits in the hall. She is barefoot and pregnant, her

eyes to her belly, her hand gently stroking it. A smile lights her face. She's made a song for me. I touch her hand and she motions to a room across the hall.

Ubangi sits alone inside. There is no furniture other than a chair and table. Cans of unopened paint are stacked in a corner. It looks like he's writing letters. A half-empty jug of red wine at his elbow. Business, whatever it is this time, must be slow.

"What took you so long, man? I could have been done gone."

"Those stairs are a bitch," I say weakly.

"This ain't the John Hancock Building, Mr. Mack. We ain't into elevators yet. I done finished designing posters for our bongo-drumming contest next month."

No doubt this scheme will be as shaky as the others. Where does he stop with all this? He stands and looks sadly out the window. Not the least bit excited by the news of the preacherman's strange gift of the church, he speaks indifferently.

"Mack, I didn't know people these days was in the business of giving away churches."

"He's just loaning it out awhile, 'Bangi. He just trying to bring a little new blood in, that's all."

"Anyway. I suppose you done heard about Wendell," he says, fanning away a fly. Turns.

"Uh-uh."

"It just happened. He's been shot."

Thirteen

"SHOT, 'BANGI?"

"That's what I heard, man. I mean, he's going to pull out of it, but I heard it messed him up . . ."

"How do you mean?"

"Now look, Mack, I'm just repeating what I heard and the dude who came up here to run it down to me was high as a kite. So maybe half of what he saying ain't true no way."

I sit on the cans of paint. Sirens shoot past on the street below. The rain hangs outside the window. "Who did it, 'Bangi? Make sense, now. Who did he say did it?"

"Two whities is all he said. Two whities in a Cadillac. He'd seen them cruising up and down the avenue for an hour before they pulled up behind Wendell and one of them shot twice. He said one of the bullets hit Wendell and the other missed."

"Two of them in a Cadillac? That doesn't sound right."

"Over the past week a lot of weird shit has gone down. Remember the night I took you to the after-hours joint? I introduced you to a cat who owned a club over on Dudley

Street, a friend of Big June's. Day before yesterday, I read where he got it in the back of the head."

"They must have been after someone else. They don't send out hatchet men for actors. Where is he now, 'Bangi?"

"City Hospital, I think. That's where they always take us." He writes on as if nothing's happened, as if I've troubled him to ask about the weather.

"I have to see him. I'll talk to you later."

"Hold tight." He licks an envelope. "I'm ready to leave too. You know I've been waiting here all day on you."

Mist settles on the street. The penny-pitchers idle from the laundromat, yawning. My mind won't leave the Cadillac, the cold eyes, the finger on the trigger . . . " 'Bangi, the mutha-fuckas should be caught. Then their trigger fingers should be cut off, their eyeballs plucked out and dollar bills stuffed into the bleeding sockets."

"You want to spend too much time on them. They ain't worth it, my man. Blow them away good-fashioned. Ain't no need for all that ceremony."

We swing past Antar's shop, but it's closed now. Did that call for him as I was leaving concern Wendell? I wonder what he and Omowale and company will do about the shooting? What about the men holding down the corners, who have never heard of Wendell and who probably would not like him—the silent, red-eyed magicians who come out of the doorways after the rain has ended and drift toward pool halls? You know, the ones scratched off everyone's list with no ready abstractions, with their guns oiled and powder dry, the ones I've been afraid of becoming ever since I've know there are two feet to stand on; one if push comes to shove, a butt if things have got messy, but stand you must. Afraid since I've known so little about what I have to fight with.

Ubangi spits into the gutter. "I heard he was going to move this Saturday too. The night man told me that."

Moving? His uncle's blood money, probably. That Cadillac again, gliding past the people getting off work, the buses, the subways. In their midst it moves, the white-eyes on the lookout for whores, these untouchables riding arrogantly. A beer can thrown at them might signify something. Their purpose is not to bring love. It isn't to point out strength. We know it. You know it too, brothers in the record store. Smack to be dropped off, local leaders to be drilled in broad daylight. Let's talk about their mamas if we don't go after them. Anything but this corny rage.

Ubangi has stopped at the corner. "I'm going to Novella's for a minute. Come on over with me, then we can make it to the hospital."

"I'm not going to the hospital, Mack," he says. "You know Wendell and me wouldn't have anything to say to each other."

"Goddam, 'Bangi! He's been shot. You don't have to make a speech. Just come on!"

"I know it sounds cold, but I can't sit up in nobody's room with nothing to say. Like everybody else, I hate to hear what happened, but I can't cheer nobody up. I mean, it ain't got nothing to do about how we got along. I just can't cheer nobody up behind this. I'd give him a gun or something, but I just couldn't sit up and talk behind the mess."

"Just sit there, then," I tell him. "But you have to come."

He just shakes his head and says he'll catch me at the club tonight.

"I won't be there for a few days. They fired me again."

"I'll call you later, then. Will you be at your old lady's?"

I nod and we turn away with nothing else to say. He's only serious about screwing up. I didn't want him to come to the hospital for any peace truces with Wendell. I've just thought that Wendell might be sparked by presences. He's said he's as lonely as anyone else, despite the cats crowding his place all hours of the night, and I'm sure they won't show up at the hospital. It had to be an accident. Wendell will play it tough, though. I can see him waving off the sentimental stuff and asking for a cigarette. I know his tough act.

From Novella's, I call the hospital. A bland voice reports that he is in serious condition. Aside from immediate family, he can't receive visitors until he's on the satisfactory list.

"Why?" Novella asks. "Why him of all people? If he's like you say, why would anyone try to kill him?"

I give her my accident theory, but she doesn't want to accept it. Assassins don't shoot the wrong man, she believes. Only the crackers she's known can shoot indiscriminately. No, simple bad luck won't count this time.

Then Little Precious comes in and tugs at my hand. "Are we still going to the zoo tomorrow?"

Novella rushes to the rescue. "One of Mack's friends isn't feeling so well, sugar. They had to take him to the hospital and Mack might have to see him tomorrow. So we'll see, okay?"

She moves to the couch and mumbles to herself, cutting her eyes at Novella. "Can I go to the hospital with you, then?"

"Hospitals smell bad," I tell her.

"I been to the hospital before, haven't I, Mama? Remember, with Amanda when her little brother was just a baby? Huh, didn't we, Mama? Your friend going to have a little boy too?"

Precious doesn't give in easily. Like her mother, she'll push you into the truth sooner or later. "I tell you what, tomorrow we'll go down to the fruit stand when I get back from the hospital. Then Wednesday we can go to the zoo."

"I hope you know what you're saying," Novella whispers. "She'll remember everything you say." But it has gotten me off the hook. Precious runs off with Amanda, who's come down for her.

"You two don't give Eileen a fit now, you hear?" But they're gone now, screaming on the stairs. My woman closes the door and smiles.

"I thought she had you that time. Precious is nobody's fool, you can believe that."

"You pulling her coat early, aren't you?"

"I have to. Now, what about the club, Mack? I heard they're opening up some new ones around here. Do you think they'll be worth checking out? Maybe you won't have to trust the hustlers then."

"Everything's set where I am. Okra will have me back on in less than a week."

"You're something else. All the stuff that no-singing Hurricane Wanda and her man put you through and you want to go back? I don't understand it."

"When I find a good group, I try to stick with it. I do the same thing when I find a good woman."

She flags it away. "Well, if you want to give them one more chance, then I just hope it works out. I just hope nothing happens to you like my daddy used to talk about. He always said a hard head makes a soft behind."

"I'll try to keep myself covered."

Novella pulls me to the kitchen, where she has to start dinner. She pours two cups of coffee. Then she hums above the music from the radio, the sway and play of her movements touching two-day-old memory: the park in the middle of the city, a wino's park streaked with evening sunshine and soft explosions of green, and littered with empty wine bottles and a rock in its dead center dedicated to a hero of some war, and we sat with Little Precious between and Novella asked if I had ever seen into forever and I, lying, said no. She told me that church has never meant Heaven or Hell to her and I should know better than to think that it has and I guessed correctly (because she smiled) that it was one of many temples of life.

We talked, too, about her music and my music and how they flowed from one spirit, one need. She said that she'd be down to hear me play (I was fired that day and hadn't told her yet). With the straight-backed strut of a deacon and shifty eyes, a man sold ice cream and roasted peanuts nearby. But the smell of the peanuts, the man and the park faded before the trust in her eyes.

"Novella, you ever wonder how we've made it so smoothly these few weeks?"

"I don't worry about it too much. You see, I know this root woman down the corner who told me how to hold you. Just cut a little of your hair off, drop it in a little bag. 'Love guaranteed for days . . .'"

She sips her coffee. "But when you first came to me with those wild ideas you had about saving everyone with your music, I had to think twice. I know now you mean giving what you can to help make things clearer. Mack, I only worry about us when you want to keep so much away from me."

"What do you mean?"

"Come on, now, you give out those little pieces of yourself like it's killing you, like I'm going to run something on you. I've been hurt too, and I know a little about payback. A woman don't often get a chance to pay back the one who ran the game on her even if she wanted to, so she gets the closest one around her while the pain is still alive. But, Mack, I can't play slick. When the feeling is there, it's there and I can't do a damn thing about it except give it. A woman can have her head bumped a lot doing that, huh?"

"There's no head-bumping to worry about. It scares me to know that I can never repay you for what you've done the short time we've been together. I want to spend a lot of time trying, though . . ."

She smiles. "My love ain't like money, Mack. It's not a loan and there's no interest on it. Why do you think that way? You see, there's so little I really know about you. For all that beautiful music and purpose inside you, why is your guard up so much? You can't see the people through your guard, can you? That Sassie Mae woman you talked about once is just one woman. I'm not her or anybody else you've ever known. Don't blame them on me."

She looks off.

"I suppose I have been standing around in the shadows, touching all my old scars, figuring the little talent I had was fragile because it was holy. I never figured that if it was so fragile, then it might not do too many people any good. You peeped all that in a pair of seconds. I bet I never had a chance."

She pushes my hand away, but not too quickly. "You want to play, I see."

"Uh-huh, let's play tomorrow and the next day until hell freezes over and time don't move no more. Just stay the woman you are."

"What else can I do if you stay the man you are?" We lie together and she's circled in my arms, in me. She coughs a short cough and I tell her, natural and clear, things that I've been afraid of telling too many times before. (Watch out you don't spoil yo' bitches, someone has warned.) The noise from someone's TV reaches through the walls.

In the next apartment, something shatters against a wall. The Richards couple, two heavyweights, are going at it again. They have four small children who no doubt are hiding behind the sofa while their parents do battle. A chair and maybe a skillet hit the wall and one of the children screams, perhaps caught by a flying shoe as she tried to get some jellybeans off the floor. More curses that melt to a long silence. The sudden scream of brakes outside and we rush for bright silent yards of easier motions. Dreams. She kisses my ear and as my hand drifts below her navel to wet softness, she strokes, stretches and kneads me. And this time, as I hear her breath come as the sweetest of all windsongs, the heavens will shake over our terrible selves.

"So here I am back North and nothing's working, Mack. The toughest dudes in the movement are scattered, ripped off, their minds silenced. Of course, there's the hope that some are underground gathering strength, but too many are tired. And the sad thing is that nobody cares. Certainly not some dude standing at his basement bar in the suburbs and scratching his ass. No, he wouldn't care. And the kids coming along now were shooting marbles when we were in the South. They think everything started yesterday and don't want to know about the days before. Man, I've thought once or twice about finishing college and going to law school. I've smoked a lot and popped my share of a few pills, but nothing was coming clearer for me that way. As corny as it sounds, Mack, without Malaika no telling what I'd be into now. I doubt if I'd be writing plays or even have the shop. We do battle like everybody else and she hasn't gotten all the way from her bourgeois thing yet, but we're getting somewhere. And that's the important thing now, man—moving somewhere because there's too much shit out here standing still.

"Anyway, that's why I gave you the Quran to read the other day. We had talked and I didn't know what else to do. It's helped me and maybe it can help you too. After all, you seem to have a helluva lot on your mind. You the only musician I know plotting to take over a church."

Antar laughs at this, stroking his beard as we wait to cross the street. Big cars lined up at the light. Hot tar and gasoline smells.

"When I first checked you out digging on our conversation in the shop that day, I said to myself, Antar, you have another convert to the holy way."

We move on toward Reverend Fuller's place, Antar going on and on. For the past half-hour or so, we've been comparing more notes on the past. I bumped into him outside his shop and thought this as good a time as any to introduce him to Reverend Fuller. I'm curious how the two of them will hit it off, though I must take care to avoid a holy war. Antar has renounced Christians for all time. Yet he keeps a long list of exceptions.

"I surprised myself, going for this church idea," I tell him. "It'll be a relief not to worry about some dude punching another in the middle of a solo. But I don't want the service to be too dead, you understand. I want people to get happy the same way they do when C. E. is up there preaching."

"When he's preaching self-hate and nigger lies?" Antar asks.

"You don't even know him, man. Cut some slack, huh?" Yet he guesses correctly as I have done before that the big car in front of the entrance belongs to Reverend Fuller.

"Good thing Omowale didn't come along," he says as we go inside. "He'd be getting himself ready to put down your preacherman, 'way down."

Reverend Fuller greets us with the smile of salvation. Thumbs his suspenders as we step inside. Gospel music is playing loudly from the kitchen. "Y'all have a seat. I was just setting here enjoying me some good music and trying not to worry about how much my wife gone spend out there shopping, heh-heh. So this is Antar?" He stops to study Antar, the beard. "Mack has told me that y'all have bumped into a few of the same people on life's highway."

Antar nods civilly. I brace myself for C. E.'s standard line about the mysterious working of things. But he's heard my thoughts and stays quiet. He offers us glasses of lemonade.

"Let's move out to the porch in the cool. Mack, on the phone you sounded like you were putting together something real fine."

"I hope so. I just want to work something where we can have all kinds of people in, people who would never come to church otherwise, sitting in here under the same roof."

"You want to work a miracle then, son. Heh-heh. If you do that, a lot of people gone want your secret. The way folks seem to be falling out of church these days is a shame."

"Black folks might be looking for spiritual alternatives," Antar suggests with the subtlety of an uppercut.

"Of course, there may be a number of alternatives," I put in. "I don't claim to have any fancy answers to lay out there, but whatever people turn to, I hope they are not blinded by it. I hope they don't use it to keep them from life."

"What are you talking about, Mack?"

"I'm talking about temples where people huddle in isolation, where they justify their actions by the fact that they can exclude others, unclean, unholy, from their secret rooms. I mean, I run up against enough bullshit—excuse me, C. E.—just trying to play my horn. Put down as a freak, a toy, a background ornament, just to get up on the stand. Then I come to the holy folks and I'm a sinner because my spirit needed no temple, because I have joined no new-style religion and tried to forget the one I knew. I share what little I have, Antar. It might not seem that way. I can't hold any secrets to justify some priesthood. I mean, most of the secrets have been blown by now."

Antar smiles. "Your spirit flows through your horn, then. Is that the point? You do it all by yourself, huh? Too hip for Allah. Wake up, Mack. To close out everything because a few things seem unfair is a mistake."

"I didn't say to close out anything. That's the useless part. I'm saying accept it all, man, the winos with the nuns, the holy rollers and unholy rollers. If I had a religion, then that's where it would be."

Antar shaking his head, C. E. crossing his legs and staring into the tops of trees.

"Mix the righteous and the unrighteous, Mack?" Antar asks. "That's very noble of you, but it is discipline which has been lacking in us, the discipline that is to struggle as a muscle is to the arm. Without it, we have no power. We are useless. That's what I've been trying to tell you under it all, man. That's what I've seen in those hot towns in the South and what I've seen in this city. That's the difference between pride and self-pity. Some can accept discipline and some can't. Those who see must help the others."

"Maybe so, but where do the chosen few go without the nasty no-good sinners? Do the chosen few huddle in the wildernesses to trade truths? Do they shy away from the funkiness of things? Their hiding out just means nothing is getting out to the people who need it. Believe or submit before you get the secret?"

"Antar, like I say, I ain't got all the answers, maybe just one or two that might work for me for a minute or two. I just want to blow some music, you know? I'll call it unity music. If I never do it again, y'all can just say that Mack did something new one day. Right now this act, this one clear act I've come to, makes a helluva lot of sense to me."

They trade looks and sip more lemonade. I've outdone myself, I've tried to keep peace between them and have made them allies. C. E., the more flexible of the two despite his age, might go along with the program. But there is very little for either of them to feel threatened by.

C. E. gets me a beer, then clears his throat. "You know, maybe a man can look at his life and see it like you see the church, Mack. Take my life, for instance. My early days was spent actin' mannish fool like I done tole you. Then I get the call and I grew to become a larger man. Not different, but larger, 'cause what was in me before done got refined and made a little better. It need to be that way when you get power because the things that come with power are sho-nuff temptin'. There a lot of preachers who be turned around by it and of course there's some who haven't. Maybe that's where the discipline come in, Antar. You need to control that part of you that want to be greedy, but you don't want so much control that you scare folks away."

C. E. leans back, sighing, thumbing his suspenders again. "I think I can see what both y'all saying." Role of middleman fits him loosely.

"You can see a lot, then, because I sure can't," Antar says.

"It's there plain as day. You're talking about changing people and most everybody wants to do that. Mack seem to be saying that ain't possible unless you allow them to change the way they want too," C. E. says.

"That means that some might choose to wallow in ignorance, to shoot up and stay high," Antar says. "If you want to be so open about it all, then there's be no reason for religion at all."

"We need a better religion that brings the best of everything together. The people can be their own gods."

That really shakes them up. Antar looks at me as if I've betrayed him, as if I've brought him here away from his territory to argue. I suggest a walk and they agree. We start down the hill toward Dudley Station many blocks away. The faces of abandoned buildings are painted with explosive gestures of heroes, named and nameless. The two holy men remark that my revelation has taken them by surprise, that I must have been struck down by it in the clear light of day. They want to call me a new man, but I tell them that I'm still out of work.

"Behind the job scene, Wendell's senseless injury, I just thought about the things we have faith in. Few of them are still standing. It has to be in the group, the past, present, future, on the group's terms, not on just the terms of the high priests and their wild-eyed visions. Then I was thinking about how so damned much that seems different is the same. Like the two of you and me."

They ignore that and move on, discussing Wendell's accident, the threats of violence on anonymous whites cruising through. It's enough that Antar will join us on Sunday. Maybe he's been shaken up a little bit and will come to church freer. Perhaps his shield of religions and revolution can be cast aside for a moment to accept what must be seen.

Fourteen

ASIDE FROM the cops, Novella and I have been Wendell's only visitors after he's been placed on the satisfactory list. He is still temporarily paralyzed on one side, but the doctors feel that with therapy he will recover. There has been no word from his family and he doesn't expect that there will be. His friends have called, sent cards, and promised to come, but have taken their time. Antar, Omowale and the others have been too busy setting up a community patrol responsible for surveillance of the black community.

At least twice before, such steps were taken, but the efforts stalled in weeks. Short memories, we have. Omowale says it will be different this time: Roxbury will be free of all devils. Yet interracial groups meet quietly over tea and put down for all time racists of all colors. Thus, alone, Wendell has spent most of the time reading.

Except for his few attempts to play the whole thing off, the visits have not been painful. It's public now: a case of mistaken identity. With his hair and his clothing, some gangsters have taken him for the leader of some nationalist group. The cops have showed him a picture of the look-alike and have called the whole thing "unfortunate." I wonder what they would say if the things had gotten the nationalist. They claim to be looking for the triggermen, but no one believes them.

"Seen one nigga and you've seen them all," Wendell has said grimly on our second visit. "If there were a reason for me—I mean me, Wendell Keyes—to get a bullet against the spine, I might at least be able to feel sorry for myself." I've been unable to say anything behind that to reassure him. The point is, he will be well again.

"You'll stay in the play, won't you? I mean, after you get out of here?"

"Hell yes! I know I'll be able to play a fantastic part too. It'll be real."

"No more Shakespeare, Wendell?"

"Shakespeare's actors weren't shot down in the streets like dogs. Whatever I learn from this, if anything can be learned outside the fact that we're niggas to be treated like niggas, even by the dumbest smelliest cracker—if there's anything to be learned, Mack, I'm going to use it. I don't know what I'll be after I get out, but it'll be a different me. Before, I thought I could be the greatest actor, now I'm convinced that I have no choice but to become one. In a hurry."

"I think I know what you mean."

"Do you really?"

"Well, once you find out there's so much accident to things, you want to hurry and get your licks in."

He nods. "Something like that. Listen, make sure you tape the church meeting. This I've got hear."

Silent in Wendell's room, Novella opens up after we've left. "I felt the same way he did a long time ago at the school I've told you about. I wasn't that brave and nobody can tell me I was. When they started spitting and tossing firecrackers and I saw those damned ugly faces every day, it was all I could do to keep from running home where things made sense. I knew the three of us skinny girls had to soak up so much for those coming behind us, but it's hard to stay in a dream, even at that age. There were fifty others in the town like us who might have come, but it came down to the three of us, our fathers really, because they did the deciding. They soaked up that mess for all the ones who didn't come that year—for our brothers and sisters and all those who would come ten, twenty years from then. And we had to believe in that, past, present and future, but most of all in ourselves. We were finding something to fight with—we had sense enough to know we were in the fight then and the best part of ourselves would remain in the fight. What you choose to fight with becomes the biggest part of you."

At Novella's apartment we pick up Little Precious, Amanda, and her mother, and start for the church.

"Did your friend have a boy or girl?" Little Precious promptly asks.

"He struck out this time. They have to fix up his side." She looks a little puzzled when I try to explain in my way that men can't have babies. It doesn't ring clear to her and I simply tell her that I hope she never has to go to the hospital except to have her own baby.

"Don't tell her that!" Novella says.

"Why?"

"She's too young."

"What's wrong with babies, when they're supposed to come?"

She shakes her head and pulls the others inside the church while I wait outside, smoking, watching the street. In large hats, Sunday-school teachers pass to go inside, eying the horn case. The church is filling quickly, and in a few minutes

Reverend Fuller will give his last sermon. Okra and the rest aren't due for another half-hour. They claim they can't sit still for a sermon, so they plan to get here just as he finishes.

A car shoots past with Crackerjack at the wheel. His hat, the tilt of his head, shoulders moving to music. His head swiveling to catch sight of fat behinds on the sidewalk. There's nothing for us to talk about any more, though he would press the point. Luckily he hasn't seen me. He'd go into the hustles he's made, what more he can do for me, and oh yeah, my man, I couldn't get down to bail you out because I've been involved in this deal that has all my loose cash tied up. His lies will gag him one of these days. I think of Fuckup, who at last report has dropped off the set to become a full-time mystic.

It has come down to Crumbly Rock Baptist Church. On this evening, as the tops of trees move slow-motion, it will be New Breed Baptist Church, and the church can make a decision and we can all move a little bit closer. We, ripples in the ripples in the ripples of holiness. We go on, substituting one church for another, one Messiah for another, one name of God for another, yet use our different positions as stones against one another. Church is, after all, any place the spirit roams free and burns us clean enough to touch, to love. It makes the distance between Antar's Revolution and Reverend Fuller's Revelations idle gossip, motions toward That Great Day When.

When the choir begins, I have to go inside. Novella has started to solo righteously. I take the seat that Little Precious has saved for me. She glows through the songs as her mother's voice touches everyone in this crowded room. Then Reverend Fuller stands and looks over the church which has filled to overflowing. He smooths his hair and begins for all of us.

"This evening, I'm thinking about a song, a work song that

our fathers used to sing in those hot fields down South, many
years ago. It goes like this:

O Lord, I'm tired
O Lord, I'm tired
O Lord, I'm tired
O Lord, I'm tired
O Lord, I'm tired of this mess.

"Now, I know you gone think it strange for Reverend Fuller
to talk on something like that on his last sermon. You gone be
thinking, what's this 'mess' he's talking about. I want to talk a
little about faith this evening, and what happens when faith
breaks down . . ."

"AMEN!"

". . . It's our faith I want to talk about—our faith in the
Lord, our faith in ourselves, our faith in faith. Now, you don't
need me to put you to sleep telling you about the condition we
in as a people. No, no, you know that already. You scrub the
floors, you pay them high notes on your furniture, and that
high rent. It's you who get the stew when somebody else be
getting the steak. But what I do want to tell you this evening,
you may not want to hear . . ."

He's smiling, and laughter bubbles from the front row,
nervous laughter at first. Restless children are snatched back in
their seats, silenced. What you going to tell them, Reverend?
Say it quietly or you will wake up Sister Williams, already
nodding next to me. Say it quickly, or Deacon Lovejoy's
daydream will wipe you out. Go ahead now.

". . . and some of you will say Reverend Fuller was trying
to talk round because the young ones like it that way. I know
what some of you will think, but I don't have to sound like
nothing I don't want to sound like, and those that know me

know that. Besides, I got more to be talking bad about than
the young folks got."

"UH-HUH!"

"Most of you know me and I dare say I know most of you.
We've been a big family together, for better or for worse, and I
come, like Caesar, to praise you, not to bury you this evening. I
remember the time the church nearly burned down and most
of you donated your money and time and we put things back
together. Those were trying times, crying times. And the time
the choir went to Vermont and those gang of farm boys stoned
the cars and a couple deacons remembered what they knew
about old-fashioned street-fighting and whipped acouple of
them good. Funny times, too. And babies, whew! If I've
blessed twenty, I've blessed two hundred. Yes, I know you and
your ways. But I'm getting sentimental and I told my wife
before this sermon that I wouldn't get sentimental. But there's
never anything easy about good-bye, not if something's meant
much to you . . ."

"WELL!"

"Never nothing easy about good-bye. A man on TV was
saying the other day that you are what you do, and he was
meaning you are what you eat, what you like, and what you
hate. Of course, there might be a little truth in what he was
saying. For a long time, folks been becoming what they hate.
You know how it can all just get down deep in you sometime.
My ole aunt said that to me once, one day that I had seen my
uncle, her big husband, not hit a little white man back.

"There were rednecks all through town that day, watching
and waiting to kill Uncle Will if he did break that man's nose,
but he never did and I saw it and she saw that I saw it, and
tried to make me understand that Uncle Will had to do that, at
that moment, in that country street. Some other day it might
be different, but that day he had to swallow his pride in front

of his wife and me. Yes, it gets way down in you sometime. It can turn things upside down and have righteous religious folks come out just like them dope-chewing fools out on the avenue right now, blocking the sidewalks. Everybody knows if you gotta spend all your time hating the brother next to you and not trying to help him out, then you need him for the wrong thing, and it's time to look at yourself hard. Why? Because you be addicted too. Addicted to another man's weakness. Can I get an Amen on that?"

"AMEN," the church says.

"Just like you start looking and acting like what you hate, the same is true for what you love . . . Love something sweet and gentle and you can become that sweet and gentle too. I've seen it. Love somebody contrary and you'll wind up contrary too. You got to be extra careful, 'cause it's all in the act. And that's the beginning of my ending this morning. All in the act; all in the living. It ain't always what you done read or somebody's done told you that's going to make you love or hate necessarily. It's more what you done seen with your own eyes, and what you've lived in your own life, and what the soul has moved you to.

"Keep the faith in the act, though your hope may be in the word. And who's to judge? We, all of us, are the final judges of ourselves. I hope in the light of judgment that our best side show. But you can't always tell. So many of us want to do dirt and leave it to the Creator to decide, hoping he was too busy to see. Some of us think it easier to believe in the Creator than in each other. Can I get an Amen?"

Reverend Fuller, who puts faith in their own gossip? You're doing only fair so far. If you don't tighten up, we may not play and leave you to your gentle flock turned to wolves at your own signal. Pull their coats. They still trust too much the lines between them—between all of us—backyard fences, tenement walls, lies they've believed from dead men. Rub their noses in the shit of ghosts, then I will come on and blow their minds back together. Music is the spirit-healer, the righteous juju.

"Say it like you mean it! After all, you got the young folks in here watching you close now. They want to know if you for real. They want to know just how serious you take this church. Let me hear you say it again . . ."

"AMEN!!"

"That's more like it. My God never liked no timid no way. The Bible said meek, it's true. But it ain't never said nothing about being invisible. So let me know you here when you say it. Help this old man out. After all, it's my last one, ain't it? Make the walls quiver when you say it, and let the ones passing outside know that ain't no jiving going on in Reverend Fuller's church. No, sir!"

"ALL RIGHT NOW. TAKE YOUR TIME."

"Thank you, ma'am, and I plan to do just that. Now, I was saying that experience is usually your best guide, your best teacher, your best friend. It ain't always easy street, though, and most of us in here know that for a fact. Sometimes we been in the same boat together, in the same boat in rough waters and seeing nothing around but more water and knowing they filled with everything that won't do no good. And when we wish up on a wind, it wants to send us into a sandbar. Oh yes, it can be that way sometime. And on top of that, just when you think about the worst that can happen to any man has happened to you already, you find yourself in the ship that's headed for destruction, the ocean against you, the wind against you, about that time it begins to rain. Raining like it ain't never rained before. And we know that done happened. It done rained on many a life here in this church for a fact . . ."

"OH, YES IT HAS!"

". . . So bad, it didn't do no good to cry. Yes, we been tried by water, sho nuff. Water is the first trial. The very first trial for all of us is that water and that kicking around in our mamas' bellies. And when we come into this world, everybody look at us and we look at everybody, thinking we done done something. That's only the beginning. But if we go back far enough, there is the water of those real ships that brought us over here, all buckled up under so much weight. They tell me that they had to throw a lot of us over to make the passage easier. Some jumped who wasn't excited by the idea of being anybody's slave. Most stayed, not knowing why, not knowing how."

"AIN'T IT THE TRUTH, NOW?"

"And we came through that."

"HAVE MERCY!"

"THANK THE LAWD, WE DID!"

"So you see, the coming out of that first trial brought us to life in a strange land."

"THAT'S RIGHT."

"Tell me, what runs through the mind when you look around and everything is strange and you don't know a soul? Except maybe the faces of those that brought you and kept you there?"

"MUST BE STRANGE, ALL RIGHT!"

"You know it is. What's to know? One thing for sure, only the strong survive. But like I say, the maiden voyage is just the first step. Let us go on a little bit. Let us look at fire. Now my Bible reminds me of three good men—Shadrach, Meshach, and Abednego. And it reminds me of a wicked king, named Nebuchadnezzar, and how he had these three men put into the fiery furnace."

"YES, HE DID!"

"Did you hear me this morning? I said a fiery furnace, a furnace with the heat of one hundred suns. Everybody knows how powerful and hot just one sun is. Think about a hundred now, and you'll know what Shadrach, Meshach and Abednego went through."

"WHAT THEY FACED, LORD!"

"There's one thing we can't forget, because if we do forget this one thing, we make Shadrach, Meshach and Abednego a story folks tell just to pass the time of day. Good people, when they was in that fiery furnace, they wasn't in there by themselves alone."

"NO, SIR!"

"They had something that could let them live through the heat of a thousand white-hot suns. Do you know what I'm talking about this evening?"

"HA!"

"They had Spirit, and his twin brother, Hope."

"YES, THEY DID, NOW!"

"And that undying love for life."

"SAY IT AGAIN!"

"I say they had Big Strong Spirit."

"WELL!"

"His twin brother, Hope."

"I HEAR YOU THIS EVENING!"

"And undying love for life. Sometimes they can just wrap us all up and just pick us up and shake us so we don't know top from bottom. They can save us when we drowning, save us when we burning up with bad thoughts, and save us on dry land. Everybody burns in they bad thoughts, burns in the memory of they bad past. But it takes a good man to give what he has done its due and move on . . ."

"MOVE ON, LORD!"

"Move on . . ."

"MOVE ON, LORD!"

He steps from behind the lectern and throws back his head to make song. Their choir joins in, Novella leading them. Then the congregation, humming and swaying with the choir. It is a song that brings screams from big sisters who have been fanning themselves. One goes off just behind me, and turning, I notice Ubangi in a back row, swaying, humming, remembering North Carolina. Then again, maybe he's just curious about my playing in a church this evening.

It's as if the church, these people, have been moving up a hill together and have stopped to rest a bit and look back over the road they've traveled. With surprised eyes, everybody is checked out, as if no one expected this strength, now getting stronger. The song ends and Reverend Fuller stands there for a second, looking into our faces. He unfolds his hands and moves back behind the lectern.

"Then after the waters of our beginning, the fire of our searching, after these comes the land. Land that is the end of our beginning, land where we find our legs for moving. Certainly the land where the rock of our church rests, the land that has held the sweat of our labor. The land we call home, though we wander and roam."

"YES, WE STRAY SOMETIMES!"

"Stray though we may, not knowing where, but thinking any place but here. And a man wants a home, I think. And if he don't, then what's his reward after the trials and tribulations he has to go through? Home and peace of mind is what I'm talking about, and the man who ain't got either one can be the sorriest of men. When you get them, you got to hold them and remember how you got them, 'cause once you lose them, it's hard getting them back."

Reverend Fuller moves onto the floor and takes up a little girl. Her many plaits are tied in red ribbons and she looks frightened to death. He walks back to the front, holding her, watching her.

"Sometimes I think they's different from us. Pure and clean and even their devilment can't come close to ours. But they is closer to God's image. No mistake that the first image of God is babies . . ."

"WELL . . ."

"Just like this little one here, looking at everything like it's new. Looking at me like I never was anything before she looked at me . . .

". . . We need a piece of land and peace of mind for those such as this little angel, bless her little heart. For those more holy than we, and who know nothing about the Bible."

Then he hands the baby back.

"That's what we need before we grow too old to wish and too useless to warn and the young ones feel sorry for us and maybe hate us too, and call us handkerchief heads for only going half the distance for them. We need these things before we sit down and claim we tired. I'd call that drowning on dry land. And who's to keep us keeping on? Spirit, Hope, Love—all those things you get tired of hearing me talk about all these years. But I add a new one this morning. Spirit, Hope, Love, and *ourselves*. That's the way I see it. The Lord is all of this, you see. For the Lord is gonna be. Anyway."

Reverend Fuller, I know why they grow suddenly quiet. Try to get an Amen now. Maybe you'll have to get it from the scarred benches, the peeling walls? Do you walk the way of the new world alone today, your last day as shepherd of a small flock? Are they afraid to let shepherds go so easily?

"For the young ones, there's a world waiting. All I can say is go and get it. Be your own gods."

He wipes his forehead and sips water from a glass on the lectern. He looks tired and a little worried. You always like to hold onto that last picture, happy picture, just like the sudden flash of memory passing a casket and you see the last happy picture, no matter how far gone, and that brings the grief. The church is still except for the whir of cardboard fans beating the air. A child cries and winos can be heard passing outside, a few drifting in. Is it Ubangi I hear now, out there sweet-talking them in?

". . . and though you might not have liked what I said this evening, I sing my own song now. I will leave you, Crumbly Rock, as I came to you—humble, with the work of how much work had to be done. I will sing loud now, for my Lord has said sing and let all hear and do not be ashamed. Sing and let them hear the sign and let them see the light . . ."

Bennie Tatum, in his pink jumpsuit, still not looking like he belongs in anybody's church, moves to the front and assembles his drums next to the altar. Winking as he goes to the organ, Okra taps my arm. The signal. Novella's voice soaring through this run-down church. Songs of the New World we're about to make. Reverend Fuller puts his hands on my shoulder and nods, then he moves on, talking to himself, smiling, and his wife watching him with a loved woman's eyes. Hurricane Wanda takes her place in the choir and from the rear, Antar has begun a chant. Next to him squats Omowale with a conga drum. Ubangi has found a tambourine from somewhere.

Just a word, Reverend Fuller, just a word. I don't know all the time what's right for people, but maybe my song can bring them together, and together we'll keep searching, looking more closely at one another. I know music has a place larger than smoky rooms, a place as large as the sky, as sure as the heart. I dry my hands after I have the horn together and wink at Novella. A manchild is coming, has to be coming, we've agreed. And, though we can only hope for the lands he will see, his voyage has just begun.

I start to play and up the aisle dances the skinny-legged woman with a man in a wrinkled sportcoat doing a heavy-footed shuffle. The man pauses to set an empty bottle beneath a bench and no one has bothered to frown because our clap-happy rap-happy selves have been burned too cleanly by song. In the beginning there is the spirit-touch.

About the Author

JOHN A. MCCLUSKEY was born in 1944 in Middletown, Ohio. He attended Ohio schools, received a B.A. degree from Harvard in 1966, then studied English and creative writing at Stanford, where he received an M.A. degree in 1972. Since then he has taught in Alabama and Illinois and is presently in his fifth year of teaching Afro-American literature in the Humanities Division at Case-Western Reserve University in Cleveland. His fiction has been anthologized and he is a regular contributor to *Black World*. He lives in Cleveland with his wife and son.